THE FIRE APPRENTICE

THE SYLVANIA SERIES

The Forest Bride
The Village Maid
The Ocean Girl
The Woodland Stranger
The Fire Apprentice
The Magic Seeker (coming in 2026)

JANE BUEHLER

Published by Emily Jane Buehler
PO Box 1285, Hillsborough, NC 27278 USA
https://janebuehler.com

Publisher's Note: This is a work of fiction. Names, characters, businesses, places, events, locales, and incidents are either the products of the author's imagination or used in a fictitious manner. Any resemblance to actual persons, living or dead, or actual events is purely coincidental.

The Fire Apprentice (Sylvania Book 5) / Emily Jane Buehler
ISBN (print): 978-1-957350-12-7
ISBN (ebook): 978-1-957350-13-4

Library of Congress Control Number: 2024918576

Western Mountains
the Iron Mine
Sylvania
to Knotty Knob and Nor Bay
Wayside
the Crossroads
the Forest Road
to Cliffside
Woods Rest
N
W
E
S
the Fairy Enclave
Gold Gulch
Woodglen and the Castle
to Sar Bay

Chapter 1

THERE'S A NEW VILLAGE BLACKSMITH," Maryanne said with a grin at Jane from the doorway. She'd returned from her errands in the village.

Jane's face heated. She shoved her fists extra hard at the dough she was kneading on the wooden table. Why did Maryanne have to tease her? *Was* Maryanne teasing her? Maybe not. Maybe Maryanne was simply excited about having a new smith in the village.

Maryanne stepped into the kitchen and unloaded the parcels from her arms onto the table opposite Jane's floury mass of bread dough. Maryanne's cheeks glowed as she smiled. She pushed the dark strands of hair off her face, tucking them behind her ear as more strands fell out of her bun. "He's just your type, too." She pinned Jane with her dark eyes and planted her stocky frame beside the table. "Dark and glowering." She winked.

So Maryanne *was* teasing her. Teasing her for being pathetic and chasing after every new man who came to Woods Rest. Maryanne didn't mean anything by her teasing. She just didn't realize how her words stung.

"The chairmaker wasn't glowering," Jane said, punching the dough. "He was friendly. And his hair was sandy colored." The apprentice chairmaker had arrived last summer. She'd found any excuse to pass by his shop, slowing her steps and peeking in the windows to catch his eye. She'd wasted three moons swooning over him before Maryanne convinced her to be more direct. But when she invited him to go on a walk, he mumbled excuses like a flustered drunkard and left town the next day.

"True," Maryanne conceded. "But he was . . . I don't know. He had that mysterious air about him. He didn't talk much."

"He was a good listener."

"And he certainly brought us enough mending work—the man wore out socks faster than a soldier on the march."

Sometimes Jane had returned the finished socks to him one pair at a time.

"Well," Maryanne went on, "you can't argue that Wells's apprentice wasn't dark and glowering. That one had more glower than the forest at midnight."

She meant the tinsmith's apprentice—he'd arrived last winter, shortly after the chairmaker left. Maryanne was right: he'd had an unbelievable scowl, fierce eyebrows, and dark hair down his back. Any rational person would have steered clear. But he'd had a scar across his cheek that fascinated Jane. It made her want to run her fingers along it—or her tongue. Whenever she passed him in the village, he glared at her, and she found herself hurrying home and sneaking upstairs to shut herself in the linen closet, away from all her housemates, so she could continue her fantasy in private.

"I still can't believe you asked that one out," Maryanne continued. "I was terrified of him."

"I was too." But she'd seen him through the window one day, pulverizing a piece of tin laid across an anvil. She'd been staring, her lips parted, as each strike of the hammer jolted inside her and thinking she might have an orgasm right there in the lane. When he'd glanced up, staring back, she'd been so sure the flash of heat and longing that shot through her couldn't be one-sided that she'd gone into the shop and walked right up to him. He'd been alone, holding the crumpled bottom of a candle holder against the anvil with a pair of tongs and gripping the hammer in his tight fist. She'd stood in front of him and gazed up into his eyes—brown—and seen some sort of helpless longing.

"Come for a walk," she'd said.

He'd blinked and his eyes had hardened, then shifted to disinterest as he stared down at her. "Absolutely not." He'd dropped the mangled tin onto the nearby table and stalked out the back door, still clutching the hammer. She'd never seen him again.

Helpless longing indeed. She was a fool. She imagined what she wanted to see and couldn't tell her imaginings from reality.

"Anyway, he's gone now," Jane said. She paused her kneading and looked up. "And I don't have a type."

"Ehn," Maryanne said, tilting her head. "The ones you notice might appear different, but they've all got something in common."

"What?" Jane asked, curiosity getting the better of her.

Maryanne grinned again. "They're all good with their hands."

"Stop!" Jane couldn't help smiling back.

Maryanne made a crude motion with her hand in front of her hips and jiggled her body, laughing. "And they have big tools and like to hammer things."

"You're one to talk," Jane said, shaking her head, "the way you and Wells go at it."

"Wells can wield his hammer, that's for sure." Maryanne stopped her suggestive movements and reached over the table. She pinched off a handful of Jane's dough and rolled it in her fingers.

"Why do they all leave then?" Jane asked, her voice small. "It's like the mere thought of me being interested in them is so horrible it drives them away." Those men who rejected her hadn't even known about her other issues.

Maryanne lowered her hand with the dough. "Jane. It's not you. Wells said that last apprentice was a disaster. He couldn't even make a tin cup without bashing it all to pieces. He had no finesse at all."

"But he didn't give up trying to do the work until I propositioned him."

Maryanne's eyebrows rose. "You propositioned him? What exactly did you say? I thought you asked him to go on a walk."

Jane shrugged before pushing her hands back into the dough, pounding it harder. "Maybe he thought I planned to tumble him in the fields outside the village." Maybe she *had* planned to.

Maryanne laughed. "He did save Elle that time she fell in the mill pond so we'll always be grateful to him for that." She stretched the dough with her fingers into a thin sheet. "That dough is done," she said, holding up the evidence. Jane's hands slowed.

Maryanne mushed the test dough back into the mass on the table and scooped it away from Jane. As she turned for a bowl, she jerked her chin toward the door.

"We've been needing a few more door hooks now that the children are getting bigger. Maybe you could run over to the smithy and ask for some?" She peeked over her shoulder and lifted her eyebrows innocently.

Jane shook her head slowly and sighed. She *was* curious. Dark and glowering . . . she didn't want it to be her type, but those were the type of men she was attracted to. That had been her type from the first man she'd ever been with through the most awful: Cedric. The fairy.

The one who'd betrayed her and broken her heart, and worse.

"Fine," she said, rubbing the dough bits off her hands and taking off her apron. She'd pushed her bracelet up her arm so it wouldn't get messy, so now she worked it back down until it hung at her wrist. It was made of a long strip of fabric from Elle's first blanket that had ripped off one day when the corner caught on a tree branch. When Cedric abandoned Jane and stole their daughter away with him, the bracelet was all she'd had left. She'd wrapped it around and around and tied a knot. For two long winters it was all she had had of her daughter, until her friend Rose had rescued Elle.

Jane glanced out the window overlooking the back garden. Beyond the rows of vegetables, the children were on the grass playing some kind of game. The older ones gave orders, running back and forth from the apple trees by the stone wall to the row of daffodil stalks by the tool shed. As Jane watched, Elle tried to follow the other children, making it only half the distance before the crowd swooped by, going in the other direction. Baby Jacob didn't even bother trying to toddle after them; he sat on his bottom, watching the action.

Elle was tough for being three winters old. Even from the distance, Jane could see the red in her cheeks from the exertion of running in the spring air. A whoop rose from whoever had won the race. The mob of children moved off toward the back meadow, scooping up Jacob as they went. Elle watched them retreat, pushing a wisp of hair off her face. She turned away instead of following, walked toward the shed, and plopped down beside the lone clump of late-blooming daffodils. She lay back beside one of the flowers and began talking.

Jane smiled as she turned away from the window. She checked that her long, dark hair was up in its bun and wiped her sleeve over her forehead under her bangs.

"What are they up to?" Maryanne asked, covering the bowl of dough with a damp towel and placing it on the stovetop to rise.

"They're heading for the meadow. Except for Elle. She's talking to a daffodil."

Panic flashed in Maryanne's eyes. Drat. Jane shouldn't have said that to Maryanne.

All the children had fathers who were fairies—fairies who'd seduced human women, fathered a child, taken the child, and disappeared. Jane's friend Rose—also half fairy—had rescued the children last spring after falling in love with a fairy prince and following him into the fairies' hidden caverns. Prince Dustan had helped Rose rescue the children and bring them to Woods Rest, where Jane and Maryanne had lived with three of the other mothers.

As half fairies, the children shouldn't be able to do the magic that came naturally to most fairies. But Rose had mastered some of their tricks and said it might be that no one had ever bothered trying to teach the children. Half-fairy children weren't common. Theirs had been sired under the orders of a horrible queen who'd wanted to use them as servants. Jane still shuddered to think of the first two winters of Elle's life.

Whenever any of the children did anything that seemed fairy-like in nature—like talking to daffodils—Maryanne panicked. Maryanne hated fairies. She never said a kind word about them and the barest mention of them raised her hackles. The other mothers were different. Ladi had made friends with fairies who lived in her new home, Woodglen, and Kitty now *lived* with a fairy in Cliffside. But Maryanne was always uneasy around fairies, even Rose's mate. She didn't want the children—her little baby Jacob and the four whose birth mothers hadn't yet been found—to learn magic.

Jane didn't mind the idea of magic, although she didn't encourage it in Elle since it upset Maryanne. Everything about fairies did. Around Maryanne, Jane avoided the F word at all costs.

Maryanne was picking at the edges of the towel on the stove.

"You know Elle's like that," Jane said gently. "The others aren't so fanciful."

Maryanne nodded.

"They're probably going treasure hunting again. You can't get more human than that."

Maryanne forced a wobbly smile. "Those coins they found last autumn certainly came in handy."

"It's odd no one ever claimed them," Jane said to keep her distracted, even though they'd been over this a dozen times. "A whole sack like that. And how did it get into the meadow?"

"Someone stumbling home drunk through the fields, I guess." Maryanne's shoulders relaxed a little. "I'm glad no one claimed them."

"And glad the grange elders let us keep them."

"That's for sure."

"Didn't you want another cultivator for the gardening?" Jane asked. "A small one the children can handle?"

"Yes," Maryanne said. Her shoulders had fully relaxed. "You're going to the smithy now?"

"I might as well," Jane replied. "If the apprentice blacksmith is going to flee the village, we might as well get it over with before people start to like him."

Maryanne smiled and shook her head. "You've not met the right man yet. Maybe this'll be the one."

"What did you say his name was?"

"I didn't. I didn't go in to meet him. I peeked through the window and saw him."

"And you could tell he was dark and glowering from a peek through the grimy window at the smithy?"

Maryanne grinned. "Darkness was oozing out of the smithy, he was so dark and brooding."

"Mm, just how I like them—oozing." Jane wrinkled her nose at Maryanne before leaving the room.

On the front porch, she inhaled the warm late spring air. Mouser opened an eye where he lay sprawled on the floorboards, then closed it. Jane didn't even need a shawl with the day warming up so nicely. She shed her house slippers and donned her shoes, leaned down to scratch the striped fur between Mouser's pointed ears, and jogged down the steps.

The trouble was, Jane mused as she ambled around the blossoming peony bush and up the lane toward the village center, even if one of these apprentices *did* want to walk with her, or to tumble her in the fields, no one could compare to what she'd felt with Cedric. Cedric—or Larch, as the fairies called him—had taken her breath away.

When she'd met Cedric—Larch—or maybe calling him Cedric was correct if she meant the sham person she'd fallen for? She had tried to think of him as Larch ever since she'd learned his real name. Cedric was a human she'd fallen in love with, a man who was kind and loving and attentive and gazed at her adoringly.

She'd had to accept he was gone. He'd never even existed in the first place. He'd been a phony person created by Larch to trick her.

Anyway, when she'd met Larch, he'd treated her like she was the most special, the most perfect woman in the world. Before him, she'd tumbled a few of the fellows on nearby farms. The kissing and petting had been lovely, but the culmination had hurt a lot more than she'd expected. And the pain didn't recede with different partners over time. None of her girlfriends had similar issues and no one could explain why she did.

Her father and brothers had expected her to bond with one of the neighbors' sons and become a farmer like everyone else in the southern region where she'd grown up. They said the romantic stories she imagined were unrealistic, that she was naive.

And then Larch stepped out of the woods like one of her daydreams. She followed him away from her home without a second thought. Being with him felt better than anything—her whole world expanded into an exciting adventure.

And the usual pain of sex was so dulled she barely noticed it, even with Larch tumbling her every night. But it was because he'd used a love spell on her, she now understood. At the time, she'd had no idea that the reason sex seemed less painful was due to a fairy spell. Or that she'd been under a love spell at all. She'd lived in bliss in his woodland cottage for a full turn of the seasons and through the following summer with her baby girl—Bluebell, they'd named her—until Larch disappeared, taking Bluebell with him. Her family had been right. She was naive and too trusting, and her fantasies were silly. Following them had cost her everything.

She had Elle back now. Larch had helped the children escape the caverns, Rose said. But that help wasn't enough to make up for the harm he had caused.

But as for a new romance? Larch had raised the bar impossibly high by making her feel things that didn't exist in real life. She wanted to find a partner who'd love and respect her, *and* she wanted the tumbling, too, but without the pain. It seemed impossible.

And no one understood. She couldn't explain to Maryanne that she missed being under the love spell because Maryanne would be horrified. She herself was horrified, and ashamed—what kind of person missed being under a spell? What kind of person missed the way they'd felt when they'd been with a villainous trickster?

Jane passed under the swaying apple trees along the lane. As she neared the village square, the sounds of the shops and market stalls echoed in the air—friendly shouts, the whinny of a horse, a child wailing. As the breeze ruffled her clothing, she took a deep breath of it in. Over the ubiquitous aromas of the grassy meadows and earthy gardens drifted whiffs of spring blossoms and frying dough. She passed the old smithy—someone was renovating the crumbling stone building—and walked under one last apple bough, its final petals of the spring scattered across the lane, before she entered the square.

One of the carpenters waved from the porch of the pub, and villagers passed in and out of the general store. In the village garden, hellebore and phlox bloomed in the grass under the shady trees, and heavy magenta peonies bobbed in a sunny corner. A young girl filled a bucket at the pump, and across the grass, a white-haired woman with wrinkled cheeks sat on the bench. Jane had the strangest sense they might be the same person, as if two scenes occurring sixty winters apart were both happening at once before her.

Jane crossed the square and headed into the sheltered lane where the smiths had their workshops. The ring of a hammer on iron sang out from the farrier's stalls at the end of the lane. In the shade on his porch, Wells slouched in a chair, munching on a plate of sausages. He dipped his chin as she passed and waited to smirk until right before she lost sight of him. Drat Maryanne; if she'd seen the new apprentice before a visit to Wells, she'd probably blathered to Wells about how she *had* to send Jane over. Maybe the whole village was watching her approach the blacksmith's shop, laughing behind their curtains.

Jane stopped at the corner of the second-to-last building in the lane, keeping back from the window. The hammer at the farrier's had gone silent, leaving only the occasional shout from behind her and the creak of a door, followed by a bang as it shut. She ran her fingers over her hair, checking that no wisps had escaped. Her back had dampened in the hot sun. She closed her eyes and took a deep breath of coal smoke and horses and the dirt of the lane.

So the chairmaker hadn't wanted her, and the tinsmith had despised her. And she'd spent two seasons pining over them. This time was going to be different. She was going to be straightforward and realistic. She was going to walk into the shop and meet the new apprentice, and if he smiled or flirted in any way, she'd invite him to go on a walk around the village at the end of the day. That was normal, right? He was new in town. Someone needed to show him around. And she wouldn't worry about what might come later.

And if he wasn't interested—or if he was downright rude—she'd turn around and walk away and that would be it. She wouldn't think of him again.

She opened her eyes, then hurried to the door.

The deep, smoky smell of a coal fire engulfed Jane as she entered the dark shop. The front of the space had two large workbenches covered with tools and bits of metalwork and notes with customer orders. In the gloom, the master blacksmith hunched on a stool by a side bench, finishing a candlestick holder with a black coating he spread on with a cloth wrapped on a stick. No one else was in the shop. Windows overlooked the silent anvils out back.

Rods of iron leaned against the walls, and a coating of black grime covered every surface. Other than wanting to give the place a thorough cleaning, Jane loved the blacksmith shop. She felt oddly at home around the tools and the glowing fires. The sparks that burst out when the smiths hammered looked like burning stars.

She scanned the open back windows one last time as she approached the old blacksmith. He looked up without stopping his task. He rarely smiled but Jane always felt as if he liked her—not that her instincts indicated anything. But he was polite and had helped her carry items home in the past.

"Good day, Master Smith. How is the shop?"

"Well enough, Miss Jane," he rumbled. "Can't say the same for the ironworks."

Jane smiled. Everyone in the village knew about the rivalry between the master blacksmith and the ironmaster. Their quarrels lasted about a moon and alternated with the times when the two of them were tumbling. "What has the ironmaster done now?"

"Lazy bastard hasn't fired up the furnace this spring. Hasn't done a bit of work. He's just scratchin' his backside and whittlin' to pass the time. Says he's going to quit the iron business and write a book now that Woodglen has a printer."

"But where will the smithy get its iron?"

Master Smith waved her words away. "He'll never quit smelting ore. He loves it too much. Besides, no one would pay good coin for a book by that ninny. Unless it's a guidebook to bein' a pea-brained dolt."

"But you said—"

"Technically it's not his fault the furnace is down. He's got no ore to process."

Jane shook her head as Master Smith got around to the truth. "Why is there no ore?"

"First load of the season hasn't come down the mountain yet. Don't know what they're getting up to at the mine. Maybe that's where the party is this spring—they're all too hungover to load up the donkeys. First wagon up never came back and the ironmaster sent a helper after it and she hasn't come back either."

"Should I hold off on asking you for anything?"

"We've got a stack of rods and plates left from last season. Should get us through until the ore arrives and is processed. What do you need?"

Jane glanced to the back of the shop again before she could stop herself. She blushed and turned back, focusing on the candlestick holder in Master Smith's hands. "We need a few door hooks, and Maryanne wondered if you'd make her a handheld cultivator. One small enough the children can use it easily."

He pointed to a row of tools hanging on the wall. "Do you like the wider tines, or the thin ones?"

Jane considered. "Thin would be lighter, right? That might help the children manage it."

"I can make you a wooden handle. Might not last as long but it would help with the weight as well."

"Thank you."

A glint came into Master Smith's eyes and he jerked his head toward the back of the shop. "Head out by the fires and ask Ro about the hooks. He should be finishing his lunch."

Heat flooded Jane's face. Master Smith had known her intentions the whole time. Was she that obvious? Or maybe she wasn't the first visitor to come see the new apprentice. Maybe a parade of single people from the village had been visiting all morning, and the apprentice—Ro—would know exactly why she'd come.

She mumbled thanks and shuffled toward the door at the back. Through the windows, the space around the anvils was empty. And then someone stepped into view.

He looked a bit like the apprentice tinsmith from the winter, with a broad build and dark hair but his hair was shorter. From outside the shop, he didn't notice her. He turned as he took up an iron tool and poked at the coals, reviving the fire after his break. Dizziness seized Jane and she sucked in a breath.

What was she doing here?

She was going to meet Ro and ask him on a walk. No, that wasn't right—she was going to ask for hooks and see how he acted toward her and decide about the walk. But she'd be so flustered, she'd never be able to make the right decision about whether to ask him!

The whole idea was ridiculous. Why would he want to walk with someone he didn't even know? Why did she even want to walk with him? Would he think she was pretty? Her hair was already sliding loose from its bun and her face burned and she sweated in her thin dress. He'd look at her and know she was sad, lonely, and desperate.

Being here this way—stalking him like prey—wasn't normal. She should turn right around and leave, and forget the door hooks—Maryanne didn't actually need them.

But then she'd be a coward, hiding from the possibility of meeting a new person. She didn't want to be a coward. Talking to him didn't make her desperate or pathetic. She had a good life and so what if she tried to meet new people? She'd lost all her childhood friends when she'd left home, and her new friends in Woods Rest were moving on and leaving. She'd be all alone if she didn't make friends. Coming here to meet Ro was no big deal. Why did she make it into one?

What *was* normal behavior? And why was it so hard for her to do it?

She opened the door and stepped out.

Chapter 2

A THIN BREEZE SWEPT THROUGH THE back of the smithy as Jane stepped out the door. Thick wooden posts held up a roof over the work area, and its stone floor was covered but the sides were open to the fields surrounding Woods Rest.

Four small chimneys were lined up in a row, each with a flat table in front of the hearth opening. The tables were at hip height and each contained a firepot, the depression where the coal fire sat. Long-handled iron tools hung from the side of each table, and each had an anvil beside it. Along the wall was a workbench with hammers and tongs of various shapes and sizes scattered across it. Forged iron leaves and flowers lay on the windowsills, thick with dust. Some day she was simply going to bring her own dustcloth and wipe them all.

Only one chimney had a pile of coal glowing in the pot, the one where Ro stood with his back to her. He used an iron poker to drag more coal onto the pile. He wore trousers and a dark shirt, and his hair was short above his neck and longer on top. It ruffled in a wisp of wind blowing through from the meadows outside the shop.

Ro called out to Benny. The awkward teen sat behind the chimney at the far end of the giant bellows that supplied air up through the bottom of the pot.

Benny lowered the pamphlet he was reading and reached up for the handle of the bellows. With one arm, he tugged it down, then up, as the bellows wheezed with air. He kept working the bellows as he returned his attention to his reading.

Jane stepped closer. Ro's head turned, his eyes sweeping over her feet before returning to the coals. "Fire's almost ready," he said. He even sounded a bit like the tinsmith. His voice was deep and quiet.

Jane fiddled with her bracelet, twisting her finger into the material, and forced her breathing to stay steady. She had no reason to be this nervous.

Ro glanced over his shoulder and when he saw her, he put down the poker and turned.

He didn't smile. But he didn't scowl, either. He gave no hint what he was thinking—no haughty look in his eyes, no interest, nothing. A leather apron covered his clothing. He had a strong jawline and his hair hung in his eyes until he reached up and pushed it behind his ear with a large, callused hand.

Skies, he had large hands. He probably knew what to do with them.

Drat. Maryanne was right. Jane did have a thing for capable hands.

"Can I help you?" he asked quietly when ten heartbeats had passed in awkward silence. She swore the rumbles of his low voice vibrated in her toes through the stone floor.

"I'm hooks," Jane blurted out.

Ro waited. He didn't laugh or scrunch up his brow in confusion.

Jane focused. "I need hooks."

He nodded once.

"For the door. For the coats and scarves."

"How many?"

How many did Maryanne want? They had five children in the house if you didn't count the baby. "Five?"

Ro nodded again and turned to the fire. "It'll be a few minutes if you'd like to come back."

Jane edged around an anvil toward the next chimney down as Ro took an iron rod from a bucket of them and thrust the end into the coals. The fire glowed where the air from the bellows blew through and greenish smoke curled off the pile of coal and whisked up the chimney. Ro glanced over as she came up alongside where he worked.

"I like to watch," she said.

He regarded her another half-beat, blinked, and turned to adjust the rod in the fire.

Skies, she sounded like a lecher. "I like being at the smithy," she explained. "I like watching the blank iron rods turn into useful things."

"You should apprentice."

Jane tried to laugh off the suggestion but a lump swelled in her throat and she ended up coughing. "No one would want me."

"I don't see why not."

"My arms aren't strong enough for blacksmithing."

"It doesn't take much strength if you know how to hold the hammer."

Her face heated again. But he hadn't said it the way Maryanne would have, suggestively, and he probably didn't mean it to sound lewd. Thankfully he didn't look up. He pulled the rod from the fire and Jane stepped back. The rod came out glowing white and crackling with sparks and she gasped. She'd never seen one do that before.

Ro looked over.

"It's pretty." Her face heated at how stupid she must sound and she took another step back.

Ro laid the white-hot tip of the rod on the anvil as the sparks abated. He reached for the nearest hammer and stepped up close to the metal. Already the glow had faded to yellow. His arm with the hammer came up and dropped.

Clang!

Jane winced even though she'd been expecting the noise and

the spray of sparks. Ro darted one look at her, as if to check that the sparks hadn't reached where she stood, and hammered in earnest, flattening the end of the rod.

He didn't hammer at it the way she'd seen other blacksmiths do it. Usually they swung the hammer in a wide arc to crash down on the iron as if they were beating a dangerous viper to death. And usually they used the biggest hammer in the shop. Ro held a medium-sized one. He stood close to the anvil and his motion was a softer up and down, but when the hammer came down it struck with force.

Talking was impossible with the noise of the clashing metal. But even when Ro called out to Benny to resume pumping the bellows and paused his hammering to reheat the orange rod, words failed her. This time when he withdrew the rod from the coals, a shower of sparks cascaded off it.

Jane squinted at the bright metal and resisted reaching out a hand as if he held out a flower to her. "What makes it do that?" she asked.

"It, um, it might be the batch of iron." He held it steady before her.

"Ro!"

They both startled.

Master Smith stood in the nearest window. "That's too much heat, lad. You'll weaken the metal. You want it glowing white, not burnin' up."

Ro placed it on the anvil. "Yes, sir."

His cheeks darkened red and he focused on his task. He shouldn't be embarrassed for his mistake. Apprenticing was all about learning. Maybe he was embarrassed she'd witnessed it. She could reassure him but speaking about it seemed likely to embarrass him further.

Jane watched how he angled his hammer at the edge of the anvil, curling the flat end of the rod into what would become the lip of the hook as the yellow heat faded to orange. Her gaze drifted to Ro's hand gripping the hammer. She'd never seen such callused hands—the marks were more like scars, as if he'd been burned by a piece of hot iron. Her gaze moved up his arm. The sleeves of his shirt were rolled up to the elbows, and each time the hammer lifted, the long muscle in his forearm hardened. She tried instead to watch how he lifted the hammer and let it fall, using the downward pull of the earth to build the force of the blow. He made it look so effortless. *Could* she do it?

He flipped the rod over, tapping the hammer lightly on the curled part to flatten the outside of the lip, and her mind leapt to a scene of those hands on her body, flipping *her* over . . .

She shook the image away. Daydreaming about tumbling a man while he was in front of you was a sure way to become awkward and ruin a conversation. And it wasn't like she could rush into the physical part of a relationship, much as she wanted to. She'd rushed into sex with Hervey, the only man she'd been with since Larch, and her old pain had been waiting and worse than she remembered it from her younger days. She had to remember to take it more slowly. Maybe if she did, she could relax and the pain would go away.

Ro turned to the fire again, rod in hand. He took up the long-handled poker with his other hand and drove its hook down into the pile of coal, collapsing the heap. He used the hook to drag more coal from the back onto the pile in the pot before thrusting the rod into the glowing center, then through it. This time when he withdrew the rod, it glowed with a broad stretch of white without any sparks. As if he knew exactly how long to leave it in the coals to heat properly. Jane bit her lip but he ignored her.

He positioned the glowing section atop a chisel-like edge mounted upright on the workbench and gave it one heavy strike, nearly separating it. He released the hammer and took up tongs to hold the curled end of the rod and wrested the rod in two.

Jane watched enthralled as he used the tongs to hold the cut piece of iron in the fire. He heated the new end he had created, hammered it to a point, and flattened it into a delicately curved tip. That would be the end she nailed to the door, once it had a hole in it.

Again Rowan withdrew the iron from the fire, this time glowing at the hook end. He dipped the curled tip into the water barrel with a hiss. It came out gray.

"Why did you do that?"

"That part of the hook's finished. If I quench it I won't risk hurting it."

He positioned the hot iron over the horn of the anvil and hammered in earnest, curving the main section of the rod into a rounded hook. He stopped to examine it lengthwise, hammered it sideways on the top of the anvil to flatten it, and continued making the curve.

Jane tried to focus on the work and not his body. When that failed she studied all the tools on the workbench and scanned outside beyond the wooden posts supporting the roof, out at the spring wheat waving gently in the field. Ro had to heat the metal once more before the hook was done.

After checking the final shape, he pinned the flat top end of the hook to the anvil with a pointed chisel, held it in place as he switched tools, and struck an extra-hard hammer blow on the chisel, punching a hole in the top of the hook. He switched back to the tongs and grasped the finished hook.

He plunged the finished hook into the barrel of water. Steam hissed out and drifted away.

Jane fanned her face with her hand. "Why are you an apprentice?" she asked. "You seem to know the craft well."

"I know only the basics." Ro withdrew the finished hook and dropped it on the workbench along with the tongs. He called to Benny and drove the blank iron rod into the fire to begin the second hook.

Jane leaned back on the cold table behind her to watch him work. She could watch all day. She should have asked for a dozen hooks. She tried to keep her lustful thoughts contained, but each time he began to shape a new hook, she felt her body being molded and shaped in his hands. Each clang of the hammer on iron vibrated through the stones of the floor and up her legs. And when he thrust the finished hook into the steaming water to quench the heat, she imagined a similar release of the tension building in her, what she would feel like with it singing through her body and shuddering free.

Three hooks lay finished on the workbench. He reached for a new iron rod and glanced her way.

His brown eyes seemed to see her for the first time, catching on her face and staring without glancing quickly away. Her breath caught and she stared back. Maybe he could sense her longing across the few paces between them, or maybe the physical labor had stirred his blood, but somehow, he was interested in her now. She felt it in the air. She was sure of it.

Ro broke his gaze away first. He lay the hot iron across the anvil. His first blow glanced off the side, showering sparks across the floor. His fist tightened on the hammer and he brought it up sideways with his arm bulging and down again, striking a harder blow than the steady smacks he had been delivering. Was that how he handled a woman? Hard like the hammer blows, or gentle with his rough, worn hands?

Or both?

Jane pressed her palms against her thighs, holding herself together. Knowing he shared her desire made it worse, harder to resist. The fourth hook clattered to the floor after he punched the hole in it. He left it there, forgetting to quench it and instead heating the rod for the fifth. He pulled the rod out, sending a shower of sparks to the floor, and bashed it twice with the hammer to put out the sparks.

He paused, panting, and Jane stepped forward.

Ro turned to her and now he *was* scowling, with dark heat smoldering in his eyes half hidden by his long hair. His lips parted.

She tilted her head out at the fields. "Walk with me?"

He stared. And suddenly he looked more like a deer that scents the hunter and thinks it's hiding by being motionless, even as the hunter pulls back the arrow to slay it. He didn't answer, just stared.

She'd been wrong, completely wrong. Again.

Tears stung her eyes as she stumbled away. She yanked open the door and fled into the shop. In the dark interior, she slowed her steps, forcing herself to a measured pace to avoid alarming Master Smith as she called out thanks. A few more steps and she reached the front door and escaped into the lane.

The bright sunshine of noontime mixed with her tears and blinded her. She stopped to catch her breath, blinking and wiping her eyes. She was so stupid. The new apprentice wasn't interested in her. She had wanted to find out, and she had her answer.

A shadow flitted across her face and she opened her eyes and peered upward.

The strangest bird was in the sky, high, high up but large enough that she could see the sunlight shining through its greenish wings. It had wings like a bat and a body like a fat snake. It circled over the village, coasting with its wings spread. Someone shouted from the square. The bird circled lower, growing even larger.

Its neck was too long for a bird. What in the skies was it?

"It's a dragon," Ro whispered behind her.

Chapter 3

ADRAGON. AN ACTUAL, LIVE DRAGON was flying over Woods Rest—no, circling over Woods Rest. Circling, as if it were about to land.

Jane turned to Ro, who stood in the open doorway behind her. He gazed up at the thing in the sky with wide eyes and his lips parted, a look of reverence.

The dragon was so close its scales sparkled green in the sunlight. Light flashed off the claws on its feet, which were tucked against its chest and underneath its belly but began extending downward. Now several people shouted in the village square. The dragon coasted down and disappeared behind the buildings across from her.

Jane's heart thumped and unease flowed through her gut. She started up the lane toward the square, hastening her steps as the shouting increased. Wells stepped out his door as she passed but she didn't stop. She exited the lane into the crowded square. Everyone was staring in the same direction.

Toward her house.

The dragon hovered above the roofs of the old smithy and the neighbors' cottages. It flapped its wings hard, propelling itself upward, up and into the sky. Its back legs were down as if it had been standing on them, and the claws on one front foot were splayed open, while the claws on the other were closed like a cage. And something was inside.

Jane ran.

The dragon flapped its wings and headed away. Her feet pounded on the road as her house came into view. It was still standing, the stones solid and comforting. Mouser was gone from the front porch.

The children's wailing reached her before she'd gotten the door open. She dashed down the hall to the kitchen. Maryanne had the children clustered around her on the floor by the door, her arms around the group of them as they clung to her and cried. All of them were crying, even Amare, the oldest at seven winters and the toughest.

"What happened?" Jane's pulse pounded as she gasped for air. She counted the heads of the children—one, two, three, four, and Jacob squashed in the middle. Five heads.

Elle was missing.

"It took her," Amare blurted out, turning his tear-stained face to Jane. "The monster took Elle."

Dizziness swelled over Jane but she held on to the doorframe until her view steadied. She didn't have time to fall apart. She had to find Elle.

She entered the kitchen and crouched beside the others. Maryanne was crying with them. Jane touched Amare's head. He sniffled, tears leaking from his eyes.

"What happened, Amare? What did you see?"

"We were in the meadow." He hiccuped. "We thought it was a pretty bird."

"It was in the sky?" Jane prompted him.

"It was flapping, and its legs came out, and Elle was on the grass."

"It picked her up," Maryanne whispered. "I looked out the window and it had its claws around her."

"She was waving at it," Deka said quietly, peeking out from behind her brother. "She smiled at it."

"It took her and flew away," Maryanne finished.

Jane sat back on the floor. A dragon had taken Elle? Dragons weren't even real—they were a myth the old folks talked about, creatures that lived in the mountains and stole misbehaving children. No one ever actually *saw* one.

But fairies had been a myth, too. Until they showed up and ruined everything.

And Jane had seen the dragon. Maryanne had seen it take Elle. This was happening. She'd only be wasting time if she went outside to call for her child.

She sucked in a deep breath and exhaled as her mind focused on one thing: rescue Elle. But how? The dragon had flown away. It could be taking Elle anywhere. And what was the dragon going to do with her? Did dragons eat people?

Jane shuddered and refused to consider it. She had to find Elle. She needed help. Someone in Woods Rest had to know about dragons—maybe one of the elders. She'd find someone who could help.

She pulled herself up using the edge of the stove. The dough in its bowl had risen against the towel covering it. Only an hour ago she'd been kneading it as Elle played safely outside. Each plate on the shelf and each shoe by the door seemed uncommonly sharp. The bright yard outside was exactly the same as an hour ago. But a dragon had come and taken Elle.

Jane turned to Maryanne and the children with their tear-streaked faces. Usually Jane was the emotional one, tearing up if she made a mistake or anyone laughed at her. But now her mind was clear as it worked to form the best plan. She'd experienced this clarity once before, the time Elle fell in the mill pond. Her emotions had vanished as she ran to save her child. The tinsmith's apprentice had simply gotten to Elle first.

Jane licked her lips. "I'll go find a grange elder," she told Maryanne, "or a peacekeeper. Maybe they know something. Maybe someone in the village saw which direction the dragon took Elle, or maybe one of the villagers who's been to the mine knows something about where the dragons live."

Maryanne stared over the heads of the children with glistening eyes. They darted to look over Jane's shoulder and widened.

"I can help."

Jane whirled toward the deep voice. Ro stood in the kitchen doorway, his hands holding the frame. Away from the smithy he looked darker, as if a black cloud of coal dust clung to him.

"I can help you find the dragon," he said, quiet and calm.

"How?"

"I've been in the mountains. I know where the dragons are."

Maryanne straightened up, herding the children behind her. All of them gaped at Ro. Maryanne was shaking as she said, "Won't it be too late?"

Ro stepped into the kitchen. "Too late for what?"

"Won't it kill her as soon as it gets back to its lair?"

"Kill her?" Ro squinted at Maryanne. "Never."

"But it had her in its claws."

Ro shook his head. "A dragon would never harm a child, human or fairy."

Jane's heart thudded to a stop and Maryanne froze. Did he know about the children being half fairies? The villagers knew, but Master Smith wasn't likely to gossip about it with his new apprentice.

Maryanne wiped the tears off her cheeks and hoisted herself to her feet. Ro had said the F word. And as usual, hearing it had brought on Maryanne's anger.

"Of course it's a fairy thing," she snapped. "I should have known. Everything bad that happens to us involves fairies."

"Maryanne," Jane said, injecting calm into her voice, "you know it's not that simple. Let's focus on getting Elle back."

Maryanne shook her head. She pointed at Amare. "Go upstairs," she said quietly. "All of you. Take Jacob." She watched as the children shuffled toward the back staircase and climbed out of sight.

She spun back toward Ro. "Why did the dragon take her?"

To his credit, Ro hadn't winced once during Maryanne's out-burst. "Dragons form a bond with children who possess fire mag-ic," he said.

"Fire magic?"

"The ability to touch fire without burning. And to infuse its power into objects. It's how the fairies make their fire powder."

"So you're saying," Maryanne said, crossing her arms, "that dragons snatch fairy children and no one minds?"

"The dragon won't hurt her," Ro repeated. "Dragons don't hurt children. They simply teach the children to use their magic. She . . ." He hesitated.

"What?" Jane asked softly when Maryanne stayed silent.

"Elle might have called to the dragon."

Her daughter talked to flowers, and now she'd called a dragon? This was what Jane got for not minding when Elle drifted off in her imaginary world or said fanciful things. Maryanne had been right.

"I should have stopped her from talking to the daffodils," Jane blurted out.

"Jane . . ." Ro began, stepping toward her, but Maryanne moved forward and blocked him.

"How do you know all this?" Maryanne asked, her eyes nar-rowing. "And how do you know Elle's name?" She turned her glare on Jane. "Did you tell him?"

"No," Jane said. "I didn't even tell him my . . ."

She faltered and grabbed on to Maryanne's shoulder to keep herself upright. In front of them, Ro lowered his hands to his sides, his fingertips lifted as if to placate a raging animal.

"You're a fairy, aren't you?" Maryanne hissed.

Ro nodded.

Maryanne pushed Jane back. "What do you really look like?"

Ro blinked and his eyes became green, the same color as the children's. As sunlight shone through the windows, his skin shim-mered, slightly pearlescent, but otherwise he looked the same. "This is what I look like."

"Why are you here? Did you know the dragon was coming?"

"No."

"We can't trust him," Maryanne said to Jane. "We should go to the peacekeepers."

"They won't know where to look for her," Ro said. "Dragons live on the tallest peaks. There are no roads to their dens." He focused past Maryanne to Jane. "I can find her."

Jane held on to Maryanne's arms, easing around her. She forced herself to peer into Ro's green eyes. She always trusted the wrong people. She had no intuition when it came to people's motives. But what if Ro actually did know where the dragons lived?

"Can you really find her?" she asked him.

"Jane, no," Maryanne said, but Jane focused on Ro.

He gazed straight back. "I swear on every rowan tree in the forest, I will try to find her and bring her home to you."

Jane dipped her head. "Thank you. But I'm going too."

Chapter 4

"YOU CAN'T REALLY MEAN TO GO," Maryanne said as Jane dug through her clothing chest for the single pair of trousers she owned. Dresses were more comfortable than the heavy pants, but if she was going to be hiking in the mountains, wearing trousers seemed smart.

"What's the alternative?" Jane asked. "If he goes alone, he might never come back. I'll go mad waiting and wondering."

"It's better than being killed by a wicked fairy in the wilderness."

"Maryanne." Jane stopped digging to give Maryanne her sternest expression. "The man's not a killer. You can't judge him that harshly for merely being a fairy."

Maryanne leaned on the doorframe, crossing her arms. "Fine. It's better than being *seduced* by an *evasive* fairy in the wilderness."

Jane laughed sharply. "He's not interested in seducing me. I practically threw myself on him at the smithy, and he looked horrified."

"Now you know what he is, that's probably a relief."

Jane didn't reply.

"I still don't see why you can't go with peacekeepers."

"Go where? They have no idea where the dragon is. You know a fairy will be better at finding it. Ro is the best option."

"Unless he kidnaps you," Maryanne muttered.

Would he? Was he luring her into the forest with his offer

to help her find Elle, only to . . . do what? Jane squelched the niggling doubt and turned back to the clothing. She didn't have a choice.

"You can't trust them," Maryanne said. "I know they're not all bad. But it's been only a turn of the seasons since they threw out their awful queen. How much can they have changed? We trusted them once and look what happened."

Jane kept digging.

"You have to admit," Maryanne went on, "it's strange he was living in the village and apprenticing with the blacksmith."

"Maybe the fairies have metalwork fences they need fixed and no one knew how to do it."

"Fairies don't even like metal."

"Maybe human goods are growing on them. Besides, I think that's a myth about metal."

"Ask him what he was doing here."

"I will." Jane pulled out the trousers, pushing the dresses and fabric that spilled out of the wooden chest along with them back in. "I'm sure we'll have plenty of time to get to know each other."

"And at the first sign of anything odd, you run."

Jane held up the clothing. The pants were shorter than she remembered, a style that ended mid-calf, but they'd be warmer and easier to move in than a dress. She folded them and sat back on her heels, giving Maryanne her full attention. "Don't fret. You heard him swear to help me. You know they can't say things like that unless they mean it."

Maryanne frowned. "Rowan trees probably don't even grow in the forests around here," she grumbled.

But Maryanne's argument was losing steam. Jane shook her head and smiled.

"Maybe his name's not even Rowan," Maryanne continued, "and he was tricking us with that 'oath.' Maybe Ro is short for . . . for Ro-dicchio."

"*Rah*-dicchio?"

Maryanne shrugged. "Ro, rah."

Jane laughed. "Fairies don't name their children after vegetables!"

"Rosemary, then."

Jane stood and slipped her arms around Maryanne. "He won't harm me. You know if he did, his new queen would have him locked up in those caverns."

Maryanne melted in Jane's arms. After Rose had rescued the children last spring, the fairies had overthrown their cruel queen and elected Rose in her place. If there was any way to win Maryanne over to accepting fairies, that way was through Rose. Since they first met her a turn of the seasons ago, they'd seen her a few times. She was a quiet person who kept out of the public view, but Jane and the other women who'd lived in the house when Rose had stayed with them all loved and trusted her.

Maryanne squeezed Jane back and let go. "That's a good idea," she said.

"What's a good idea?"

"I'm sending a message straight to Rose to ask about this Rowan fellow. She'll know if he can be trusted, and if anything's amiss, she'll send fairies into the wilderness after you."

"Maybe she'll send them anyway," Jane said. "I don't know how the two of us are going to find a dragon."

"I'll send a message to Ladi in tomorrow's mail. And Ladi has that fairy friend who can send a bird to Rose, or whatever they do."

"Thanks, Maryanne. If he tries to seduce me, I'll hold out for a rescue."

"Don't you dare fall for him."

"I told you, he's not interested."

"But *you* were. He might change his mind once you're out in a forest alone and sleeping side by side under the stars."

"I doubt it."

"Then promise. Promise you won't fall in love with him."

"Fine," Jane said to end the conversation. "I promise."

Jane dressed in the trousers along with suspenders to hold them up and a plain linen shirt. She finished packing her satchel with a few items and carried it down the stairs to the kitchen. Maryanne had packed sandwiches for her, along with dried fruits and nuts and a packet of flat crackers that would last a few days, so she added the food to her bag along with a drinking gourd. She found the children gathered quietly in the front hall.

"I'm going to find Elle," she told them, imbuing her words with a confidence she didn't feel. She took the wool coat off its hook. If she and Ro were going into the mountains, she might need it, whereas Maryanne would be fine without it this spring. She draped it over her satchel.

"Is she all right?" Amare whispered.

"I think so," Jane said. "The blacksmith's apprentice knows about dragons and he says she is."

"She was smiling," Deka said as she had earlier. "She was happy when it picked her up."

Jane held back the shudder that wove through her at the image of the dragon's claws closing around Elle. Was Ro right? Were dragons truly harmless? How could she trust what he said? She forced a smile at the children before grabbing a scarf and leaving.

Everyone was outside, either watching the sky or watching Jane walk by. They must've seen where the dragon landed and known something was up, but they hung back on their porches. Did they know the dragon had taken Elle and that the blacksmith's apprentice had been a fairy in disguise? Well, they'd find out now. They'd probably think she was reckless to go after the dragon. Or to go off with a fairy. But no, most villagers didn't have the history with fairies that she and Maryanne had, and so they got along with them fine. Maybe the master blacksmith had even known Ro was a fairy.

But why had he hidden the color of his eyes, the sure sign of a fairy?

No one was trying to stop her from going, anyway. The neighbors nodded from their porches and the crowd in the village square parted before her. A wagon hitched to a tired-looking horse waited in the center, and Ro stood alongside the driver, one of the local farmers. The bed of the wagon was piled with the last of the winter cabbages and crates of spring carrots.

Someone tugged on her pant leg. Shamus, one of the more rambunctious children in the village, was beside her.

"Was it really a dragon?" he asked with wide eyes.

"Yes, but there's no reason to—"

"Wow," he whispered, letting go of her. "Can I come with you to see it?"

Before Jane could answer, his mother broke through the crowd and hauled him away.

Ro came up beside her and led her to the back of the wagon. She placed her satchel in and sat on the board before scooching back and pulling her legs up. The wagon had enough room for her and Ro, and she could lean on the crates. He climbed in after her, holding a large pack with straps.

People called out good wishes as the wagon jerked into motion and trundled out of the square.

She had seated herself tilted toward Ro, whereas he'd sat facing straight backward. From the side, his long hair hid his eyes. He wore the same clothes he'd had on earlier and his feet were bare, tucked in front of him with his ankles crossed. Fairies weren't accustomed to wearing shoes. The soles of their feet grew tough enough to walk barefoot in the forest. He must have put shoes on in the smithy to hide his identity. Or maybe a smithy was dangerous enough that even a fairy would wear shoes there.

She shifted her bottom so she also faced backward. Much of the crowd had drifted away. The wagon continued at its sluggish pace and her shoulders twitched with a longing to climb over the cabbages and slap the reins on the poor horse's back.

"Do you really think Elle is safe?" she asked.

"Yes."

Ro's assurance was all she had. She forced her shoulders to relax. "We could walk faster than this," she muttered.

"We'll make it to the crossroads by nightfall."

She waited.

"We wouldn't start up the mountain road until morning anyway. It's better to save our energy while we can."

The mountain road led west from the crossroads. Jane had passed it last moon when she'd accompanied Liza to her new home in Knotty Knob. It had been overgrown and menacing. And Elle was up it somewhere.

"But Elle will be alone overnight."

Ro sighed quietly. "The dragon won't let anything harm her."

The dragon. Right.

Jane leaned against the crates and watched the village square recede behind the wagon. Soon the waving stopped and only Shamus watched them roll away. They passed the cottages along the northern road, with fields spread out to the edge of the forest. The cottages dwindled in number and the trees came closer.

She had to think about something other than Elle or this slow-rolling pace would make her scream or smash something. How was Liza doing? She hadn't replied to any of Jane's three letters. Jane continually noticed Liza's absence in the house. Of all the friends she'd made since leaving her home and surviving the fairy love spell, Liza was the one who understood her. Liza had understood her longing to have Cedric back, and her inability to let go of the romance of fairy princes and magic, even as the awfulness of what the fairies had done sank in. For many seasons after his betrayal, Jane had imagined Cedric coming to find her and bringing their child, confessing he truly loved her and had never stopped loving her, that he'd been locked away by his mother the queen and physically unable to come back to Jane.

But gradually, the daydream had soured. Liza had moved on, courting a farmer from Knotty Knob who'd come through Woods Rest the previous autumn. After six moons of courting, Jane had traveled with Liza to visit his home—and to ease her own worries that he'd turn out to be another swindler preying on her friend—and Liza had bonded with him and moved to Knotty Knob, leaving Jane alone in Woods Rest. Maryanne had whatever she had with Wells—some sort of mutual agreement involving a lot of tumbling—and Jane had nothing. Unless she counted her failed attempts to flirt with every new man who came to the village.

Of course, she had Elle. And they were going to find her and bring her home. But Elle was a child, not a friend her own age she could really talk to.

She stole a glance at Ro. He sat rigidly, not slumped against the crates like her, and he could have been sleeping for all the noise he made.

"Which name do you prefer?" she asked. "Ro or Rowan?"

"Rowan," he said without turning.

He clearly didn't want to talk to her, but they were going to be stuck together for days, if not longer. She couldn't tolerate things between them being awkward the whole time. Would talking make it more or less awkward?

"Why did you use a nickname?" she asked.

"I didn't."

Jane blushed. It was true—Master Smith had been the one to call him Ro, and Rowan hadn't been present to correct him. She was making this more awkward with every breath.

"Then why did you hide your eyes?" she asked. He couldn't shift the blame for *that*.

"It's easier if no one knows."

"How so?"

He exhaled and finally looked her way. "Maryanne is uneasy around fairies," he said. "I've no wish to upset her."

Jane focused on her hands in her lap. After a moment, she said quietly, "Don't mind Maryanne. She was badly hurt. I know it's not your fault."

Another awkward silence followed, interrupted only by the creaking of the wheels on the packed dirt road and the occasional snort of the horse. The grasses alongside the road waved in a slow breeze, and the sun shone in the west over the treetops. As they entered the edge of the forest, leaves rustled and Jane inhaled the cooler air and the pungent scent of growing things. She shifted her seat to stop her bottom from going numb and found herself facing Rowan again.

"How are we going to find the dragon?" Jane asked.

"We're going to visit another dragon and ask directions."

What in the skies? Jane studied his profile, waiting.

Rowan didn't elaborate.

"Another dragon?" she prodded.

"I know the way to his den. He may be able to tell us who has Elle."

"How do you know a dragon?"

"It's a long story."

"We've got time."

"It's a long, *personal* story."

"Fine." Jane rested her cheek against the crate of carrots. She tried to stay quiet. The wagon wheel creaked, once, twice as it rolled. A dozen times. "So you can talk to animals?"

"Just dragons."

"You can't do birds and things like Prince Dustan?"

"Not well."

"I thought all fairies could do that."

Silence.

A worry stirred in Jane's mind. "What about Elle?" she asked.

"If she possesses this fire magic, she can talk to the dragon, right?" If Elle couldn't communicate, how would the dragon know if she was hurt or needed something?

Rowan's shoulders tensed. "I don't know."

"But if Elle was able to 'call' the dragon, she must be able to speak with it."

He inhaled deeply and let it out. "No one knows how the bond works. Fairies with fire magic used to come along once or twice in a generation, and each time, a dragon would show up to teach them how to use it. But it's been decades since anyone was taught."

"Why?"

"Because of the queen." He obviously didn't mean Rose. "She wouldn't let anyone go, even when the supply of fire powder ran low. We didn't know if the dragons would come back."

He turned to her at last, tucking a long strand of hair behind his ear. "Elle is young to be a fire apprentice. After all the winters the dragons were ignored, hers must have been excited to find her. It won't matter if they can't communicate perfectly. The dragon will take care of her."

"What will happen if we don't find them?"

"She'd finish her apprenticeship and the dragon would bring her home."

"How long would it be?"

"Maybe a season or two?"

Jane couldn't believe what she was about to say. "Do you think we're wrong to take her back?"

He blinked at her before shaking his head. "I'm sure she's safe. But we should check on her. It might be better to wait until she is older." He continued quietly. "Unless you don't want her to learn the magic at all."

Did she have a choice? Now that she was faced with it, the thought of Elle using magic unsettled her. But if Elle had truly called the dragon . . . didn't it show that Elle wanted this? She was only three, too young to make such a decision. But Jane didn't want to hold her back if she had a skill she loved and could excel at. She didn't want Elle ending up like her—drifting through life with no skills and no purpose, at least not beyond raising Elle.

"What exactly would she learn to do?"

"With fire magic, someone can touch flames without harm."

"You mean she can't burn?"

"No, she can be hurt by fire. But she can use the magic to control it. If a tree were on fire, a fairy trained in fire magic might be able to absorb the flames and save the tree."

"How do they make the fire powder?" Jane had seen Cedric, no, not Cedric, Larch use it many times, sprinkling it onto a single log that would burst into flame and burn for days in the hearth without being consumed.

"The fairy works together with the dragon. They absorb the dragon's fire and put it into something that can be carried and used easily—usually sand."

Dragon fire. Jane had forgotten all about the fact that dragons were supposed to breathe fire. What if it burned up Elle by accident?

"If it's been decades since a dragon came," Jane said, "how do the fairies still have fire powder?"

"We're almost out of it."

Jane furrowed her brow. If the fairies wanted more of the stuff, they might try to use Elle to get it.

"The last fire magic user is very old," Rowan continued. "She has offered to try to call a dragon and return to the mountains to work, but it would be a hard journey for her."

"Maybe the fairies should learn to build fires with firewood," Jane murmured.

"They know how. They don't like all the healthy trees it kills."

Jane glared at him but he wasn't regarding her.

Self-righteous fairies with their we-do-everything-better mentality. She shifted her seat again, away from Rowan, and leaned her legs against the far side of the wagon. Leaning back on the crates, she held up her bangs and let the cooler, shady air brush her skin.

They passed deeper into the forest with trees thick on either side and only a narrow strip of sky overhead. The sky remained blue but the forest was dark. The sun would set soon, and Elle was out in the mountains all alone. Well, all alone with a dragon. Would she be frightened? Jane shivered and tried not to think of it.

"Why do you call her Elle?"

Jane startled. Now he wanted to talk? She surveyed the woods to gain a moment before she spoke. She'd had enough thoughts of Larch today. But she wanted Rowan to talk to her, so . . .

"We named her Bluebell when she was born. But when Rose brought her back to me, Maryanne insisted we give the children new names. I chose Murielle but it never felt right to me. Elle loves flowers, and one time in the forest, she ran ahead and led me to a patch of bluebells. I think it's supposed to be her name. I didn't want to upset Maryanne, though, so I started calling her Elle. It could be short for either name."

Rowan had spoken voluntarily. Could she ask him more questions? What other fairy magic could he do, if he couldn't communicate with animals? He could change his eye color—could he change his whole appearance? Could he make enchanted objects using his magic, like the nearly invisible thread made of spider silk Rose had told her about? And why had he wanted to leave the fairy village and learn blacksmithing?

But she remembered his recent words about the dragon—"a long, *personal* story"—and her conversation faltered. Instead she asked, "Where will we sleep at the crossroads?"

"Do you have any coins?"

Jane shook her head. "I didn't like to take them when we always need things for the children."

Did he have coins? Fairies could always find a way to earn some using their magic to help humans. Did he plan to stay at the inn near the crossroads? Would he pay for a room for her? What if the inn had only one room available?

What if it had only one bed?

Rowan flicked his hair off his face. "I guess we'll be sleeping in the hayloft then."

Chapter 5

THE INNKEEPER GRINNED AT JANE across the counter. "My hay-loft's getting more action than I am." Jane's face heated like her cheeks were on fire. The innkeeper had offered the inn's stable to them at no charge, which was apparently common these days—although the innkeeper made it sound like travelers were using the hayloft for a tumble instead of a night's rest.

"Thank you for letting us stay," Rowan said in his low voice. Jane tilted her head, watching him use that seductive tone on the innkeeper. Earlier she had half-jokingly wondered if he cast a spell simply by speaking to her, using that voice to convince her to be reckless and travel with him. But he wouldn't do the same to the innkeeper.

Unless he was using a spell to get them a free place to stay.

"Take the lantern," the innkeeper said, gesturing to a lamp flickering on the counter, "and hang it inside the stable door. It'll give you enough light to get settled and I'll come by and get it in a bit."

Rowan thanked her again and lifted the lantern off the count-er. He wore his pack over one shoulder. Each time he moved it, it made odd clinking noises. Jane tried not to think about chains.

Jane picked up her own bag and followed him out the door. Dusk had fallen and moved on to darkness even before their wag-on ride had rolled to a stop in the center of the crossroads. The outpost looked exactly the same as it had when she and Liza had come through last moon. A handful of houses stood at the intersection, along with a newly built general store with a light inside, showing mostly bare shelves. The inn had been here longer and included a small dining room where a few customers drank ale and played music.

As she followed Rowan off the porch, she peered down the road heading west, the one they would take up into the mountains tomorrow. Beyond the light from the store and a lantern hanging over the inn's porch was a wall of solid black. A few night insects called, but the forest seemed to be sleeping. Until an owl screeched and Jane startled and tripped. And Rowan—suddenly facing back toward her—put out a hand to catch her. She blushed again.

She muttered thanks and watched where she was stepping. Around the side of the inn, a path wide enough for a wagon led to the back with the outhouse and pump and the stable. The lights of the outpost faded to only their lantern, and she trailed her fingertips along the rough wooden boards of the inn's wall to keep herself steady. In spite of the relative silence out front, the backyard was even quieter without the noise filtering out of the dining room. Once the sunlight had gone, the temperature had dropped, but hay was supposed to be warm so hopefully they'd be able to sleep.

The stable was a long wooden structure on the far side of the grassy yard from the inn and outhouse. Woods towered behind the building. The lantern illuminated a solid wall of wide vertical boards until Rowan scanned with the light and found a door. He lifted the lantern onto the hook inside and stepped all the way in.

Was she being reckless? Sleeping in a hayloft with someone she barely knew—a male someone, and a fairy? But Rowan didn't feel threatening, in spite of the fact that he might be carrying a pack full of chains. His actions today didn't suggest he'd make advances toward her tonight. And truly, a hayloft wasn't *that* romantic. It was probably an itchy place to sleep. Jane followed him, leaving the door ajar so the innkeeper would have a sliver of light to see by.

Daytime warmth still hovered in the stable and the musty smell of hay and animal dung filled her nostrils. A lone horse snuffled in the stall beside the entrance. A large sliding door on the left would open to allow a wagon into the space. The center floor was empty, with a few barrels pushed up against the back wall, and deep shadows filled the empty stalls.

A ladder down the end on the right led up into the center of the loft. To the sides, in the dim light that reached that far, lumpy bales of hay were stacked less than halfway to the rafters now winter had passed, but the entrance by the top of the ladder was clear. Jane moved her satchel strap across her chest to wear the bag on her back and followed Rowan through the stable and up the ladder.

Someone had obviously slept in the place before. While most of the hay was baled, the area against the back wall had a thick layer of loose hay across the floor. Rowan headed straight back into the shadows. Jane lingered in the light. But once the innkeeper retrieved the lantern, pitch darkness would fill the stable, so what were a few shadows? If mice or birds nested in the hay, she'd have to face them sometime. She sighed and followed him.

He dropped his pack to the floor with a clang. "Are you tired?"

The moment he said it, Jane yawned.

"I have things to tell you but if you're too tired I can wait till morning."

If she had been tired, she wasn't now. "I'm not too tired."

"Sit," he said quietly.

She slid her satchel over her head and knelt in the hay opposite Rowan. Her nose twitched from the dusty air, but the stable was dry and having shelter was comforting. Who knew where they'd be tomorrow night.

She glanced across at Rowan. He'd seated himself with his legs crossed and rested his elbows on his knees. He bit his thumbnail before stopping himself and lowering his hand, which he studied, one thumb rubbing over the other. He *did* have a scar there, at the base of his thumb—a dark slash that couldn't be merely a callus. His hair had fallen forward and hid his face. Until he looked up and caught her staring at him.

She shifted onto her bottom and tucked her legs beneath her, trying and failing to act calm. "What did you want to tell me?" she asked, and it came out overly perky.

Rowan sat up, tugging on his shirt neckline. "I imagine it's hard for you to trust a fairy," he said, watching the floor. His voice was barely audible. "I want you to trust me."

What could she say to that?

"I'm sorry I hid what I was when I came to your village."

Something about the way he said "your village" prickled at Jane's shoulders. As if he'd come there . . . for her.

"I don't want to have secrets."

Jane barely breathed as she waited for him to continue.

"I have things to tell you," he repeated. "If they make you want to go home, I'll find a ride for you in the morning and I'll go into the mountains alone and find Elle."

Dread followed the tingles up her shoulders and down her chest.

He ran a hand through his hair. "I know Larch," he murmured, avoiding her face.

The name was jarring but not surprising. "He was the queen's son," Jane said. "I imagine all the fairies know him."

"We were close as children."

"You were friends?"

He nodded.

"Are you still?"

Rowan hesitated. "I no longer respect him."

"Is he living nearby?" Jane asked, herself hesitating. "I always wondered . . ."

"He's in the forest near Woodglen."

That was where Rose lived. Jane had never wanted to visit Rose's new home because of a deep-down apprehension of seeing Larch again. And she would never take Elle back there, near the place where she'd been imprisoned. Although Rose didn't live in the underground caverns where Elle had lived. She had a treehouse out in the forest. Which sounded rather nice, except Larch might be nearby.

Jane had never asked Rose what happened to Larch after the fairies rejected his mother as their queen. But she'd assumed he might live in their forest enclave. Still, having it confirmed that he lived a day's ride from her unsettled her. He'd seemed worlds away since he'd abandoned her.

She couldn't stop herself from asking, "Was he ever trapped?"

Rowan's brow furrowed.

"I mean, was Larch ever imprisoned by the fairy queen the way Prince Dustan was?"

"No," Rowan whispered. He clasped his hands together again and the fingers of one rubbed the other. "He was always free to go."

Her daydreams about "Cedric" returning to her, telling her he'd wanted to be with her all along . . . They never would have come true. He'd been free the whole time but he hadn't wanted to see her.

Rowan's expression had darkened. His lips parted as if he might speak but then closed.

"For a long time I hoped I could see him again." She ran her finger along her leg, along the seam in her trousers. "It doesn't matter now. I never want to see him again."

After a pause, Rowan said, "There's something more."

She waited.

He paused to take a deep breath, almost silently but so slowly she knew he was bracing himself to speak. He kept his face down. "When we were boys, I did something that upset the queen. She would have punished me but Larch intervened. I always felt I owed him everything. He took advantage of my gratitude. I did everything he asked, season after season. When the queen ordered him to sire a child for her, I helped him."

Jane's insides twisted, and the sandwich she'd eaten on the wagon ride threatened to come back up. She drew deep breaths, trying to stay calm.

"How?"

Rowan's knuckles were white, with one hand fisted over the other. "Larch was never adept at magic. His lack of skills embarrassed him and he hid it. When he needed to use magic, I'd cover for him." He licked his lips. "I'm not especially skilled at magic either, but I practiced making potions. Most of the work of making a potion is in the ingredients and method and only a little magic is needed. I could sometimes come up with a potion Larch could use in place of his own magic."

Dread crawled over Jane, paralyzing her in front of him.

He stayed hunched over but looked up at last. "Larch wasn't strong enough to cast a love spell, not like the one Dustan used on Rose. He was petrified of failing the queen. And he didn't think he'd be able to trick a human woman into lying with him, and staying with him, without magic."

Jane's head was ringing and her body curled in. Rowan's forehead crinkled and his lips parted. He didn't continue and she didn't want to hear what he would say, but watching the guilt in his eyes was worse.

"Go on," she whispered, wrapping her arms around herself.

"I made the potion Larch used on you. He put it in a drink he gave you. I'm sorry. I wish I had never helped him."

Jane hugged herself, unable to think a coherent thought. Larch. His love spell—a potion. He'd given her wine. He'd stolen Elle from her.

She hadn't wanted a child. She hadn't been ready and she wasn't a very capable mother—not like Maryanne, always playing with the lot of them. Jane liked it when Elle occupied herself talking to flowers, and she could have a moment's peace. And look what had happened—her little girl—kidnapped by a dragon. She was a horrible mother.

But she wouldn't give up Elle. She had gotten Elle back. And as much as they had suffered being apart, if Rowan hadn't made that potion, she wouldn't have Elle.

Rowan sat frozen and silent, but the flare of his nostrils as he breathed gave away his tension. She forced her own breath in and out until she could sit up straighter and focus on him.

"Don't be sorry for me," she said. "I wouldn't change it, not now."

He stayed rigid but bowed his head. "Do you want to ask me anything?"

After how reticent he'd been all day, offering an open invitation to answer her questions must be difficult for him. She didn't want to pry into his personal life. But he had walked into hers.

"Why did you come to Woods Rest?" she asked.

"At first I was curious. And I wanted to make amends."

"Curious about . . . ?"

"About you." He *had* come for her. Suddenly Jane was glad he kept his head bowed. "I learned where you lived after Rose came to the caverns," he continued. "So once the fairies were free to go, I thought maybe if I saw you and Elle, saw that you were happy, I'd feel less guilty for the part I played in deceiving you."

"And making amends?" she asked.

"I thought if I lived in the village, I could keep an eye on you and Elle and offer help if you needed it. I didn't want to get close to you, just to be nearby. But I didn't think you'd be comfortable with a fairy living in the village so I hid what I was."

"Why now, though? It's been a whole turn of the seasons since you were freed. Did you honestly happen to show up the day Elle gets kidnapped by a dragon?"

"No. I mean, the dragon was a coincidence, yes. But no, I didn't just show up." He rubbed a hand on the back of his neck. Jane had uncurled enough to watch him. He exhaled and looked up and into her eyes.

"I came to Woods Rest late last summer. I had enough magical ability to change my face slightly and lighten my hair. I got an apprenticeship . . . with the chairmaker."

Jane's jaw dropped. "But . . . You . . ."

He hurried on. "When I met you, I tried to be friendly only because I didn't want to be rude. But you kept coming by to visit me and I didn't know how to stop you. It would have been wrong to become friends with you when you didn't know who I was." The words rushed out and color rose in his cheeks. "When you asked me to spend time with you, I panicked. It wouldn't have been right. I was only in Woods Rest to help and I'd been deceiving you. So I left."

"That was you?" Jane said, her mind struggling to catch up.

"Yes. As was the tinsmith's apprentice last winter."

Jane's mouth fell open.

"I thought I'd do better that time. I made myself appear menacing, and every time I encountered you, I tried to be rude. I thought it was working."

"It wasn't his personality I was attracted to," Jane muttered. "So why did you return again? The tinsmith rescued Elle from the mill pond. And you've had two seasons to see that Elle and I are . . . fine." She'd planned to say they were happy, but at the last moment it had seemed like Rowan would know she was lying.

Rowan rubbed his hand across his jaw. "I don't have much magical skill. I have no purpose at the fairy enclave, not like the other fairies. But in Woods Rest I could make a difference. I could play a small role in caring for the children Queen Oleander harmed, even if I played that role without anyone knowing."

When Jane didn't reply, he continued. "I had a better plan this time. I was going to tell you I had a sweetheart in another village. That way I could live in Woods Rest without risking feelings developing between us—or between me and any of the other villagers.”

“I’m afraid the early gossip was mostly to do with your appearance,” Jane said, “not your eligibility.”

“I didn’t realize word would get around so fast that a new person was in town. You startled me when you arrived this morning and I forgot my story. I came after you to tell you.”

Jane pushed a strand of hay across the floorboards. He *knew* she had gone to the smithy to check him out. “You must think I’m pathetic.”

“I don’t think that. But I’m sorry if I made things worse for you.”

After a moment, Jane shrugged, remembering the past few seasons and how life had . . . *brightened* a little for the first time. “You made life more interesting at least.” She realized where her thoughts were going and her face heated. All those stolen moments in the linen closet after seeing him in the village. That had been *Rowan* she’d been fantasizing about. She wished she could groan aloud.

And now Rowan was watching her think about how she had fantasized about him. She forced her thoughts to the present. “Well, until the part where I propositioned you and you rejected me.”

Rowan hung his head. “It wasn’t you. Truly.”

He’d been hanging around the village on and off for almost a full turn of the seasons. She tried to recall the two apprentices but remembering their faces was difficult—she kept seeing Rowan’s instead. But she remembered perfectly how the tinsmith’s apprentice had pulled Elle from the pond. And the chairmaker’s apprentice . . .

“All those holes in your socks?” she said.

Rowan rubbed the back of his neck again. “You said no one needed mending and your savings were running low.”

“We couldn’t imagine how you were wearing them out so fast.”

She recalled the past autumn and winter. What else could she remember? "Wait—did you leave a sack of coins by the stone wall in the meadow behind our house?"

He nodded, staring out into the darkness of the stable.

Jane had already embarrassed herself in front of Rowan earlier that day at the smithy. She'd asked him to walk with her, with her intentions—tumbling him in the fields—plastered across her face. To think she'd also propositioned him as the chairmaker *and* as the tinsmith, the tinsmith who'd been *rude* to her, was downright mortifying.

And they had a past connection thanks to Larch. Rowan had helped Larch seduce her. The reminder brought the ringing back to her ears and left her breathless again.

This, all of this, definitely counted as odd. Maryanne would want her to return home immediately. Maybe she *should* go home and let Rowan find Elle on his own. He'd probably travel faster without her. She had no reason to think he'd take Elle and run. Unless he took her to use her for her magical abilities?

But Elle hadn't yet learned to use her magic. And Rowan snatching someone's child? After how he'd spoken about Larch just now? Unlikely.

But what if Elle was scared of him? How would Elle know leaving with him was safe if Jane didn't go too?

Jane shook her head. "I can't think straight. Can we sleep and talk more in the morning?"

"Yes, of course."

Rowan uncrossed his legs and reached for his pack. As the contents clinked and shifted, he pulled out a thick blanket. The edges of the blanket sparkled in the dim light. It must be some fairy thing, maybe magical thread to hold it together. Jane found her own blanket and moved a few paces away on the hay, leaving the warm spot where she'd sat. She lay down on her coat and stretched the blanket over herself as Rowan did the same. They both lay on their backs, staring overhead.

A minute later, someone entered the barn with scuffling foot-steps. The shadows lurched as the lantern was taken off the hook. The light faded to blackness and the door banged closed.

Jane sighed out the tension in her shoulders, sinking into the hay and willing it to warm up. The day had been warm with sun. But the cold of winter hadn't completely gone, and a chill draft crept into the stable. Without sunlight to warm them, the boards beneath her held the coolness of the past few moons. Rowan rustled in the hay nearby.

Jane yawned. She couldn't see a thing so she closed her eyes. She rolled onto her side and pulled her thin blanket tighter. She'd go to sleep and in the morning she'd figure out what to do.

But she couldn't stop seeing Rowan the way he'd been as he confessed his secrets to her: hunched over as he wrung his hands and apologized. Her thoughts grew muddy as she yawned again.

"I would have fallen for Larch regardless of the potion," she said into the quiet stable. "It wouldn't have mattered if you hadn't helped him. He'd have been able to trick me regardless."

Rowan didn't reply.

Sleep came but not for long. The air grew colder with the night and while her body warmed the hay, her blanket wasn't enough to warm her top side. She should burrow into the hay but she wasn't awake enough to make the effort. She rolled over, warming her cold half in the hay as the heat escaped her warm side. Finally it worked and her body was warm all over. With streams of moon-light shining through the cracks of the barn wall, she sank into unbroken sleep.

Jane felt the pale, warm sunlight on her face. She peeked open an eye. Dust motes drifted in the narrow beams shining onto the hay. Jane was so delightfully warm. Across the floor, Rowan's breathing was steady with sleep.

She could go home and Rowan would find Elle. Doing so seemed like a big commitment from him, regardless of all he'd said about assuaging his guilt and having a purpose. But on the other hand, he really did seem like Elle's best chance. How many other fairies had a dragon they could visit to ask for directions? Rowan was the best person to do this.

But she didn't want to go home. What she'd said to Maryanne was true—she'd go mad with waiting if she let Rowan travel on alone. She should be with him when he found Elle in case Elle needed comforting. Besides, how could she make the best decision for Elle without seeing this dragon and where it had taken her?

But could she trust Rowan? Her instincts were telling her yes. He'd admitted to his role in Larch's deception. He seemed truly sorry. And Rose had told her how all the fairies had been lied to by the old queen. They'd been told humans were barely more intelligent than animals, and that human women didn't care about their young any more than a housecat did. And they had never spent time with humans to learn any differently. The younger fairies had grown up with those misguided beliefs. No one knew any better until Dustan fell for Rose, realized the truth, and spoke up about it.

But she always trusted people when she shouldn't.

Well if she shouldn't trust Rowan, then she shouldn't trust him with Elle, which meant she should go with him anyway. She stretched and relaxed her body and rolled onto her back. Something warm and smooth rubbed against her chin. Jane reached for it.

Something dark was woven into the threads of the blanket. It was the size of a coin and shiny like the inside of a seashell but black, and when her thumb rubbed over it, it radiated warmth. More of the shiny chips lined the edge of the blanket.

This wasn't her blanket; hers was underneath it. The top one was Rowan's.

She caught her breath and listened. He still breathed evenly as if he were sleeping. She leaned slowly up until she could peek at him over her bed of hay. His dark lashes rested on his cheeks, his face exposed but the rest of him buried in the hay. She lay back, glad he'd kept himself warm.

She pulled his blanket up over her chin. And without thinking, she pulled it farther and sniffed it. It smelled comforting like warm clothing and Mouser's fur. She snuggled beneath it to wait for him to wake.

Chapter 6

ROWAN WOKE SOON AFTER THE sun rose, casting glaring beams of light into the hayloft. As he stirred, Jane sat up. Only then she was sitting, watching him yawn and rub the sleep from his eyes as bits of hay stuck to his shirtsleeves. Embarrassed to be staring, she gathered up the two blankets and focused on folding them and stashing hers in her bag as Rowan emerged from the hay. When he murmured a good morning, she mumbled out a thank you and handed him his folded blanket.

She awkwardly told him she wanted to continue on the journey and he didn't try to dissuade her but merely nodded. They ate the last of Maryanne's sandwiches before Jane tied her hair up and followed Rowan down from the loft.

The morning was bright and cold as they trudged to the front of the inn. The road leading west into the mountains looked inhospitable, with its rutted surface and overgrown borders, but in the early sunshine it no longer seemed menacing. But regardless, if Elle was up that road, Jane was going up it, too.

Rowan gave one glance back at her and set out across the Forest Road and onto the smaller byway. A piece of straw clung to the back of his head and she reached out to pluck it off but stopped herself. She couldn't go touching his hair without permission. The straw fluttered as she followed him along the righthand track of the road, which was flatter and drier than the muddy left side. The motion of walking and the breeze shook it loose at last and it drifted off him and toward the ground, missing her fingers by a smidge as she reached for it.

She studied the back of Rowan's head. His hair fell in soft locks with a gentle curl. But they were cut short at the bottom. Jane shook her head and scanned the forest towering over them on both sides. The lefthand track dried enough to walk on so she hopped over to that side and hurried forward to walk beside Rowan. He didn't react.

She kept pace with him for a few minutes. The road stayed flat and the two tracks were more open than they'd appeared from the crossroads. All around were leafy trees and a chorus of birds sang as the sun pierced through the canopy. The forest smell was damp and rich with the spring scent of new growth pushing up from the earth.

Occasionally a branch blocked the road and Rowan would reach to toss it aside or kick it out of the way. As a new one appeared Jane hurried forward to move it. "Why doesn't anyone maintain this road?" she asked as they walked past.

"They do."

She waited. When he didn't continue, she said, "Really?"

"The ore for the smithy comes this way. As long as the wagon can get through it's good enough for the humans."

"What about the fairies?"

"They don't need a road."

Right. The sanctimonious fairies would never clear so many trees and disturb the wildlife with a road. But they had no problem using the roads the humans built.

"Do the fairies come this way in their . . . pursuits?"

"Sometimes."

Jane sighed and gave up trying to engage with him. "Master Smith said his shipment was late," she muttered. "Now I can see why."

Rowan kept walking.

As another patch of mud appeared on the lefthand track, Jane fell in behind Rowan. Words kept bubbling to her lips and she forced them back. Rowan was so silent it seemed likely her incessant talking would annoy him. But talking was in her nature. Especially when she was nervous. The sun was rising—soon it would be a full day since the dragon had taken Elle. Where had she slept? What had she been eating?

To stop herself from fretting over Elle or talking to Rowan, Jane peered into the surrounding forest. The trees were in full leaf, green and thick, so she couldn't see too far in among them. Birds called and flitted between the branches. The leaf litter rustled as squirrels searched for food. A slight breeze stirred the topmost branches but the air around her was still. But the road they trekked along was shaded and would be for most of the day, given the narrow strip of sky overhead, so hopefully she'd stay cool.

The land had appeared flat when they set out, but they crossed a brook on a rough wooden bridge and the water flowed swiftly beneath them as it ran downhill. And her legs tired as the minutes passed.

"Thank you again for the blanket," Jane said.

Rowan grunted.

"The dark bits along the edge—they were warm?" she asked.

"They store the sun's heat."

"I assume magic is involved."

He didn't reply.

"Is that magic the same as the fire magic?"

He shook his head. "Sun magic is also rare. But it doesn't involve a dragon."

"Can you do it?"

"No."

"But you can change your appearance," she said.

"Only a little."

"When you were the chairmaker's apprentice, you looked completely different."

"Changing my face or hair is easy. I can't change my size. I can't become invisible."

Jane pressed her lips shut, thinking. "Dustan used a potion to change Rose's appearance. Couldn't you make one that would work on yourself?"

"I don't make potions anymore."

His tone warned her not to continue. He'd said he was gifted with potions, yet he'd stopped making them? Was it because of her and the love potion he'd made for Larch?

The road sloped more steeply uphill. Jane saved her breath for the effort of walking. She tried to pass the time by retelling herself her favorite stories. Not so much the fables and tales from her childhood, which seemed faded and phony, but the real-life tales of the people she knew.

Like the day Maryanne met Wells: She'd been making baskets for the villagers, and he'd come to the house to commission one. But everything he said sounded so sleazy she thought his request for "a basket to put my tools in" was a proposition for sex. Of course, they ended up tumbling anyway, after she'd whacked him over the head and called him a litany of nasty names. Wells was a bit of an oaf but if he made Maryanne happy, Jane could overlook it.

Rose's love story from last spring was her favorite. Dustan had seduced Rose with the help of a love spell. But unlike his brother Larch, Dustan had quickly realized Rose and the other humans were different from what he'd been led to believe. Instead of continuing with his seduction plan, he'd helped her escape from a tyrannical father and despicable fiancé and eventually freed her from the spell, believing he would lose her. But they'd found their way back to each other. Jane smiled, thinking of how Rose seemed to glow with happiness when she said Dustan's name.

Rowan's pace never slowed and Jane made sure to keep up with him. She'd insisted on coming and she didn't want him grouching about her slowing them down or resenting her. But skies, her feet were getting tired. And the road had more and more rocks embedded in it, poking up at all different heights, making the walk more treacherous. How did he walk on this road in his bare feet? His soles must be used to it. Her shoes rubbed against the backs of her heels but she didn't dare take them off. How long would someone have to walk barefoot to get used to it?

Hopefully whoever drove the wagon bringing ore down from the mine had a thick seat cushion.

As the sun cleared the treetops and shone down from the top of the sky, Rowan stepped off the road into the shade. Thank the skies. She'd been sweating from the climb even without the sun. Maybe it would pass over to the trees on the other side while they rested.

Under the trees, a soft carpet of pine needles spread over flat ground. Coming off the road, she could tell how steeply the road sloped by comparison to this wayside where the ground leveled off. A circle of rocks near the center contained the ashes of past cooking fires, and a smooth, old tree trunk alongside the firepit made a seat. A squirrel nosed around the ground but as they entered, it darted up the nearest tree.

Rowan strode to the firepit, lowered his bag onto the trunk, and sat.

"I have bread we can eat for lunch," he said, digging in his pack.

Jane sat beside him and put her hands together in her lap. She bit her lip as he pulled out a loaf wrapped in cloth, a wedge of cheese, and a short knife, and moved his pack to the ground. He lifted his eyes to regard her.

"I don't mind if you talk."

Her cheeks flamed hot but Rowan turned back to the bread as he opened the cloth. He cut a slice off the end.

"I don't have to talk," Jane squeaked out.

"I don't mind."

"I don't want to annoy you."

He started on the second slice. "I like it when you talk."

Jane's whole face burned, and her neck and breast and possibly her toes. He liked it when she talked? But he never responded! She leaned away from him so he wouldn't see her blushing and pretended to hunt in her bag for something but he only went on cutting slices of bread. She retrieved her water gourd and sat up. Rowan handed her a slice of bread with cheese.

"Are you actually a blacksmith?" she asked.

He shook his head as he worked on the cheese.

"But you know the basics."

"Someone showed me once."

"A human?"

"No, a fairy."

"Why did they show you?"

"I was younger. I needed to hit something."

Jane smiled. "I know that feeling." She took a bite of her bread and cheese.

He didn't reply.

"You had a forge? In the . . . the place where you all lived?" She was unsure how to describe the underground caverns in the forest where the fairies had lived under the old queen. Rose said many of the fairies had felt imprisoned there. The word "village" seemed too nice.

"Not a proper smithy. A makeshift one."

"How did it work?"

He blinked a few times, staring off. "We built the fire in a basin of rocks with an opening in the bottom for the air to blow through. The caverns have several chimneys that allow smoke to escape—in the kitchens and a few other rooms. And we hammered against a slab of metal. It was loud."

"What did you make?"

"Hooks."

She waited.

"Fairies don't use metal objects much. If we needed a tool, we'd more likely get it from a human smith." He stopped cutting the bread and sat up to eat. "There's a proper forge in the forest now. It's in a rocky courtyard to the north of the gardens."

An idea came to her. "I wonder . . ."

Rowan lifted his eyebrows.

"Would using dragon fire affect the process?"

He tilted his head, questioning.

"I mean, blacksmiths use a coal fire because it burns slowly. So what would happen if you used a fire made with the fairies' fire powder? It burns so long." She frowned. "But I've only seen fire powder used on a stick of wood, and the fire is no longer dragon fire after it's put into sand, is it? Sorry, that was a stupid question."

"It's not." He studied the bread in his hand, nudging the slice of cheese into the center with a finger. Even that finger had a scar on it. "A fire made with fire powder burns more evenly than any human fire and lasts longer. And you can use coal as the fuel instead of wood. So yes, you could use it in a forge fire." He took another bite.

"Is the result better?"

He shook his head. "The result depends only on the smith."

Jane paused her questions to finish her first slice of bread and cheese.

Rowan laid a second slice on the cloth for her. "You could do it," he said as she picked it up. He'd said something similar yesterday in the smithy. Her inclination was to deny it again. But Rowan didn't speak like a flatterer. He spoke so little that the words he did say seemed true. And why would he say that about her if he didn't believe it?

"Everything Maryanne and I do for money—the mending and cheese-making and weaving baskets. I like those crafts but sometimes I want to smash something. When she stakes the tomatoes in the garden, she gets me to drive the stakes in. Sometimes she has to stop me because I'll keep going and bury the stake too far down or splinter it in two. We can barely get them out at the end of the season. I would love to try blacksmithing."

"Talk to Master Smith when you get back."

What did that mean? Wasn't he going to stay on as the apprentice? Jane frowned, but she didn't want to ask.

"Do you know Rose?" she asked instead. "I haven't seen her since last autumn."

"I spoke to her before I left the forest the first time."

Jane inhaled sharply. Had Rose known about Rowan coming to Woods Rest?

But he quickly added, "I didn't tell her exactly where I was going."

Her shoulders relaxed. "She might not have let you go if she'd known what you were up to. Telling her 'I'm going to stalk your friend Jane and make her mend all my holey socks' probably wouldn't have gone over well."

He met her gaze and for the briefest moment, his eyes narrowed at her teasing. He frowned and closed his eyes. "It was hardly stalking," he muttered.

Jane had the strangest sensation in her chest, a bubbly lightness. She thought about Larch, about the unforgiveable things he'd done, and their history felt distant. Like it had happened to someone else. It had always been so close to her before. "I suppose," Jane said, not believing the lighthearted words coming out, "that's true by fairy standards."

This time, Rowan stared so hard her confidence failed.

"I'm teasing?" she said.

He shook his head, continuing to watch her, but his face softened.

"I've never joked about it before—about fairies or what Larch did. I've never been able to think of what happened with Larch without becoming upset. I'm not sure what's happening to me that I'm making jokes about it."

"Maybe you're healing," he offered.

She frowned. "There's still plenty of me that's a mess."

"How so?"

She hadn't expected him to ask. She put her untouched bread back onto the cloth and smoothed her hands over her legs, thinking over her answer.

"I can't find the feelings I used to have," she said. "When I was younger, love seemed exciting. And then, well . . . It wasn't perfect. But then I met Larch and we had . . . what we had. And now nothing ever feels as good as it did that time. When I was under the spell, I mean. But that wasn't real, so . . ." She shrugged. "I'm left wanting something I can't have."

Rowan's face was scrunched. "I thought you were over him?"

"Not him. I'm definitely over him. I shudder to think of the person I was, the person he wanted me to be. I don't want to be her ever again."

Jane frowned, trying to figure out exactly what she meant. "I mean the feeling of being in love. It was all consuming and heady, like floating or flying like a bird. Love will never feel like that again."

"Maybe it's not supposed to feel like that," he said. "Maybe it's not supposed to feel the way a spell or love potion makes it feel."

"But that's the problem. It's *not* supposed to feel that way. But however it *is* supposed to feel, it will never compare."

Rowan didn't reply. He'd finished his lunch and was picking at a thread on his trousers. Jane took up her second slice of bread and ate it. Too late, she realized her comments would only make Rowan feel worse about the part he'd played in Larch's deception, since the love potion that had left her ruined for non-magical relationships had been his doing. Not that his guilt was her responsibility. But it had been nice talking with him while it lasted.

Chapter 7

AFTER THEIR BREAK FOR LUNCH, Rowan and Jane returned to the road. He led her into the trees on the far side to fill up their water gourds at a stream he somehow knew of and they continued on.

A short way up, the double track ended at an empty wagon standing abandoned.

"The wagons for the mine stop here," Rowan said, running his fingers along the edge of the wooden sides. "It's strange they've left one. Usually they come back down with the ore." Beyond the wagon, the path gave up all pretense of being a road. As if he heard her wondering, Rowan added, "They use packs on mules to carry the ore from the mine to here."

Jane didn't reply as they started up. After a few paces, she was already puffing from the climb.

How did he know so much about this area? It probably had something to do with his long and personal story about knowing a dragon.

After five minutes on the narrowed path, Jane didn't have the breath to talk even if she wanted to. The climb was steep and she had to watch every step she took. Someone had wedged flattish rocks into the path to give it some semblance of being the way to follow—the rocks were too orderly to be random—but it only barely resembled a human-made path. So many stones protruded from the ground at odd heights and angles that each step required care. In places water trickled down the rocks as if it might actually be a creek bed that had dried up for the summer. The places where it did flatten into a dirt path were pits of mud she had to skirt around.

A few times, Jane had to stop and use her hands to push herself up a steep step. Or in one place, where the path crossed a sheer rock face, she took baby steps to cross it, sure her feet would slide out from under her at any moment. Rowan never struggled—he strode along the path and balanced easily as he stepped up the rocks without needing his arms. But somehow he remained the same distance in front of her no matter how slowly she went. Maybe he slowed his pace to match hers. She never caught him looking back. But he could probably hear her panting behind him.

On the narrow path, as she walked under the bushes, they grew down just enough to brush against her head. After an hour, wisps of long hair were tickling her neck. One kind of bush eventually dominated the greenery. It had twisty branches and large, oval leaves in a deep, waxy green color. The leaves splayed out in rings with a clump of small, paler green fronds sticking up in the center. It must be some mountain species.

How far did they have to go? Would it be another day of this tomorrow, or three more days? Or ten? Did Rowan know? If she asked, he might think she was complaining. She had to treat this situation like basket orders before the winter solstice celebrations— you never knew how many were going to come at you, so you simply wove one after another until the orders stopped coming.

Sooner or later he'd have to stop for the night. Hopefully it would be soo—

Jane's foot slipped from a rock and twisted sideways and a pain shot through it. She landed on her knees, taking the weight off her foot. She'd cried out without meaning to.

Rowan crouched before her.

"What happened?" he asked with concern.

"My foot slipped."

"Does it hurt?"

"No." She held it off the ground.

"Let's see if you can stand on it. May I help you up?"

She nodded.

Rowan reached his hands to her sides and lifted her as he stood. A memory flashed in her mind of Larch doing something similar, that second day when she'd been following him through the forest and they'd come to a downed tree. Only Larch hadn't asked first; he'd picked her up and swung her over the trunk like it was all a game. At the time she'd found the action romantic, but now it seemed presumptuous that he hadn't asked.

When she was upright, she lowered her right foot gingerly toward the ground. The moment it touched, the pain flared again and she winced. Rowan's hands tightened around her.

"It hurts," she said.

"You might have twisted it. There's a place we can stop ahead."

Could she make it? Maybe if she crawled. But Rowan slipped himself under her right shoulder and lifted her weight up with his arm around her waist. He took a step and she hopped after him.

"It's not far," he said.

As slow as slugs, they made their way up the steep trail. Rowan took steps one by one and waited for her to catch up. His arm was hard against her side and warmed her through her shirt, and if she turned her face toward him she caught the scent she'd sniffed on his blanket that morning. She kept her hand firmly on his shoulder, hanging on, but several times she caught herself wanting to squeeze him a little more than necessary.

When they came to mud or a large rock across the way, he practically lifted her over it. Would it be easier for him to simply carry her? He should be able to with those bulging arms he had. Was it rude to ask? Maybe he didn't suggest it because he thought she wouldn't like it.

He paused as they caught their breath.

"Would it be easier to carry me? You know, piggyback or whatever."

"You'd have to wear my pack."

"I can do that."

His grip around her loosened and she balanced on her uninjured foot. She withdrew her arm from his shoulder to give him space and shifted her satchel to hang by her hip. He hefted the pack off with a clang and helped get it onto her arms, over her own bag, without tipping her sideways. When he eased it down onto her, it hung on her shoulders like a dozen sacks of flour. What in the skies was he carrying, a set of cast iron cookware?

He turned away and crouched down before her.

Skies, his back was broad. And once she climbed onto his back a whole lot of her body would be pressed against him—from her legs wrapped around his hips to her face beside his neck. But he was waiting and she couldn't back out now and besides, taking a ride would get them to their stopping place faster.

She leaned over his back and put her arms around him.

His hands found her thighs and clamped on to them as he stood, lifting her from the ground and drawing her legs around him. The bags pulled her backward but he compensated, hitching her up once until she settled against him. She eased off on her hold once she was balanced.

Rowan resumed climbing the trail.

Riding on his back was as jarring as hopping had been. But it was jarring her in an entirely different way. How had she not anticipated this? She tried to keep her mind off the sensations—the thud of his footsteps shaking her inside her thighs and the temptation to nudge herself against his back. It had been so long since she'd pressed herself up against a man. Would it feel as pleasurable as she imagined?

She had some nerve calling Rowan a stalker earlier. She was the lewd one. Here he was carrying her when she was injured, and she was imagining humping his back.

Jane leaned her cheek against him and tried not to think.

Rowan stepped off the trail at last. They were at another wayside like the one where they'd had lunch, with an identical firepit, log and all. Her right ankle had begun to ache with a dull throbbing. Rowan leaned forward and slowly let go of her legs, allowing her to slide down his body until she stood behind him, balancing on her good foot. He took the bags off her back, set them down, and held her hand as she hopped to the log and sat.

Her ankle was swollen.

Rowan was eyeing it. "Can you get your shoe and sock off?"

She carefully undid the laces. He immediately squatted down to help ease the shoe off. For a moment the pain returned. As long as she didn't touch anything, she could pretend the injury wasn't that bad. Before he could start undressing her, she peeled the sock down and off.

"Well, at least your foot's not swollen," he said. "Tell me if this hurts."

He pushed at her foot and she felt nothing—well, nothing other than his fingers touching her. She shook her head. He pushed a few more places, pressing her foot this way and that. She kept shaking her head. He let go of her and touched the ground to balance himself, straightening up to peer into her eyes.

"I think it's only a twisted ankle."

"Did you apprentice with the healer before the chairmaker?" she asked.

He almost looked like he almost smiled. "It's just the basics."

"Thank you for helping me."

"I'll make a poultice to reduce the swelling and we can bind it for the night."

He stood and retrieved his pack. Around them, the light was dimming and a chill was creeping into the air. Trees and more of the twisted bushes with the waxy leaves formed a ring around their clearing, but directly over the firepit was open to the sky, which had faded to a deep twilight blue. Maybe they'd have stopped to camp here anyway, even if she hadn't injured herself. They'd just have arrived a bit faster, with more daylight left.

Rowan poured water from his gourd into a corner of the firepit and stirred with a stick that had been leaning nearby. He scooped out a handful of wet dirt and ashes, turned to her, and smoothed it up against one side of her ankle. His other hand did the same on the other side.

The muddy ashes were surprisingly cold. The water from the stream had been cold but his gourd must insulate water better than hers. Rowan kept his hands on her leg, looking at the ground.

"Do you want me to hold it?" she asked.

He shook his head once. "My hands are already dirty."

The sky darkened a little more.

The chilled poultice didn't warm. A soothing relief stole through her ankle. It wouldn't be cured but it felt less angry than it had. At last he lifted his hands.

"It's mostly dried," he said. "Keep it on and I'll start a fire."

She expected him to reach into his pack for a pouch of fire powder, to use the way Larch had many times, but instead he stood and marched into the trees. As she held the dried mud, branches snapped in the darkness. He returned with an armload of fallen wood and broken tree limbs.

He used a regular, human-made steel and flint to light the fire, feeding in small bits of moss and twigs until a flame caught. He stacked the wood he'd gathered beside her.

"Keep feeding it and I'll gather more."

He kept telling her what to do, but somehow it never sounded like he was giving her an order. The words were bossy but his tone was low and quiet. As she headed off again, she let go of one side of the poultice and picked up a branch to hold in the fire until it caught. The small flame cast out a wave of heat before she tossed it on top. The poultice slipped down. It no longer felt cold at all. Jane peeled it off her skin on each side and lay it on the ground. She added a few more sticks to the fire, careful not to press on her right foot.

Rowan appeared silently from the shadows with another armful of wood. He unloaded it and moved to her right side. "Can you get your leg up here?" He leaned to pat the log. As she twisted sideways and lifted her leg, his hand caught under her calf and eased her leg over the log and down until her foot rested gently. He took a kerchief from his pocket. His rough fingers slid out from beneath her ankle, pulling the kerchief after them. In a few quick motions, he'd tied the cloth tightly around her ankle. He stood without a word and stalked off into the shadows again.

Jane kept her leg up and turned back to the fire. Night animals were starting to call, and overhead the first stars were peeking through the leaves. She hadn't been in a forest like this in many seasons, not since . . . not since Larch. Didn't humans ever end up out in the forest at night? Or was it a fairy thing? Or maybe, her boring life was what kept her at home in the village, making baskets and hanging laundry. Never having an adventure.

Well she was certainly having one now.

Should she be? Look what had happened the last time she'd abandoned her settled life to have an adventure. But she hadn't had a choice this time. She was here to rescue Elle.

Rowan reappeared from the darkness with one more bundle of wood. He set it down without speaking and left. But he quickly returned, cradling something in his hands. For a heartbeat she imagined he had a rabbit or some other helpless creature, but of course he wouldn't have that. Fairies didn't eat the animals they could talk to.

He held mushrooms and onions.

"I assume you know what you're doing," Jane said, pointing at an orange mushroom. "I don't know that kind."

"They're fire mushrooms."

"Fire mushrooms?"

"I don't know the human name. They only grow near dragon dens." He spread the cloth with the bread on the ground and set out the vegetables.

"So we're close to the dragon?"

"We should reach him tomorrow."

"Does he have a name?"

"I called him Axe. He seemed to like it."

Jane's brow furrowed. "How old were you when you met?"

"Ten winters. Keep feeding the fire."

Jane glanced down. The few twigs she'd lit had almost burned out. She reached for a few bigger ones and dropped them into the pit one by one. Before she could ask more questions, Rowan left again.

She fed the fire more carefully this time, and by the time Rowan returned, she had a few larger branches crackling in the flames. She was distracted tonight. At home, she could keep a steady fire going all morning when they needed one. If she ever did ask Master Smith to take her on as an apprentice, at least she'd have that skill to offer. Although a fire made with coal would behave differently—she'd have to learn how to manage a coal fire.

Rowan sat beside her, adding to the pile of mushrooms. They were the flat, wavy kind that grew in clusters on the sides of logs or other hosts. He got out a short knife and began whittling down the end of a relatively straight stick into a sharp point. His thumb was twice the width of the stick but he handled it gently, rotating it as bits of wood flew off into the fire. When he had a sharp point, he skewered a few mushrooms and handed it to her. She held it over the flames.

"It's easier to roast things if the fire's burned down," he said, "but I'm too hungry to wait."

"Me too."

He gathered up several of the spring onions with their long green fronds and wiped off the dirt clinging to them, pinching the roots off too. His fingers nimbly braided the greens together.

Jane pulled her gaze away from his working hands and jerked her skewer up, rescuing her mushrooms from a flaming death. Drat. It was always the hands that got her. Rowan leaned forward and hung the bundle of onions on the end of her skewer. He began to prepare a second stick.

When she held both skewers, he cut the rest of the wedge of cheese, and soon they were finishing off the bread and cheese and eating juicy mushrooms and onions straight off the fire. The mushrooms were tasty with a pungent, meaty flavor. Jane kept the fire small to make the wood last. Outside of the flickering flame and the small glow around it, the woods had gone dark. Stars filled the sky overhead.

"There's a spring nearby," Rowan said as she pulled the last mushroom off her skewer and popped it into her mouth. "After you wash up for the night I'll refill your gourd." He took a long drink from his and splashed water over his fingers, wiping them clean and drying them on his pants. "I'll re-bind your ankle," he added, "and then I'll leave so you can get ready for sleep."

He had a plan. Of course he did. She'd wondered how she would manage taking care of her personal needs with him nearby and herself unable to walk into the woods for privacy. With her bad ankle, she'd imagined herself crawling into the thickest bushes to pee and hoping he couldn't see her through the leaves. But he'd thought of what she needed.

He took up his knife and began cutting a wider piece of wood than he had for the skewers. When he'd produced two relatively flat pieces, he moved to sit on the log beside her ankle and undid the kerchief. The dying firelight flickered on his face, smoothing out the rough edges and making him look like a fresh-faced young knight in a tale.

"How does it feel?" He gestured at her ankle.

"Much better since the poultice."

"Tell me if it hurts." He gently slid his hand beneath her ankle, pressed into her skin, and held the two halves of the splint up against her, fitting them behind her ankle bone on either side. The skin on his fingers was rough like a laundryman's or a farmer's. Every time the smallest bit of him scraped against her, she felt it up her calf and down to her toes.

She had to stop thinking about the scuff of his hands on her skin. It was too easy to lose herself daydreaming, imagining him sliding his hands up her leg. She didn't want to be inappropriate when he was only trying to help her with her injury. "It's useful to know how to do this," she said to distract herself. "I'm sure the children will be spraining things soon enough. So far we've only had scrapes and bruises."

He held the splint firmly as he wrapped up the kerchief, pulling it tight. "Oh?"

"Maryanne usually handles healing-related crises. She's the one who's gifted at mothering. She was born to do it. I'm always ten steps behind where I'm supposed to be."

"You're probably doing fine," he said. He wrapped the kerchief around her ankle again to swathe a larger area. One hand was wrapped clear around her leg, holding the tight kerchief in place.

Skies that hand was large. And he held her leg so tightly she wouldn't be able to kick it free if she tried. "But not like Maryanne," she rambled on. "Mothering comes naturally to her; she loves it. She seems perfectly content raising five children and sneaking out to tumble Wells three times a quarter-moon."

"Wells? I wondered why he was always getting new baskets."

Jane frowned. What did Rowan have to do with Wells? Oh right—Rowan had been Wells's apprentice last winter. "What do you mean, new baskets?"

"Maryanne would come into the smithy," Rowan said, "and Wells would say, 'I need to show you the length of the tools for the new basket' and they'd disappear upstairs for half an hour."

Jane grinned. "You didn't realize what they were up to?"

"Well . . ." He grimaced. "Maybe they made a lot of noise looking at his, um, tools."

Rowan had to be joking. He had to have known what they were doing—from what Maryanne said, she and Wells were noisy lovers.

And now Jane was thinking about tumbling again. Because Maryanne would come home from those daily rendezvous and blather on about Wells this and Wells that, his giant size, and how they'd done it on the kitchen table and cracked it down the middle and then he'd had her up against the doorway or over an empty ale barrel that rolled back and forth as he thrust into her, and on and on. And Jane would laugh and smile and try not to let on how jealous she was that Maryanne had someone to romp around with, and that Maryanne was able to do all that tumbling without any pain. Her stories were what Jane wished for, for herself. But she'd never be able to do all that, not with the way her body wouldn't work right.

Rowan pulled the kerchief extra snugly and tied the tips in a knot. He kept holding her bound ankle in both his warm hands. What if he started rubbing her leg or . . . or massaging her foot . . . or stroking her—

"It was too soon for me," Jane blurted out. "I wasn't ready to be a mother." Rowan tensed and his hand was still touching her, tightly, so she babbled on. "I love Elle but if I could do it again, I would wait. Well, obviously, if I could do it again I wouldn't be tricked by a fairy into leaving my family to follow him into the woods with no thought to the future. But I also wouldn't stop drinking bitter tea because he assured me fairies had some magical ability to prevent pregnancy."

A shocked silence followed her words.

Rowan's hands had clamped on to her leg. His splint was effective, though, because she felt no pain. He blinked and loosened his grip as he lowered her foot back to the log.

"He told you that?"

She nodded, trying not to cry. She'd been foolish to believe something like that.

"I'm sorry," he said.

"He must've worded it carefully since it's such a glaring lie, but that's what he implied. By the time I realized I was pregnant, the love potion had me so addled I don't think I cared."

Rowan stood and studied the ground. A lit ember glowed nearby and he flicked it back into the crackling fire with a bare toe. "I meant to mention this before but I didn't know how. I can boil water for you to make tea."

Her eyes smarted again at his kindness. "I didn't bring any bitter herbs. I packed so fast thinking of Elle that I forgot. Even Maryanne forgot. But it's not like I need to drink any right now since I'm not . . ." Skies this was embarrassing.

They passed a few beats in silence. Night insects and perhaps a few frogs cheeped in the dark, but the chirping wasn't as loud as it could be, not like the pond in the village when the frogs were really going at it. An owl hooted in the distance.

He held out a hand. "Let me help you to the edge of the clearing."

Awkwardly, she got to her feet and let him support her to move away from the fire. He brought her to a poplar sapling she could hang on to and crossed to the far side of the fire to disappear into the darkness. Knowing the darkness cloaked her as well was a comfort. After she'd taken care of her needs, she hopped slowly back to the fire and found her toothbrush.

When Rowan returned, he didn't comment on anything she'd said earlier. He pulled two woven hammocks from his bag and hung them from the trees. She didn't protest when he gave her his blanket with the heated chips, which he'd laid in the sunshine while they'd rested after lunch. She handed him hers to replace it. He had her wrap herself in the blanket before sitting sideways on the hammock so her underside wouldn't get cold in the night air. With one pivot, she turned lengthwise and lay back, and the hammock curled around her.

"All set?" Rowan asked.

"Yes."

She was warm and her muscles were so tired, and lying in the hammock felt decadent. But her mind was too awake. Tonight was Elle's second night away from home. Was she all right? Did she miss her mother? After the first two winters of her life, serving the fairy queen, what if she thought being taken from home like this was normal?

Jane listened to the rustling of Rowan lying down. She should have asked him how far away they were, but surely he'd have told her if he knew. They had to reach his dragon friend first and then they'd know where Elle was. Rowan's movements ceased and he was silent, but she lay awake into the night.

Chapter 8

JANE WOKE TO THE SMELL of . . . something delicious. Of course, she was so hungry, stale biscuits would probably smell delicious. But this involved a fire, if she wasn't imagining the scent of smoke in the air.

The folds of the hammock closed over her face and the tightly woven threads kept out the light. She nudged aside the edge, blinking in the morning sun. The brightness of the daylight surprised her. She twisted slowly to peek out in an effort not to dump herself onto the ground.

Rowan sat beside the firepit, stirring something in a small tin bowl in the coals. He barely had a fire, just embers, and the pile of wood he'd gathered was gone. A tin cup with no handle rested on the log beside him. The chill air nipped at her exposed face but the bright day promised to warm soon. The birdsong was a chorus.

She started to sit up and halted. She'd been so tired last night she couldn't remember exactly how she'd gotten into the hammock without falling.

"Rowan?"

He looked over. For a moment, he felt closer than he usually did. His eyes were wider and his lips parted before he pressed them shut and swallowed. She could see the green of his eyes even from several paces away.

"I'm not sure how to get out of the hammock. I don't want to fall on my ankle."

He pushed the bowl out of the embers before standing and

coming to her side. He helped her sit up and wiggle off the woven mesh, catching her when she wobbled on her left foot. She lowered her other foot to the ground.

He waited with his hands on her sides. This close, she could smell his skin, although the smoke of the campfire permeated all their clothing.

"It's tender but there's no pain."

"Try walking on it."

As she tested it out, he supported her weight, moving across the clearing with her. What a relief to walk again. If her ankle hadn't improved overnight she'd have been stuck—she'd have had to let Rowan go on without her, or else make Elle wait even longer for her rescue.

Once she'd settled on the log, Rowan tilted his head at the cup beside her. "I made tea. That's yours."

The cup warmed her hands as she lifted it. She sniffed and a zingy aroma filled her nostrils.

"What's in it?"

"Sassafras root, pine needles, and a few violets I found."

She tried a sip. It was warm and peppery. "Thank you."

"I made oats but I've only one bowl. You can have some first."

Jane shook her head, sipping the tea. "You eat first. I'm not fully awake yet."

Rowan lifted the bowl to his lap and had a few spoonfuls. "You can stay here," he said, "if you're worried about your ankle."

She lowered the cup.

"I'll be back by tonight."

"Are you trying to get rid of me?" He'd been secretive about his past with this dragon they were trying to find. Maybe he didn't want her to meet the dragon.

He met her gaze and quickly looked away.

"You'd be faster without me," she said.

"I don't mind how fast we go."

"Do you *want* me to stay here?"

"I thought you might not want to continue."

She straightened up. "I do want to. If you don't mind."

"I don't mind."

After a few minutes, he stopped eating and offered her the bowl. She held out her hands.

"I almost forgot," he said. "I found some berries." He turned to scoop them off the top of his pack.

Jane narrowed her eyes, staring as he sprinkled the tiny wild strawberries into the remaining cereal. He'd *forgotten*? Why was she certain he'd waited to give the berries to her? She couldn't see a way to argue with him so she accepted the bowl with a simple thank you.

When they eventually set out, with their gourds filled and the splint removed from Jane's foot, Rowan led her up the trail only a short way before stepping off to the left. Nothing marked the spot, and he moved under the trees without any trail she could make out.

"How's your ankle?" he asked.

"Okay. Once we got moving it felt good as new. Is it far to the dragon?"

"Not as the crow flies." Something about the way he said it felt ominous.

But the way they walked was easy going, with moss covering the ground to cushion their feet and only a few places where they had to detour around undergrowth to keep on course. Through the trunks to the west, boulders littered the ground as it sloped upward on their right, and the trees and bushes to the left thinned as if the land dropped off. Squirrels chittered from the branches as they passed and once a chipmunk darted off a rock and disappeared beneath a mossy stump. No branches snagged at her hair, although today she had braided it and tied off the end with a ribbon instead of tying her usual sloppy bun, hoping to better keep it out of her face as they walked.

When the sun eventually shone through the branches overhead, it wasn't where Jane expected it to be. She'd lost track of their direction, but the sun was behind them to their left as if they now headed west instead of south.

"What are these bushes?" she asked as they passed under more of the twisted branches she'd been seeing along the trail.

"Rhododendrons."

She touched the center fronds as she passed a cluster of the bushes. A few dried-out strands with a reddish color clung to the leaves.

"Do they bloom?"

"Yes."

"What do they look like?"

"Pretty."

Was he teasing her? "That's not helpful."

"You might get to see some."

"How?"

"They should still be blooming at the top of the mountains."

The top of the mountains? Weren't they already at the top? Jane bit her words back and kept walking.

Sunlight shone in front of them and grew brighter as they approached. Rowan slowed and Jane came up beside him and started. The forest floor dropped away and a vast valley spread before them. The trees stretched on endlessly—so far that it seemed she should see Woods Rest or even the towers of the castle in Woodglen. But all she saw were treetops under a blue sky. To the right, the way forward abruptly ended with a vertical wall of rock towering up on the south face of the mountain.

Why had Rowan led them this way?

He glanced down at her, and his eyes had a spark she hadn't seen before. "Now comes the fun part."

A sense of foreboding settled in her gut.

"It's not too late to back out if you want to stay here."

Was he daring her to continue? She lifted her chin. "Lead the way."

He didn't move, towering over her like the boulders. His lips moved and—

Jane stared.

Rowan was smiling at her.

"This will take a moment," he said, and he slid his pack off and crouched beside it.

Jane snapped her jaw shut. He'd actually smiled. For the first time. Why? What made him smile, here of all places? Her chest warmed and her own lips smiled in the wake of it.

Rowan opened his pack and pulled out a coil of rope. It was thin but it might be crafted of that special magical thread the fairies made that could hold an extraordinary amount of weight. When Rose had been a princess and trapped in the castle, she had climbed out of her tower window on a ladder made of the stuff when Dustan was courting her—or rather, seducing her. The ladder scene was one of Jane's favorite parts of Rose's love story.

Rowan handed her a wide, tightly woven belt with several iron buckles along it. "Wrap that around your waist as tight as it will go," he said. "Like this." He stood, took off his coat, and rolled it into a bundle that he wedged into his pack. He fastened a second belt around himself, snapping the buckles rapidly. She took off her own coat and scarf but she couldn't follow how he did the belt. He next tied the end of the rope to his belt before checking for snags and tying the other end around a tree trunk. He tucked the rest of the rope into a pocket.

He faced her, eyeing her waist as he rolled up his sleeves. "May I?" he asked.

She lifted her hands away. He undid the buckle she had fumbled with and cinched the belt tighter, then snapped several buckles shut. The belt had an odd metal loop on the front. He tugged on it and she stumbled into him.

"Sorry," he said, catching her and setting her upright. "I wanted to make sure it was tight." Her fingers had grabbed on to his bare forearms. She lifted her hands and tried not to think about how hard his forearms were.

He let go of her and turned to the wall of rock. He started forward but quickly turned back to her. "Stay here," he said. "I'll come back for you."

And he stepped onto the rock. Jane gasped, paralyzed. He'd wedged his bare toes into a wide crack, but his hands seemed to be gripping the flat face of the rock. Below him, the sheer face continued down, down, down. If he fell . . .

He worked his way out on the rock wall one smidge at a time, until he reached for a higher knob and pulled himself up. How did he know where to go? And more importantly, how was she ever going to follow him? As he moved, he let out the rope so it trailed down the wall and over to the tree where he'd secured it.

Once he got moving, he went more quickly, climbing from one handhold to the next. His body sprawled across the rock with his limbs at odd angles, reaching for protrusions she never would have noticed.

Had he done this before? He was familiar with the area and the sources of water, and he seemed to know where the handholds on the rock were. And he'd said he knew this dragon. So why had he come here to visit a dragon in the past? Did the dragons have resources the fairies could use in addition to their fire?

Or had Rowan come to learn fire magic?

He pulled himself onto a ledge twenty paces over her head, kneeling and working with something out of her sight. He stood with the rope in his hand and fiddled with his belt, tugging on the rope a few times. He stepped backward off the ledge.

Jane squeaked. She would have screamed but he caught himself before she could get it out, somehow standing tilted at the edge of the ledge with the rope stretched tightly between his belt and the rock in front of him. What in the skies had he fastened it on up there?

He leaned backward farther and began walking down the wall.

His right bicep was flexed and his fist gripped the thin rope, which was stretched taut but grew longer the farther he came down. He pushed with his toes and swung sideways toward her before dropping the rest of the way and stepping off the rock and onto the ground.

Did the rope possess some other form of magic, aside from being strong? The length in his hand connected to an iron piece he had fastened somehow to his belt's front loop. The rope wrapped in a neat double loop around the iron piece. His tight grip on the rope must have stopped it from spooling out faster. Jane peeked up at his face.

He was smiling down at her. "Your turn."

Her stomach churned like the oats had changed their mind about being eaten.

"Unless you no longer want to go." His warm smile had the edge of a smirk on it. "You could wait here and I'll go up alone."

"Absolutely not," Jane managed, fisting her shaking hands.

"Pack your coat and put on your bag."

She did as he ordered, slinging her satchel across her chest to wear it on her back. Rowan unclipped the iron piece from his belt and slipped the loose rope off, then retied it into a firm knot. He hooked a finger into her belt (skies, those hands!) and pressed the iron piece against the loop on the front of her belt, and the side of the oval pushed open and snapped shut, attaching it to her. He tugged on the rope, but this time she planted her feet so she didn't stumble into him.

Jane touched the iron piece, pressing on the springy part until it opened and letting it snap shut. "Did you make this?"

"I shaped the iron."

"How?"

"Smithing."

"How did you make this part that snaps closed?" It must have some tiny mechanical spring inside it.

"Maple made that. With jewelweed seedpods."

"Jewelweed . . . ?"

"And magic."

Right. Magic. But why jewelweed?

Rowan stepped aside, leaving Jane a clear path to the edge of the drop. She gaped up at the rocks and at the rope trailing loosely from her belt to the top and back down.

He cleared his throat. "Tell me at once if you feel lightheaded. Up this high, the air gets thin and sometimes it makes people dizzy."

"Okay."

"I've got the other end of the rope." He slowly drew it in until it went taut on the way up to the ledge and back, and tugged gently on her center. He wrapped it around his hands a few times. "I'll take it in as you go up. If you did fall, I'd catch you. And if I slipped somehow, you'd only fall a short way before the tree caught you."

Jane nodded, trying to still her shaking hands. "How do I know where to grab?"

"I'll talk you through it. The worst part is the beginning. It's meant to look impossible so no one will try it."

"Why?"

"Dragons don't like visitors."

Right. The dragon. In her fear of climbing the cliff face, she'd completely forgotten there'd be a dragon at the top.

"Ready?" Rowan asked.

"Um, sure." Jane wiped her sweaty palms on her shirt.

He pointed to the rock. "See the place with the darkish tint? That's a place you can grab. You'll have to step out to reach it."

Jane lifted her foot. The belt at her waist pressed against her back, letting her know Rowan had the rope ready to catch her if needed.

She stepped forward onto the narrow crack, and for a moment her head spun and she risked tumbling off but the belt held her up. With a whimper, she placed her other foot in the crack and pushed herself to the left, moving her first foot and reaching for the spot

Rowan had shown her. Her fingers closed on the barest edge of rock, but it was enough to hang on to and she could lean forward slightly. Her toes were wedged tightly in the crack. If only she'd taken off her shoes, she'd be able to detect the edge of the rock more easily, although if she had, her feet might get scraped up and make things harder.

The rope in front of her loosened. "Do you see the large knob where I pulled myself up?"

Jane turned her head, getting her bearings on the wall. "Yes."

"If you move yourself along the crack bit by bit, you should be able to switch the hand that's holding on and reach the next handhold, and the next, until you are under that knob. Go nice and slow."

Jane felt her way along the crack with her toes until she could reach the first handhold with her right hand. She moved farther and patted the rock with her left fingers until they found a protrusion she could grasp. A breeze riffled her hair, blowing the sweat off the back of her neck. She kept her gaze up, away from the view opening behind her—and below her. Rowan had said this was the worst part.

She reached the third handhold. The knob came next. Eagerly she stepped toward it and her foot slipped. Her stomach lurched, but her fingers clenched around the smaller protrusion and the rope went tight in front of her, holding her safe until she got her toes back onto the wall. She swallowed. More carefully, she stepped out and reached for the knob.

Rowan walked her through the next step of pulling herself up and finding the next toehold, then the next and the next. Climbing was painstaking work. Without a guide, she'd have clung to the cliff face for hours before she located the places she could grip her hands or wedge her toes. After what felt like an hour, she pulled herself up onto the ledge and onto her knees. The rope trailed off her and passed through an iron loop driven into a crack in the solid rock before hanging down to where Rowan held it at the edge of the forest.

Jane touched the metal loop that had been holding her up when she'd slipped. Who had driven it into the rock like this?

"Are you all right?" Rowan called.

Jane turned onto her bottom and slid backward until she was safely seated on the ledge. She signaled down to him. As the rush of the climb wore off, her legs pounded in fatigue, and her fingers and palms were red and indented with the texture of the rock she'd clung to.

"Undo the clip on your belt and attach it to the loop up there," Rowan said.

Jane carefully pressed the lever to open the clip and slid it off her belt. She hooked it through the loop in the rock and let go, and the lever snapped shut. Like the snap of a jewelweed pod shooting its seeds out when the children squeezed them. She smiled. That was how the fairies had made the hook snap shut. She tugged on the rope to check it and show Rowan it was secure.

He put his pack on and untied the other end of the rope from the tree, threaded it through his own special climbing belt until no extra remained, and tied a knot. He coiled the extra and wedged it into a side pocket on his trousers. Letting go of the rope, he stepped onto the crack again and moved up the rock following the now familiar path. No wonder his fingers were so strong, if he did this regularly. How often did one visit a dragon? Barely a minute later, he pulled himself onto the ledge. He wasn't even sweating or breathing heavily.

He exhaled and relaxed as he sat beside her. His legs swung where they hung off the rock, like a child riding on the back of a wagon. "It's a fine view."

Jane tore her gaze away from him to scan the valley spreading all around. A ridge of tree-covered hills ran along the righthand side, probably the western side of the valley, but when she checked the sun, it was high overhead and didn't help her with directions. "That's the south?" she asked, pointing.

He nodded.

"Where's Woods Rest? Can we see it?"

He pointed farther left than she'd have guessed. "The Forest Road curves away to the east. It's that way."

"All I see are trees."

"The village is a small clearing relative to the forest."

"Spoken like a fairy." Jane smiled to show she was teasing.

He pressed his lips together and didn't reply.

"What about the castle. Can we see that?"

"On a clear day you might. There's too much mist today." He pushed himself to his feet with no effort, seeming unconcerned that he might topple off the edge. "Ready?"

Rowan helped Jane to stand. He unclipped the magical spring-clip from the rock and coiled the remaining rope, stashing it in his pocket.

"Where did the iron loop in the rock come from?" she asked.

"I drove it in the first time I came."

"You drove it in?"

"It's best to be safe. Besides, it's more fun to come down using the rope."

Fun? She lifted her eyebrows.

He smiled. "I'll show you on the way down."

Ugh. "Why didn't you leave the rope, since we're coming down?"

"I don't like to leave a rope at the bottom in case anyone comes along and sees it. Humans have all kinds of weird ideas about dragons—that they hoard gold and have magical scales. It makes the humans a danger."

"I've never heard of anyone even seeing a dragon," Jane said.

"That's because they hide."

"So how do you drive a piece of iron that far into rock?"

"With a hammer."

Jane squinted. "How old were you?"

"Twelve."

"Skies," she whispered as Rowan reached for the rock behind them and shimmied up it. He turned to give her a hand and pulled her up after him.

"This part will be easier."

After the sheer face of the cliff, climbing over the boulders above it was a cinch. Rowan lifted her up in a few places where he had to scale a wall but could reach down to her. The trees they'd left behind disappeared below the rocks as they climbed above the treetops. Nothing grew where they were climbing except scrubby bushes clinging to cracks in the rock and more of the fire mushrooms, which were unlike any Jane had ever seen, now that she'd examined them in daylight. Most mushrooms grew in moist places, feeding on dead logs or the mossy earth, but these were clinging to the rocks. They formed thick clusters of twenty or more caps with furry-looking gills underneath and they seemed to glow from the base, although when she blinked and looked again they were simply a brilliant orange.

She touched the edge of one mushroom cap they passed. "How are they growing here?" she murmured.

"The dragons make them grow. They breathe fire on certain places in the rock and leave it porous so rainwater can gather and the mushrooms can thrive. They spread into the forest but you never see as many as you do at a dragon den. And you find them only near a dragon."

Of course he knew. Know-it-all fairy.

"Why do dragons grow mushrooms?"

He stopped at the base of the next boulder and scrunched his brow. "To eat them?"

"I thought . . ." Jane stopped. She already knew she was wrong.

"That dragons ate cows and deer and people?"

She couldn't meet his gaze. "Yes."

He shook his head sadly. "Humans."

"Are you actually joking?"

He snorted. "No. Let's go." And he started up the next ledge.

Twice more they used the ropes to climb, each time using iron loops fastened in the rock. Rowan would tie the rope at the bottom, scale the wall, thread it through a loop at the top, and lower himself down. He'd fasten the rope to the spring-clip, fasten that to her, and hold the ropes as he guided her up. And after she attached the spring-clip to the loop in the rock at the top, he'd untie the rope at the bottom, attach it to himself, and climb up to join her.

Jane ran her finger over a loop as she waited. If Rowan had hammered them in, he must have expected to use them again—to visit the dragon often. Had he? Or was this his first visit since he'd been twelve winters old?

Each time they ascended, the top of the peak seemed just beyond them. But as they reached the top a new layer of rocks would appear above them. Until finally they came out on a flat rock with no further height to climb, surrounded by rocks loaded with a thick layer of the orange mushrooms—but she still didn't see a dragon. Below, a tree-covered slope stretched to the north and ended. That must be the hill they'd been climbing from the crossroads. It continued upward to the west. Behind it, other rocky peaks like the one they were climbing towered in the distance.

"Could Elle be on one of those?" Jane asked, looking out at the sea of trees and rocks.

"She shouldn't be far. The dragon wouldn't want to carry her any longer than needed."

So that was a yes. Elle was on top of one of those towering peaks. Hopefully the dragon wouldn't let her fall off.

"Jane."

She pulled her gaze in from the view.

"Are you . . . um, calm about meeting Axe?"

"Calm?" Her voice ended in a squeak.

"If we make too much noise, we might startle him, and if he flies away I can't talk to him."

"Oh. You don't want me to scream and fling a shoe at him."

"Correct."

Jane licked her lips. "I can be calm."

Rowan turned and stepped up on a rock. Once he did it, she saw a row of rocks climbing up like a staircase. It passed between two boulders—he turned sideways to fit through. Jane followed close behind. As Rowan exited the passage, something moved beyond him.

She stopped at the end of the tight space, waiting as Rowan stepped down into the . . . courtyard? It was a circular area with a flat floor of rock. A long scaly tail curled out of a dark, gaping hole at the far side. The tail twitched on the floor. Jane stopped breathing, watching the tail. The dragon tail. It was green and shiny, covered with hand-sized scales. Rowan looked back. He motioned for her to stay and continued forward.

"Axe?" he called out gently. As if the dragon were a child he was waking from a nap.

The tail lashed up and down. When Mouser's tail moved that way, he was cross and about to attack someone.

But were dragons like cats? Or more like dogs? Was the lashing tail friendly, like a dog tail?

Jane stepped back into the passage so the boulders surrounded her.

Rowan called again and this time a scuffling sounded in the cave, and the tail was pulled in. And the front of the dragon came out.

It had a giant head, as tall as Rowan, with pale yellow eyes and faded green scales covering its snout, and a small ridge down the middle, from its eyes over its head and along its neck. Its neck went on and on to the massive body filling the cave entrance. It shuffled forward on two stout front legs (with claws!) until its folded wings cleared the cave and flexed open slightly, as if it were balancing but didn't want to open them all the way. And it was sniffing Rowan.

Its snout was right up against him, snuffling his clothing. Rowan stood motionless.

Was he able to communicate with it? With him. Rowan had called Axe a him.

Axe drew back his head to study Rowan from top to bottom. He lowered his bulky body to the stone floor and folded back his wings. Rowan sank down before him, and he had a hand on Axe's snout. Like he was petting the dragon.

"That's not why we're here," Rowan said softly.

The dragon exhaled. Thankfully no fire came out, with Rowan sitting right in front of him.

"It's too late," he murmured. "We can't stay here."

The dragon snorted hard enough to ruffle Rowan's hair.

"It's too late," he said again, and he reached up to wipe his eyes.

Was Rowan crying?

Jane lowered herself carefully and quietly to sit in the passage. She leaned on the boulder and hugged her knees. Witnessing this reunion she didn't understand felt awkward and intrusive. She closed her eyes and waited.

A few minutes later, Rowan touched her shoulder. She blinked up at him standing before her. And behind him, the dragon was watching her.

"Come say hello."

Rowan took her hand, helped her up, and led her into the courtyard. He kept ahold of her hand. Maybe he worried she'd bolt if he didn't hang on to her. They stopped in front of the drag-on's huge face.

"This is Jane," Rowan said, as if they were in a parlor about to have formal tea. "Jane, this is Axe."

Jane curtsied slightly. Heat from the dragon's exhales washed over her.

"He's told me where Elle is," Rowan said.

"Can he understand our words?" Jane asked.

"No. Maybe his name and a few others."

"Will you thank him for me?"

Rowan was silent and the dragon's eyes darted over to him. The eyes moved quickly for such a lumbering body. Jane couldn't imagine Axe swooping over Woods Rest and snatching Elle the way the other dragon had. Was he older? Or did dragons always wake up with creaky joints? As soon as they were back in the forest, she was going to ambush Rowan with questions.

"He's happy to help us. He didn't realize how young Elle is. But he understands your concern. And—" Rowan's voice cracked once, and he swallowed. "He understands we can't stay."

The dragon was watching her again.

"Could we come back?" Jane asked. She turned to Rowan. "We could come back to visit with him for longer. After we find Elle and sort everything out."

Rowan gazed at her with his lips parted. He shut them, blinking a few times. He smiled softly. "He would like that."

With one last glimpse at Axe, Rowan turned away from the dragon. He gestured for Jane to go first across the courtyard. She stepped once toward the exit before Rowan pushed into her, stumbling against her back and grabbing her around the waist to stop her from falling over. He let go of her quickly, apologizing for tripping.

Jane peeked back. She could have sworn Axe was grinning.

Chapter 9

LIMBING DOWN THE PEAK FROM Axe's den went more quickly than going up. Jane still scrambled slowly over boulders, even with Rowan offering a hand. But when they came to a sheer cliff face, Rowan set up the rope and bounced his way down in a few heartbeats.

Once he was down, she untied the rope from the loop in the ledge and threaded it through the same loop so it could move back and forth. She lowered the free end to Rowan and pulled up the end with the special spring-clip dangling from it. She clipped it to her own belt and climbed over the edge while Rowan held the rope tightly. He lowered her down as she clung to the rope and used her legs to stop herself from knocking into the cliff wall.

It was not "fun" at all.

Rowan caught her elbow and stopped her from twisting as her toes landed. She wobbled and crumpled to sit until her limbs stopped shaking, but her hands still shook as she unclipped the rope and passed it back to Rowan. He pulled it through the loop above them until he had it coiled in his hands and they moved on.

She held in her questions so she could concentrate on getting down the cliffs safely.

Axe had told Rowan that Elle was one peak away. He had felt the other dragon's enthusiasm as she flew off to meet Elle—Axe seemed to think Elle *had* called to her—and he didn't sense anything wrong since they'd returned. He referred to the other dragon as Sunshine, but Rowan couldn't tell if that was a dragon name or something Elle had come up with and Sunshine had shared with Axe. Knowing her daughter, Jane strongly suspected the latter.

Sunshine's peak wasn't far from their location, but it was tall.

They'd refilled their gourds from a basin of rainwater outside Axe's den. Rowan thought it was safe to drink—maybe the thin mountain air and colder temperatures kept it pure. And Rowan had filled his sack with fire mushrooms. He told her he hadn't wanted to take them, knowing Axe needed them too, but wanted to please Axe by accepting the gift.

As soon as her feet were on the moss of the forest floor, Jane pounced on Rowan. Figuratively.

"Why was Axe sniffing you?"

Rowan coiled the rope one last time. He bent to wedge it into his pack beside all the mushrooms. Jane crossed her arms, waiting. She wiggled her toes as Rowan slowly closed up his pack. He exhaled as he stood and put the pack over his shoulders.

"He was identifying me."

"He's not blind, is he?" Axe had stared right at her.

"No. He hadn't seen me in a while."

Jane pondered that as they set off through the trees. If Rowan's appearance had changed that much since Axe had last seen him, he must have been young at the time. Twelve, he'd said—he'd first come when he was twelve. Was that the only time he'd been here? He was striding quickly ahead of her.

She hurried after him. "How were you communicating with Axe if you can't do it with animals?"

"It's easier with dragons. They're very intelligent."

"Do you have a bond the way Elle has with Sunshine?"

"I've known him a long time."

"Does that kind of bond happen only when there's fire magic?"

He didn't answer.

She'd better steer her questions back into safe territory before Rowan shut down completely. "Is Axe old? He seemed . . . slower than Sunshine."

"He is old. Contrary to human myths, dragons don't live forever."

"Are there a lot of dragons?"

"Not here."

"Then where?"

"Most of them live deep in the western mountains. There are hot mineral springs that benefit them. They only come to the edge of the mountains when—" His words cut off.

Jane kept silent.

"Only a few come this close to our civilization," he finished. He hurried forward.

Jane jogged along behind him but didn't ask anything else. What was his history with Axe? It seemed obvious they had a bond, and Rowan possessing fire magic was the most obvious explanation, but if that was true, why didn't he know how to use it? He'd said he was not especially skilled at magic—had he tried to learn and failed? She wanted to know but not enough to upset him by asking.

Before the sun set, they reached the main trail and descended to the clearing where they'd camped. As Rowan approached the firepit, he stopped. His shoulders stiffened and he glanced about quickly. Jane came up beside him.

"Someone's been here," he said.

"How can you tell?"

"The wood in the fire. I left our skewers and a few branches stacked against the edge for tonight, and they've all been knocked sideways."

"It could have been an animal?"

"Maybe."

"Or someone coming down from the mine?" Master Smith had said his ore was late. But nothing indicated a load of ore had passed down the trail that day—like mule droppings or broken branches. The forest was as quiet as it had been all along. She searched the fireside for the hard shell of mud she'd used as a poultice the previous evening. She couldn't see it or even its broken remains.

Rowan dropped his pack to the ground and turned to her. "Jane. Please, you can't tell anyone the way we went today."

"I won't. Of course I won't. You said dragons don't like visitors."

"It's more than that. If anyone knew he was there, they'd try to reach him. Humans—"

"You said. They think dragons have hoards filled with riches and magic to steal. Rowan, I swear, I won't tell anyone where he is."

She'd taken his hand while talking. She squeezed it and the panic in his eyes receded.

"No one will hurt him," she said.

"Thank you."

Tonight Jane was able to help gather wood for the fire, and they had the feast of mushrooms from Axe. Within a few minutes, Jane was lighting a fire as Rowan skewered the mushrooms. He left her roasting them to find more onions.

They ate quietly, supplementing the meal with the nuts and dried cherries she had packed. Now that she was sitting and the adventure of climbing the tall peak and meeting a dragon had passed, Jane was fading. Her arms and legs ached and as the fire warmed her, she slumped down where she sat and jerked herself awake. She flexed her sore limbs. They had to climb again tomorrow—how would she ever manage?

Rowan glanced around the clearing as darkness fell. He'd been doing so repeatedly as they ate. His eyes were alert and his shoulders tense—not like her body, ready to fall off the log. He must be worrying about whoever had come through the campsite. But it was most likely an animal—maybe a raccoon sniffing the firepit for any food they had dropped the previous night.

Rowan left her by the fire to hang one of the hammocks in the trees, leaving his blanket in it. When she dragged herself up and approached, he indicated it was for her.

"I'm going to sit by the fire a little longer," he said.

Jane took care of her bedtime routine and finally was able to stop moving as she lay back in the hammock. For a moment after lying down, she could barely move to shift her body to the center. She summoned the willpower to use her weary muscles. She'd slept in her clothes the previous night, too awkward with her injured ankle to do any more, but tonight she pulled the suspenders off her shoulders and undid the buttons on her trousers, trying to get comfortable. If only she could sleep in her underthings. But she wasn't about to start stripping off her clothing with Rowan nearby.

This was Elle's third night away from home. But they knew where she was. They might even be there tomorrow. Jane had to be patient only a little longer.

The flickering light of the fire filtered through the weave of the hammock. Instead of giving in to the pull to close her eyes, she watched the light fade as the fire died down, and she listened for sounds of Rowan going to sleep, but the clearing was silent. She lifted her fingers to the edge of the fabric and peeked out. He sat beside the pit, where embers glowed dark and red.

He'd seemed so lighthearted when they'd begun climbing the rocks but pensive since they'd finished. He must be mulling over their visit with Axe. When she'd offered to return to Axe, she hadn't reasoned through what she was saying. She'd felt desolate seeing the solitary dragon and the words had come out. But she meant them. She would like to see him again. And if she went, Rowan would go too, and that seemed important somehow but she couldn't think clearly anymore.

Rowan looked lonely. She could get up to sit with him. But she was so drowsy. She blinked slowly. He looked despondent sitting there alone by the dying fire.

Rowan softly called her name. She inhaled cool air and turned over in the hammock. He called again and she clumsily pushed herself upright, breaking into the light of morning. She smelled the chilly forest air and rubbed at her eyes.

Rowan stood by the firepit. "I'm sorry to wake you," he said in that low voice of his. "We've a long day."

"What time is it?" Her throat was raspy from sleep.

"An hour past sunrise."

"I can't believe I slept so long." Her sleep had been heavy and dreamless.

"You worked hard yesterday."

"Did you sleep?" she asked, eyeing Rowan's clothing. Not that she expected him to bring pajamas on a trip like this. But his clothing wasn't rumpled and the second hammock wasn't hung.

"Some. There's tea." And with that, he strode away into the trees to give her a few minutes of privacy.

When she settled by the fire, she scanned over the pot and cups in the hot coals. Rowan had made oats again, enough for two so she sprinkled some of her dried cherries in so he would have to share them. She started eating her half, avoiding the cherries. When he returned, she passed him the bowl.

After they had eaten and packed their things, they headed up the main trail and past the place where they'd left it the previous day. Axe had told Rowan to go to the apex of "the people trail" before turning off to reach Sunshine's peak. As they continued on, they passed the remains of a broken wagon wheel. And then a ripped-up leather shoe. And a bit of rusty metal sticking up from a clump of grass. Rowan's shoulders tensed with each new object. Humans had left the trash along the trail, he would say; typical humans. But he was probably right. Even when the fairies used human tools or other technology, they were careful with it and they'd never dump it in the woods when it stopped working.

Soon after they'd started climbing, they rounded a bend and came to a small signpost. Letters carved into the wood read MINE and to the right of the post, a trail wound off into the trees. This trail was wide and flat, weaving between stumps and saplings and out of sight. They stopped at the turn.

"Is there any reason to go down there?" Jane asked.

"No. I'd rather we didn't."

Since he was trying to keep the dragons' locations a secret, it made sense to avoid letting anyone know they were here. But he hesitated, peering down the path.

"Rowan?"

"It's awfully quiet for a mine."

"Have you been before?"

"No. But I imagined a mine would have humans shouting orders at each other and a lot of metal machinery clanging."

Typical fairy response. Although Jane would have thought the same thing. Breaking chunks of iron ore out of rock, or whatever iron miners did, seemed like it would have to be noisy. "Do you think something's wrong?"

"I don't know."

He turned uphill and continued walking.

After the turn to the mine, the trail grew more difficult. A channel of rocks of all shapes and sizes cut through the bushes and Jane had to use her hands to scramble along. As the slope steepened, climbing it actually became easier because she could pull herself upward over the rocks rather than trying to hop from one to the next on her feet or to crawl over them horizontally. It made sense the trail wouldn't be improved west of the iron mine because no one had a reason to come this far. But a trail led onward, however wild. Maybe at one time, someone—humans or fairies—had had a reason to journey over the mountains on this route.

The trail narrowed to dirt between saplings and curved around a large boulder. As she came out on the far side, the bushes opened to reveal a sheet of rock sloping down to an abrupt drop-off. Jane halted, staring in horror.

Rowan was three steps onto the rock. He glanced back and slowed. "Hang on to the branches," he said. He moved to the top of the slope and reached for a branch hanging over it and another as he crossed. He didn't need to hold on like that and was doing it to show her. She crept onto the sheer rock, leaning out for a sturdy-looking branch before leaving the safety of the dirt trail. She placed each foot carefully, checking its grip before moving her weight onto it, and never let go of one branch until she had the next in her fist. It took fifteen paces to cross. Rowan waited on the far side and continued into the bushes as soon as she stepped off the rock.

Across the drop-off was a view of the ridge of green mountains running up to the north. Jane gazed out as she caught her breath. None of the rocky protrusions like the ones she'd seen from Axe's peak were visible here. They must be to the south, like Axe's, and to the west of this hill they were climbing.

She followed Rowan into the bushes. She couldn't see any trail at all, just rocks and leaves and tree trunks, but he strode along as if he were following a path. The rhododendron bushes returned in larger and larger patches until she was passing through a tunnel of them, clambering between boulders that the bushes clung to and spilled over.

"How can you tell where the trail is?" Jane panted.

"There are markers."

There were markers? She hadn't seen a single thing that wasn't a rock, leaf, or branch since they'd left the mine.

A moment later, Rowan slowed. He pointed to a fat dribble of orange sap on a tree trunk.

"That's a marker?" She reached to run her fingers over the hard surface as she neared. It wasn't sticky at all, as if it had dried into a solid resin.

"It's meant to look natural."

"Did the fairies make them?"

"Yes."

"Don't the markers wear off?"

"Eventually," he said. "Someone comes through to repaint them every dozen summers or so."

"How do you make the paint?"

"Pine sap. And magic."

Of course. Magic.

Sunlight glinted on the golden sap. Jane searched overhead for the sun as Rowan continued forward. A beam caught her right in her eyes and she blinked it away and followed him.

The continuous tunnels of rhododendron bushes shaded them as they climbed. The effort of climbing warmed her from the inside, but the shade grew chillier the higher they went. She gasped for air. But not enough that she would worry Rowan about it.

The first day of climbing had made her feel strong, but the resulting stiffness and aches were compounding. Her whole body was one big ache, from the soles of her feet to the tops of her shoulders. If only she could talk to Rowan to pass the time. She didn't have the breath to do it.

"Here," he said, stopping and reaching into one random bunch of rhododendron bushes. As Jane caught up, she peered through the thick leaves. His fingers touched lightly on a cluster of magenta blossoms in the center of a ring of leaves. The bright pink amid all the greens and browns of the trail sparked joy in her breast. Each flower looked delicate, with petals as thin as silk, but together the blossoms radiated out from a central point to form a ball of flowers bigger than one of the summer melons that farmers brought in from the plains at Woods End.

"That's beautiful," Jane whispered.

Rowan withdrew his hand and slowly resumed climbing. Jane dragged herself away from the flower. But soon they passed another, and another, and another the higher they climbed. She watched for new blooms with each new bend of their route.

And suddenly she stepped out of the bushes onto a rock and the whole world seemed to open up. Green mountains spread to the west before her, ridge after rumpled ridge, so far into the distance that the farther ones were blue and beyond those they faded into the sky at the horizon.

Wind whipped at her bangs, cooling her of any heat she'd built up on the climb. After a hint of pine and the scent of damp growth, the cold in her nostrils obliterated the smell of the forest. Pink blossoms dotted the bushes along the top edge of the rock she stood on and she spotted a few of the orange fire mushrooms. They must be nearing Sunshine's den. The sun beamed high overhead.

The trail dropped in front of her, running over another sheet of rock, downhill for the first time since they'd left the outpost at the crossroads. Twenty paces ahead, it disappeared back into more blossom-covered bushes with a splotch of resin on the rock beside the entrance to the tunnel. Dark-green pointed pine trees and the rounded tops of hardwoods rose over the leafy rhododendrons.

"Is this the top?"

"Yes. We can take a rest."

Rowan stepped onto the broad expanse of uneven rock and found a seat, stretching his legs before him. He rotated his ankles in a few circles and stretched his back. Jane carefully followed him onto the rock and lowered herself beside him.

"I'm down to hard biscuits for lunch," he said. "They're plain but filling."

Rose had described the fairies' travel biscuits once. They were deceptively simple looking but filled with nuts and mashed up dried fruits and seeds that gave a person the energy to walk all day. Which was exactly what Jane needed.

Rowan unwrapped a stack of the bar-shaped biscuits and peeled one off for her. She took a bite—her teeth stuck in the dense biscuit. She had to work her jaw to move her teeth and rip the bite off. She munched through its strange taste of salty sweetness while gazing at the view.

The distant mountains must be taller than this one they'd just climbed. To the north the tops rose above the tree line, and the most distant rocky peaks were capped in white snow. She didn't see snow on the western peaks but they were pointier on top, except for a cluster with strangely flat tops.

As if he read her mind, Rowan pointed at the group. "Do you see the volcanoes?"

"That's what they are? The ones without points?"

"Yes. The bits of cloud around the tops are vapors drifting from the thermal vents."

"Have the fairies traveled that far?" She'd heard of volcanoes but she'd never known anyone who'd seen one.

Rowan shook his head and didn't answer for a beat. "That's where Axe is from," he said at last.

"Where the mineral springs are?"

"Yes."

Rowan had avoided talking about Axe before, but he stared westward with a wrinkle in his brow and Jane couldn't resist asking. "Will he return there soon?"

Rowan stared so long without moving that she thought he wouldn't answer. His gaze dropped from the mountains to his empty hands in his lap. "He has to. He needs to visit the springs but he . . ." Rowan's lips pressed tight and his fingers curled into fists.

The silence grew heavy. "How far can we see?" Jane asked to break the silence, and without meaning to, she looked to her left. The mountains to the south were smaller domes, all covered in trees until they disappeared from view.

"Maybe forty or fifty leagues?"

"Not far enough, " she whispered.

"For what?"

Her cheeks heated even with the stiff breeze. Did fairies have extra-keen hearing? "Nothing." But when he waited, she sighed. "For a moment I imagined we might be so high I'd see past the edge of the forest. This far west we might be aligned with the Gulch."

"The Gulch?"

"Gold Gulch."

He shook his head.

"It's a tiny outpost on the south edge of the forest, up against the mountains. Someone found gold there once which is how people ended up there, but the gold is gone and the families who remain are farmers."

"Is that where you're from?" he asked quietly.

She nodded and ripped another bite off the biscuit.

"Do you miss it?"

Did she? She missed joking with her brothers and the comfort of having her father nearby. But her father had always been melancholy and she'd guessed losing her mother had caused it. And since her mother had died giving birth to her, she had always feared she was what made her father sad.

And it had been lonely in their cottage, several leagues away from the nearest neighbor. Day in, day out, always the same chores and work, the same company.

They'd had seasonal gatherings in the small village center. Those had been exciting. People would camp for several days and the youngsters would sneak off together to talk and kiss and possibly tumble each other in the bushes, finding who they liked and might bond with. That's where she had first tumbled someone. And continued to tumble others, several times as the seasons passed. Afterward she had gossiped with the other girls about their experiences.

The others had been eager for more, ready to mate with whomever they'd most enjoyed in the bushes. But Jane had felt rushed to pick someone without feeling like she *knew* any of them. Yes, she wanted someone who was fun in the bushes—or, ideally, in a bed—but that wasn't all she wanted in a life-mate.

Everyone had assured her the pain of the first time would pass—no one else seemed bothered by it, they were so excited by the pleasure of the encounter. But for her, the pain didn't pass and no one could explain why. Even the other girls' mothers hadn't found a solution, merely advising her to relax or to use a little cooking oil to smooth the way in or to try a different position. But nothing had worked.

Rowan had asked if she missed it. "Only sometimes," she replied.

"Have you been back since . . . ?"

"No."

"It's far to travel."

"It is."

He didn't respond.

"I couldn't believe I walked all the way from the Gulch to Woods Rest. Later, when Ladi showed me on a map where I was, I couldn't believe it. Woods Rest is the nearest town to the cabin where—" She stopped. "You probably know . . . I mean, you . . . um, never mind." What was she thinking? Poor Rowan. Just because he'd been friends with Larch didn't mean he knew about the "romantic" cabin in the woods where Larch and his brothers brought their victims.

Rowan picked at a piece of orange fruit on the corner of his biscuit.

"It feels like we've walked that far today," Jane said to change the subject.

"We're almost there," he said.

"And by 'there' you mean . . . Sunshine's den?" Jane asked hopefully.

"The bottom of the climb up to it."

"Right." Jane had another bite of her biscuit and kept her groan inside.

Chapter 10

WHEN THEY'D FINISHED THEIR BISCUITS, they had a long drink and refilled their gourds from a deep puddle of rainwater gathered in a dip in the rock. Rowan knelt to repack his bag so Jane used the time to shake out her braid, running her fingers through her hair and letting the wind cool her scalp. She lifted her bangs to wipe her sweaty forehead. She gathered up her hair and rebraided it tightly, binding the end and tying the long braid into a knot at the back of her head. If they were going to climb again, she wanted her hair safely out of the way.

At the apex of the trail, where it plunged into blooming rhododendron bushes to head east, Rowan stopped and studied the surroundings. "Axe thought Sunshine's den was on the south side of this trail, on a peak near to his. We'll have to get there as best we can." He pushed aside branches and ducked into the opening, holding the branches until she had them in her hands and could creep in after him.

Walking through a forest where—probably—no one had ever walked except squirrels and chipmunks was strange. They were the first people ever to see this tree, or that rock. If the forest held any secrets, they might uncover them. In places, they had to detour around underbrush. Rowan would check the sun after each detour and realign them onto his path to the south. The ground sloped upward but only slightly.

They passed through a clearing where the extra sunlight had

produced an especially gorgeous cluster of blooming rhododendrons. When the trees closed in more densely and blocked the light, the forest floor cleared of growth. Only a few of last autumn's leaves littered the bare expanse of moss, as well as a few small boulders, and they could walk more quickly. She moved up beside Rowan.

Even this high in the mountains, birds twittered in the branches. The squirrels were shyer than the ones who hopped around on the grass in Woods Rest. Here they scrabbled around the tree trunks with clicking claws to stay out of view. A small reddish one sitting on a high branch glared down at them with its tail up stiff and vibrating. It let out a volley of fast cheeps, continuing to scold them as they passed below.

"He's warning his friends that we're here," Rowan said. "I tried to calm him, but I'm not sure anything got through, given my weak skills." He smiled ruefully.

"You probably could have learned if you'd been allowed in the forest when you were younger," Jane said. She hated to see him think that he was lacking.

"Did you consider smithing when you were younger? Was there a shop in your village?"

"No. Nothing like that in the Gulch. It's not much of a village."

He kept watching her as they walked side by side.

"Most of the farmers could mend a horse's shoe, but we didn't have a proper smithy. We had a building for gathering and a few merchant carts came through each summer. But otherwise the Gulch is only cottages on farmsteads with long stretches of road between them. Our farm was up against the edge of the forest, several leagues off from the village center."

"Would you like to go back?"

"Maybe to visit. I wonder about my family. My brothers must be bonded by now. But I felt too ashamed to return after . . . after what happened. And then Elle came back to me, and it seemed too hard to travel all that way with her. I don't think I'd want to raise her there. I did send a letter so they'd know I was all right."

"You did nothing to be ashamed of."

"I trusted someone when I should have known better."

"You trusted someone who took advantage of you," Rowan said with a hint of an edge in his voice. "He is to blame, not you."

"But it's exactly what my family said would happen. They said I shouldn't daydream the way I did. They expected me to bond with one of the neighbors' sons and become a farmer like everyone else. But I couldn't."

"None of them attracted you?"

The rumble of his voice saying those words heated her inside. Jane swallowed and forced her thoughts to their conversation. "Maybe at first? I did like some of the young men. But we'd fool around and that part . . . wasn't so enjoyable." Her cheeks heated.

"They were disappointing?"

She had been disappointed but the problem had been her, not the young men she'd known. But how could she explain *that* to Rowan? "I suppose. But I'd imagine someone instead—a handsome stranger appearing in our yard and falling in love with me and taking me away on an adventure. So when I met Cedric—Larch—it felt like my daydream was coming true."

"How did you meet him?"

Jane turned to Rowan in surprise. He wanted to hear more about Larch? She'd never told the details to anyone. Her friends in Woods Rest had each had her own, similar story and hadn't needed to hear of another heartbreak.

But he watched her as he walked, as if waiting on her answer.

"I was picking berries in the woods behind our house," she said. "He seemed to appear from nowhere, and I should have been alarmed but he was so solicitous. He kept his distance as he spoke, and I thought he was handsome. He said he was traveling through and had stopped to rest in the shade. His story made no sense because he was far off the road—my daydreams had never been logical. That's what made it seem wondrous, though: I'd imagined something nearly impossible and it had happened."

Rowan was still listening, breaking his gaze away only to check the ground at his feet. When he again turned to her, unsmiling but not unkind, she found herself continuing the story.

"He helped me pick berries and asked about my life. When the sun got low, I said I had to go, and he asked me to meet him there the next day. He told me not to tell my family—he insisted he wanted to meet them, but only after we spent more time together. I just wanted to see him again. I went the next day as soon as my brothers and father were out in the fields. I knew they'd be working until sunset."

She took a moment to remember. For so long, it had been the happiest day of her life. Even after Larch betrayed her, and after she understood he had enchanted her with a love spell, she still remembered the feeling of joy she had had that day, until finally after many seasons, the memory had faded.

"Larch had a picnic spread in a sparkling glen—now I know he used some fairy trick to make it sparkle—and he gave me wine, which was so sophisticated. I felt odd after drinking it, but I thought it was the alcohol. I'd never drunk much ale. I was kissing him within the hour and hungry for more but he wouldn't give in, promising only to give me more if I'd leave with him that night. And I wanted to—I had no thought to how it would hurt my family. I'd like to blame the love potion for that because I hope I wouldn't have been so callous. He sent me home with a basket of berries so I could say I'd been working all day. I never even wondered when he'd gathered them."

Her throat tightened when she thought of her last sight of her family, all those seasons ago. "I don't know how I faced my family that evening and kept my secret hidden. After they were asleep I packed my clothes and sneaked out. I left a note so they'd know why I'd gone, if not where. The moon was rising and everything felt romantic. Larch met me at the edge of the trees and led me into the forest and he had a horse. It never seemed odd he suddenly had a horse—but again, I hope the love potion made me so stupid. I was only glad we weren't using the road where someone might stop us."

Rowan faced ahead as they walked. But if he wanted her to stop he didn't say, and she couldn't stop now.

"We walked some of the time and each time my legs began to ache, he'd stop and kiss me until I was too distracted to care. He must have known people would come after us because he kept us moving through the night and past dawn, until I was sleeping against him on the horse. He didn't stop until night came again. That night I lay with him on a blanket on the forest floor, and he gave in to my begging. And it was better than it ever had been . . ."

Had it been better? She hadn't anticipated the pain because she'd been besotted with "Cedric." But she had felt the usual sting-ing, rubbing feeling as he entered her, only muted as if the edges of the pain were dulled. Maybe the love potion had made intercourse easier, too. And she hadn't cared about her enjoyment because she'd wanted to please Cedric so badly. At the time she'd thought it must not hurt as badly because Cedric was "the one" for her, her true love, the most amazing lover of all time.

Blech.

Rowan walked beside her in silence.

"Anyway," Jane said, "after that, he wanted me all the time. I thought he must be as mad for me as I was for him. But now I know . . . he was trying to get me pregnant so he could take the child and be done with me."

Jane's face heated the moment she stopped speaking. Once she'd started remembering, the whole story had poured out. All her foolishness and the reckless decisions she'd made. Maybe she'd been under a love spell once she drank Larch's wine, but she hadn't been that first day when she'd fallen for his phony charms and decided to lie to her family and sneak out behind their backs.

"You were young," Rowan said as if he knew she was blaming herself again.

"I was stupid. My family was right. I had my head in the clouds and my daydreams led me astray. And the absolute worst thing that could have happened did. If it weren't for Rose and Dustan, I'd never have gotten Elle back."

"All you did was go to meet with Larch. That's not a terrible thing. The rest of it was the love potion."

"But the magic can't completely change you—that's what Rose said. It only enhances the feelings you already have. I must have wanted him some."

"That's not hard to understand. He was handsome and charming and offered the excitement you craved."

"But now I don't know who to trust." She could hear the whine in her voice but couldn't stop herself from continuing, letting all her frustration out. "Maryanne says I should think strategically: who'll be a kind father to Elle and a decent partner. Is that the way to do it? That sounds like my family again, telling me to ignore what I feel and choose one of the neighbors and be done with it. And should I feel something in the beginning, or will that come after? I don't know what it's supposed to feel like when someone is a suitable match. I think about it all the time until I'm looping in circles, confused. How can I tell who's right for me? How do I sort out liking how he looks, or feeling attracted to him with my body, or if I like talking to him, or if he's logically a good match, or—"

Jane cut herself off and her face burned. Why was she babbling on about this? Rowan walked alongside her without speaking, clearly embarrassed, his eyes trained on the ground in front of him.

"I'm sorry," she said.

"You've nothing to be sorry for."

Tears pricked her eyes. He was always kind, but she felt ashamed for her past and for spilling it all out like that.

Jane stayed quiet as they walked a little farther. She listened to the birdsong and tried to enjoy the smell of fresh mountain air. She needed to calm down before they were climbing up another cliff or she'd slip and fall.

One birdcall grew louder, a rapid cheeping with a trill at the end. A pair of birds with an orange splotch under their wings perched on a low branch ahead. "Cheep-cheep-cheep-chi-i-i-i-i-it!" one called before they took off together and swooped to the next tree. "Cheep-cheep-cheep-chi-i-i-i-i-it!"

Rowan followed their flight. As Jane and Rowan progressed, the pair stayed with them, always moving to the next tree.

"What are they?" Jane asked.

"Towhees."

"Are they trying to tell us something?"

"I think so."

The birds flew farther ahead, landing on a tree to the right. As Jane and Rowan neared, the ground dropped and split. A rocky chasm opened as the view widened and ahead the trees dwindled with a view off the south side of the mountain. Rowan stopped, scanning the forest on either side of the cleft.

"Cheep-cheep-cheep-chi-i-i-i-i-it! Cheep-cheep-cheep-chi-i-i-i-it!" both birds sang together. They broke into a harsh, squawking call, hopping between the branches of their tree.

Rowan took a tentative step toward them and they trilled and flew to a farther tree. He followed them along the right edge of the chasm. "I think they want us to go this way."

"That's . . . nice of them?"

Rowan smiled. "Axe must have asked them to come. To show us which way to go along the side of the mountain."

Jane smiled at the reminder of the older dragon who was helping them. Next time she saw him, she'd do more than thank him. Maybe she could bring him baked goods or maybe he liked having his scales scratched. Rowan would know what Axe liked.

She followed as Rowan resumed walking. From behind, she couldn't stop noticing how attractive he was—from his dark hair with its soft locks that cut off at his neck, to his broad shoulders that dwarfed the large pack on his back, to his lean hips and sturdy legs striding over the hard ground. But Woods Rest had plenty of sturdy, broad men. Rowan was different. His stillness, that calm way he handled everything, appealed to her. His low, quiet voice that was somehow commanding, and the attentive way he listened, and how he always excused her faults, declaring that she was young or had not failed when she trusted someone. He made her believe him: maybe she wasn't hopelessly flawed.

The ground narrowed into a lip along the base of a rocky cliff. To her left, the land dropped away with sickening steepness. Once they started onto the narrow path, the towhees chirped a few times and flew away.

As they progressed around the southern edge of the hillside, the largest trees cleared completely to show the view to the south. One rocky peak to the left towered above the treetops.

"Is that Axe's den?" Jane asked.

"Yes."

Rowan moved slowly and Jane took each step carefully. The drop wasn't sheer—if she fell, she could grab one of the saplings clinging to the steep slope. But hopefully this section of the trail wasn't long. Occasionally rhododendrons and other bushes hung down over them, clinging to cracks in the rocks, and more and more fire mushrooms appeared. This side of the mountaintop was shady at least, so no sunlight glared in her face as she picked her way along.

The steepness below them lessened and filled in with boulders, piling upward, and a tall peak appeared as they came around the mountainside. It was as wide as the entire village center in Woods Rest, much wider than the rock column they had climbed yesterday. They walked until they reached its base.

Rowan peered up at the towering peak. It was so steep it seemed to lean over them and the chill of the perpetually shady stone filled the air. Up high, mushrooms clung to the rocks, along with mossy patches and scraggly shrubs, but the first hundred hands or so was a sheer wall.

Rowan slid his pack to the ground. "I'm going to see what's on the other side." He shed his coat and stepped onto the boulder at the base of the peak. He climbed across the rocks, growing smaller and smaller until he disappeared around the distant endpoint.

Jane dropped her satchel beside a bush. She pulled her coat off, enjoying the cooling breeze, and lay it on the soft moss at her feet to sit on. She sorted through her remaining food. She had a packet of crackers, but the fairy travel biscuits served much better to provide energy for a climb. The dried cherries were gone but she had a napkin filled with apple rings and another of pecans. Her water gourd was half-filled. Otherwise, all she carried was her toothbrush, her blanket—Rowan gave it back to her each morning and took his, probably because his was much heavier—and a clean set of underthings, which didn't seem worth changing into if she couldn't bathe first.

She spread the blanket on the ground and laid out the food on it. She nibbled on a cracker, closing her eyes to wait.

After a while, Rowan reappeared on the opposite side of the peak from the direction he'd left in—he'd completely circled it. He climbed over the last few rocks at the base. "There's a better place to go up on the back side." He stepped onto the solid ground, eyeing her row of supplies.

"This is all I've got left," Jane said. "Do we have enough supplies to go up and back?"

Rowan dropped down beside her, crossing his legs. He dragged his pack over with a clang. "I've got plenty of hard biscuits and oats," he said. He tugged out his blanket and gourd, followed by a stitched fabric sack (the oats, she guessed, based on the dust filtering out the seams), the packet of biscuits, and his knife. The two belts they'd worn while climbing to Axe's den came out next, and the length of rope with the spring-clip on the end. The two hammocks. Something long and hard tumbled out: a dagger in a sheath. Jane startled but Rowan only moved the dagger to the side.

He took out more rope, this time thinner and shinier. It must have even more of the special fairy thread in it to make it shimmer like that. Hopefully the magical thread made it strong enough to get them safely up this peak.

He pulled out more of the thin rope. And more. How did he have all of this in his pack? And then he pulled out a large iron hammer. And a handful of flat iron pieces with a loop on the end of each, and more of the magical spring-clips.

Jane gawked. No wonder his bag had nearly toppled her over when she'd worn it. "You've been carrying that hammer this whole time?"

"We might need it to get to the top."

"You mean, to get me to the top, don't you?"

He pushed his hair behind his ear and turned his face up to hers. She was used to him watching the ground so when he did regard her, his gaze was riveting. In the shady spring day, his green eyes mirrored the treetops, filled with life and hope. What would they look like as spring passed into summer? In the warm sun instead of in cool shade?

He smiled slowly. "I could climb to the top without ropes," he said, "but it's safer not to."

Jane's cheeks warmed. Why? Nothing about his words suggested anything smutty—it was the same as if Maryanne had said, I'm going to buy fabric. But the way he said it, staring into her eyes with his voice soft and curling around her, made her think of crawling across the two paces between them and pushing him down on the moss.

"I suppose it's not so bad if I slow you down, if it keeps you safe," she said, trying to keep her voice steady and light.

   Jane Buehler

There. Nothing suggestive about that at all. But her cheeks only got hotter.

Rowan blinked and looked down, still smiling. "I'm not sure how high it is or what the climbing will be like. We could wait until the morning to start if you don't want to risk sleeping up there."

Sleeping up where? On the side of a cliff? She squinted up at the towering rocks. "Do you have a plan to 'sleep up there'?"

"I do."

Jane hadn't seen Elle in three days. Knowing they'd been journeying toward her had kept her patient, but being this close she didn't want to wait around for morning.

"Let's start," Jane said.

Rowan wedged his coat and blanket into his bag. "Let me carry your water," he said, deftly whisking her gourd off her blanket and into his pack with his own. The hammer and other goods followed. "We might have tight spots to squeeze through and it'll be easier to manage if your pack is light."

Jane bit back a protest. He was the expert here. She wouldn't try to sort out what was logical behavior and what was Rowan trying to make her comfortable at his own expense. He probably wouldn't even notice the extra weight.

She repacked her bag, folding her coat and scarf with the blanket at the bottom because she was sure to warm up once they started climbing. She left it on the ground as she stood. Rowan held out the belt. "Do you remember how it goes?"

She took it and wrapped it around her waist, cinching it tight and closing the first buckle. "Like that?"

He watched her hands. "Yes."

She fumbled with the next buckle and the rest until they were all fastened. She tugged on the front loop to show him it was secure. Because if he reached for her to test it, she might do something stupid.

Rowan donned his own belt and pack and started onto the

rocks the way he had come, passing between the peak and the green hillside to the north. Around on the western side, the sheer face gave way to a slanting tumble of boulders. On the low side of the slant, broken rocks continued outward for a few paces before ending at the drop off the side of the mountain. Using his arms as well as his legs, Rowan clambered up the patch of boulders. At least if Rowan or she fell backward, they wouldn't go over the edge. They'd land on a pile of jagged rocks instead.

Jane started up after Rowan, watching where he gripped and where he placed his feet and copying him as best she could. Climbing this way wasn't hard and they reached a ledge within a few minutes. Rowan followed the ledge back toward the forest the way they had come. The ledge ended above the sheer cliff they'd first seen but off to the north side so they couldn't see where they had started from, below. As the rock continued up from where they stood, it became more cracked and knobby than the sheer face below.

"We can go up here," Rowan said, kneeling and opening his pack. He motioned to Jane to take a seat. He took out the hammer and one of the iron pieces with the loop and slid his fingers along a crack in the rock, concentrating. He poked the flat end of the iron piece into the crack in a few places. After a few tests, he positioned the iron piece and raised the hammer. Jane cringed as he brought it down. The ring of metal on metal filled the air. The first strike drove the piece in but Rowan kept pounding on it, deeper and deeper. At last the hammer went silent.

"Won't Sunshine hear us?" Jane asked. If they spooked the dragon, she might fly away, presumably taking Elle with her.

"Hopefully we'll be quieter when we get close. I can try to communicate with her as we near."

Rowan tried wiggling the loop and it didn't budge. He tapped lightly on it with the hammer, testing if it could handle a sudden pull downward, before threading the hammer through a strap on the side of his trousers. He tied a length of rope between the new loop and his climbing belt. "It will stop me from crashing to the ground if I go over the edge," he explained. But as he stood to face the new wall of rock, the threat seemed to be that if he fell he would crash onto the ledge, not tumble off it.

Leaving his pack, Rowan gripped a protrusion and pulled himself up the wall. Jane scooted back to watch. He moved much more slowly today, sometimes stopping for a minute or more as he searched for handholds and footholds. This stretch was a long way up, so far that he crossed the line where the mountaintop's shadow ended, climbing into the sunshine. When her eyes began to tire, Jane stopped watching and instead worked out the crick in her neck. The air was chill in the shade and she forced in the deepest breaths she could, never quite getting enough air. When she next checked the cliff, Rowan had disappeared.

The hammer rang out, distant and tinny. After a minute of the noise, silence fell. Jane shielded her eyes and peered up, waiting.

Rowan tipped himself over the edge of the cliff, clutching a rope with one hand and letting it out as he walked backward down the rock, the same way he had at Axe's. As he let out the rope, it seemed to shimmer and disappear in the light as it twisted and turned. He walked down into the shade and closer until he stepped off the wall onto the ledge beside her, smiling.

"You honestly enjoy this," Jane said.

He unwound the turns of rope from the spring-clip, grinning, before unfastening the clip, tying the rope firmly to it, and passing it to her.

Jane clipped herself to the rope and ran her fingers up it. It was thin as a knitting needle and faded in and out of view with the tiniest motion. "This rope has more of the special fairy thread."

"Yes."

"Why did you switch?"

"It's stronger. We might have longer distances to climb today."

Longer distances. Wonderful. She waited for instructions.

Somehow Rowan remembered the holds he'd found that led to the top because he guided her up the cliff, step by step, taking the slack out of the magical rope as she went. Her arms had begun sore and now they ached but she had no choice but to continue. The alternative was asking Rowan to lower her down and waiting for him at the bottom.

When at last she pulled herself onto the ledge, she lay on the rock to catch her breath and let her head steady. She wasn't dizzy—she could see clearly. But her mind seemed to be catching its breath, too. She could have fallen to sleep right there. She'd reached the sunlight. It shone warm on her face and heat radiated from the rock under her body, but the sun was moving lower. The edge of the sunlight had shifted as she climbed and was right below the ledge.

Rowan was waiting. She pushed herself up to sitting with her bottom firmly on the rock and her legs dangling off. She unclipped herself and fastened the spring-clip to the new iron loop he had hammered into the rock. Rowan untied the rope at the bottom, coiled up the extra, and started up after her.

The mountaintop still blocked most of the view to the north with the sun skating over the rim. Rowan moved quickly up the rock. Jane reached for her water and remembered Rowan was carrying it. Her heart sank as he climbed onto the ledge beside her.

"Rowan, I forgot my bag."

"Where?"

"At the bottom. I was so nervous about the climb I forgot to put it on. I'm sorry."

"It's all right. I should've noticed you weren't wearing it. Do you want me to go back for it?"

After all that work? And they were already racing the sun—how much time would it take for Rowan to go all the way back down? And he had her water. "I can do without it," she said.

Rowan only nodded, coiled up the rope, and immediately turned to the next section.

They scaled two more cliffs with Rowan searching out a path each time and hammering a loop in at the top, then coming down to guide her up. He left the thin ropes hanging each time they moved on from these resting points. Why? Was it to escape quickly if something went wrong with Sunshine? Or maybe it seemed less risky to leave the ropes here, at the top of the mountain where no one ever came and already partway up the column of rock. Plus the rope was nearly invisible if you weren't searching for it.

The sky's blue was deepening as the sun neared the horizon, draining the light from the sky, and a snippy wind blustered through Jane's bangs where she sat waiting for Rowan to climb up to her. This ledge was fairly deep and she sat with her back against the cliff, trying to absorb the warmth of the stone and escape the biting wind. Because she faced west, the sun had been on the stone for a while. She kneaded her fingers, warming them and rubbing out the soreness from gripping the rocks. The sweat from all her exertion was damp and chill on her neck and she shivered. Drat. Her coat was with her bag.

Rowan clambered onto the rock in front of her. Even he seemed tired. He dropped his pack and crawled over to her.

"How do you feel?" he asked.

"Cold."

"We should stop here. The light's going to go once the sun sets, and I'm not sure how much farther it is."

"Okay. My, um, my blanket was in my bag."

"You can have mine."

"But you'll freeze! It was my mistake to forget it."

Rowan's voice remained patient. "Do you have another idea? Aside from me using the blanket and letting you freeze?"

Jane blushed. At least blushing warmed her. She could hear Maryanne ranting in her mind as she said, "We could share?" She winced, unable to meet his gaze.

"I don't want you to be uncomfortable," he said quietly, "from the cold or otherwise. I have my coat."

"No, I don't mind." She sat straighter, trying to sound calm and ignoring the specter of Maryanne. "It might be awkward, but it's more important we stay warm."

"All right," he said, swallowing. "We can share."

Chapter 11

JANE BIT HER LIP AS Rowan crawled across the ledge away from her. Had she really offered to share a blanket with him? That meant they'd be sleeping . . . close together. Jane swallowed.

At the edge of the ledge, he unclipped the rope from his belt and rose up on his knees, opening his pack.

"I don't suppose you have some magical way to stop us from rolling off the ledge in the night?" she asked.

Rowan regarded her a moment too long before pulling out one of the hammocks. As he spread it lengthwise along the ledge she moved out of the way. Crouching at one end, he slid his palm over the rock above it, as if examining the bumps and roughness. He did this motion a few times until his fingers settled on one place. He had an object in his other hand—a round thing like a walnut. He leaned to look past her briefly and pried the two halves open. Something stretchy inside resisted his pull.

Jane checked over her shoulder and saw empty open space. What had he looked at? The sun had set, leaving a yellow glow over the distant mountains.

Rowan had the walnut shell open and he dabbed a finger into a gooey substance inside it, turned, and spread it onto the cliff. He lifted the end of the hammock and pressed it into the goo.

It held.

"What is that?" Jane asked as Rowan crawled past her to the other end of the hammock and began the motions again.

"Fairy glue."

"What's it made of? Slug slime and magic?"

"Was that a lucky guess or did Rose tell you?"

"Wait, it's actually made from slug slime?"

"And magic."

Was he making fun of her? "How do you get it? Scrape it off slugs?"

"They wouldn't like that. We scrape it up after they pass. It's especially potent if you harvest it after they've mated. Plus they make a lot of it when they, you know, have slug sex."

He had to be teasing her. "Have you watched slugs have sex?"

"Yes."

Jane lifted her brow.

"It's quite romantic."

She shook her head. "How does the glue work? Can I move the hammock?" She pointed at the first place he'd hung it.

"You can try." He sounded challenging, more smirky than she'd ever heard him.

Jane tugged on the hammock. It held to the rocks. She gripped it in both fists and pulled.

"Careful. Don't fall backward and topple over the edge."

Jane let go of the hammock. It truly was fastened to the face of the cliff.

"How will we get it off in the morning?" she asked.

"Slug glue works only from twilight through the night. Once the sun rises it dries out and falls off."

"So we need to wake up before the sun or we'll fall off the peak?"

"Only onto the ledge. That's why I hung it down low."

"Can it truly hold both of us?"

"A patch of fairy glue can hold many horse-weights. And we'll have two patches."

"And the hammock?"

"Woven with fairy thread."

"Of course."

Rowan unfurled the hammock enough to spread his blanket inside. Jane caught the end and helped. He handed her a travel biscuit and her gourd and they had a quick meal as the evening chill settled in. Thankfully Rowan came up with a method for her to take care of her bodily needs by clinging to one end of the hammock and hanging her bottom off the edge of the ledge. After describing it, he turned away and intensely concentrated on slowly coiling a length of rope from his pack as she awkwardly followed his instructions.

She shivered as she straightened her clothing and placed her shoes up against the cliff so they wouldn't fall over. She tucked her loose suspenders into the top of her trousers so they wouldn't get hung up on anything. Like Rowan. And she unbound her hair and ran her fingers through it to comb it out, with help from the stiff breeze.

He ducked his head. "Ready?"

An uneven laugh escaped her throat. He turned. She inhaled slowly and waited.

Rowan stashed his pack by her shoes and sat sideways on the hammock, pulling the fabric out under his thighs. He positioned his seat on the back side of the hammock against the cliff, turned, and lay back, pulling his bare feet in. He held out the side for her to sit on, and she copied his motions and lay down beside him. Her shoulder dug into his bicep and he smelled nice, like his blanket had when he'd first given it to her. And he was warm. The blanket was under them and hanging out of the hammock. She pulled the edge of it over and around her body.

It was so uncomfortable.

"I might try turning," Rowan said. His arm moved up away from her side and he shifted until his back pressed against her. His back was also warm. She wanted to turn with him and wrap her arms around him. *That* would be comfortable.

Instead, she turned away from him.

Lying back to back was better. Her face was against the hammock but she could breathe well enough through the woven material. Hints of cold wind whispered through, but she was warm where the blanket swathed her and Rowan was a furnace against her back. She yawned. She wanted to flip over. She always flipped over once before she fell asleep.

But if she flipped over she'd be practically holding him. One move and she'd seem like she was rubbing up on him. But if she didn't flip over she'd never be able to sleep. And the circumstances were dire. They were sleeping in a hammock hanging on the side of a cliff, for skies' sake. And besides, she'd only promised Maryanne not to fall in love with him. She hadn't promised anything about not cuddling against him. For warmth, of course.

Jane hitched her hips over and her body followed. She did it once more and faced his broad back. She resisted putting her arm around him and simply snuggled against him.

Rowan shifted.

Was he uncomfortable? What if *his* face was pressed into the hammock? Or what if, on his side, the hammock was up against the hard cliff wall and his face was mashed into *that*?

"Are you comfortable?" she asked, yawning.

She could hear the gears of his mind coming up with a reply that wasn't a direct lie. "I don't mind it," he said.

"Here." She tugged on his shoulder and his body followed, turning over toward her. She nosed her way under his arm and he put it around her, under her head. He ended up back on his back but now she faced him and curved against his side. The hammock forced her legs to straighten against his and she pressed the tops of her cold toes on his warm skin. "Is this okay?" She yawned again, settling into him and closing her eyes.

"It's fine," he said softly. He pulled the blanket over her.

The wind whistled over the rocks outside. Jane listened to it in the dark, along with Rowan's quiet breathing. His chest rose and fell against hers. Everything was warm, from her feet nestled against his calves to her cheek lying beside his chest. As soon as she settled down and closed her eyes, the memory of gripping the cliff walls returned, as if she were reclimbing it. Last night she'd been so tired she'd slipped into slumber a moment after closing her eyes, but lying against Rowan held away her exhaustion.

They were so close to Elle. They'd reach her tomorrow. Rowan really *had* been able to find her. Would they take her home? Or let her stay and apprentice with the dragon? Jane would have to stay, too, if Elle stayed. She smiled, imagining a look of horror on Maryanne's face if they returned without Elle and said they'd left her behind alone.

But if she stayed, how would they get home when Elle finished her apprenticeship? The dragon might take Elle home but it probably wouldn't want to carry her. Could she get down this peak on her own? Maybe Rowan would come help her when the time came. She snuggled into the warmth of her hammock bed and put the thoughts from her mind. She had to meet the dragon and see Elle first.

No forest sounds reached them, only the soft wind. Rowan's chest expanded slowly. As it deflated, his whole body relaxed beneath hers before his breathing resumed its even pace. She hugged him close with her free arm as the rock wall towered before her again, knowing he would guide her safely up it. His hand came to rest gently on her back.

Jane dropped. Panic reared up but arms tightened around her. She wasn't falling. She'd only been dreaming of cliffs and climbing. She was lying motionless on someone with arms holding her safe and she was wrapped in warmth.

She rested her cheek against the warm fabric and relaxed, stroking its softness with her fingertips. She was in a hammock, she slowly remembered—that's what the falling feeling had been. Rowan had said the slug glue holding up the hammock would wear off at dawn, and the hammock would fall a hand's width to land on the ledge beneath it. The hammock had fallen but she was safe and she hadn't even landed on hard stone, only on . . . Oh. Oh no.

She was lying on top of Rowan.

Her pulse accelerated as she came awake. How long had she been on top of him? Skies he felt nice beneath her and with his hands on her back. If she pretended to be asleep, would he keep lying still and holding her? He could probably tell her heart had started racing, though, pressed up against his own. And her fingers splayed against his chest might have been caressing him.

Jane lifted her head and his hold on her loosened. The crown of her head brushed the hammock, splitting open the gap at the top. Her hair was pooled all around her shoulders on Rowan's chest. Morning light shone into Rowan's green eyes watching her.

Her breath caught and she became the deer startled motionless by the hunter. He was flat on his back with his head lifted up to gaze at her. His long hair hung to the side of his bare forehead and his lips made the sweetest bow. She resisted the urge to crawl up his body and kiss them. She forced her own lips to move. "Are you all right?"

He blinked, staring. "Did you sleep well?" he answered instead.

"Yes. Are you injured?"

"Why would I be injured?"

"From the fall."

His eyes crinkled at the corners. He jerked his head to the side, gesturing for her to move. "Off," he said, closing his eyes and resting his head back. But he said it so gently he might have been saying, Please come kiss me.

She pushed her fingers against the hammock fabric and reached an arm out to find the ledge, shuddering when her hand met freezing air and stone. But she couldn't delay, not with Rowan lying under her. She got a knee out, too, only now she was halfway straddling him and as she pushed herself sideways, she rubbed against a hard bump and oh, skies, that had to be him! She scrambled away, out onto the cold, hard stone.

Frigid wind surged around her, whisking away all of the blanket's warmth in the morning breeze. But all she could think of was that bump—Rowan's arousal. It had to be. Had it happened because of her lying on him? Maybe not—some men woke that way every morning. But if it *had* been because of her, what did that mean? He'd acted petrified when she'd asked him out in the smithy. Had he changed his mind? Or maybe it wasn't her specifically but he wanted a tumble and having a body lying on top of him and—she had to admit—snuggling against him had affected him.

Rowan's coat came around her shoulders, warding off the cold. He stood beside her and was already turning back to the hammock. She thanked him without looking up and huddled on the ledge. Maybe he'd think she hadn't noticed his erection. This didn't have to be embarrassing for either of them. She would put the memory of his—she swallowed—of his morning situation out of her mind.

She held the coat closed and backed against the wall as Rowan moved the hammock away. Far away to her left, to the south, wan sunlight shone across the misty treetops of the forested valley. Before her, fluffy stretches of cloud filled the sky down to the western mountaintops and patches of mist spotted the shadowed valleys. Their western-facing ledge was deeply shadowed, but the sun must be shining on the other side of Sunshine's peak. It would be hours before they were warmed by the light, though, unless they climbed around to the eastern side.

She shivered and pulled Rowan's coat tighter. He was rolling the hammock into his pack, wearing only his shirtsleeves. "Your coat—"

"I'm fine."

She bit her lip. Was it worth arguing? He wasn't shivering and he'd be climbing again soon as he scouted out the next stretch of the cliff. She slid her arms into the sleeves and thanked him again.

Rowan polished off a travel biscuit and set off. Jane waited on the ledge, nibbling on her breakfast and watching the clouds shift as the sun rose. The remnants of mist burned off on the forest to the south and the sky overhead cleared to a brilliant blue. To the west, the clouds sank down from the mountaintops, coalescing into a solid wall of fog over the valley even as sunshine filled the empty sky. She rolled her neck and hands in circles, leaned side to side, and rotated her ankles, working out the stiffness.

Rowan dropped onto the ledge beside her. "Ready to start?"

She wasn't but she couldn't tell him that. He never complained about anything, and he didn't even have to be here. She rose to her feet and gave him back his coat, knowing she'd soon be sweating with the effort of climbing.

They climbed the entire morning. Sunshine had taken Elle to a remote peak where no one would molest them. It showed the dragon was careful, which was auspicious. But the thought of Elle at the top of this tower of rock filled her with anxiety. After a midday meal of more hard biscuits, Rowan returned from climbing with a smile.

"We're almost there."

"Did you see Elle?"

He shook his head. "Sunshine's den is at the top of the next climb."

"But—"

He touched her arm. "It's hidden. We'll find it when we reach the top."

Jane nodded. Her heart was hammering. Elle would be fine. She was up there and she'd be fine.

"Sunshine may be waiting for us," Rowan said.

"How do you mean?"

"She might hear us coming."

Jane snorted. Rowan did everything silently. He meant Sunshine would hear Jane coming, but he was too polite to say it.

"So what do I do at the top?" Would she come face to face with a dragon without Rowan there to translate?

"Stay by the trees. I'll be right behind you."

"Trees? Up here?"

"You'll see." He indicated the end of the rope as he tied it to the spring-clip and handed it to her to fasten to her belt. The rope ran up and back, as usual. "She has some sturdy trees growing up there. I used them for the ropes. I didn't like to drive a spike into her den without asking. Or to wake her with the blow of a hammer, to be honest."

Jane started the climb. She was getting better at finding the handholds, sometimes gripping them even before Rowan called out directions. She climbed until her head broke into sunshine as she crested the top of the rock. The rope ran a few paces across the ground to loop around a trunk in a cluster of trees covered in pale pink blossoms. Apple trees! On top of the barren rock? Only the top wasn't barren—plants grew everywhere. But no dragon was in sight, and she saw no sign of Elle.

Jane crawled onto the top of the peak, glad of the warm sunlight although the stone under her hands was cold. She unclipped the spring-clip from her belt and lowered it down to Rowan before examining the entrance to Sunshine's den.

Color covered the top of the peak. Twisted pine trees mixed with delicate green bushes created an unusual landscape—were those blueberry bushes? Thorny branches with russet-green leaves and white petals arced across the rocks—those were blackberry! Beside the three apple trees, a deep pool of water shimmered in the breeze, surrounded by soft grass. And orange fire mushrooms covered the vertical sides of every rock, from the wall behind the apple trees to the larger boulders all around. The wide space was like a very disorganized human garden. Jane remembered Axe's sparse den and ached to think of the isolated dragon lying in it all alone.

Sunshine and Elle must be here somewhere among the trees and boulders. Jane pushed herself to standing and moved away from the edge toward the apple trees, stretching her muscles in all the ways they hadn't been used while climbing. Rowan appeared without a sound and climbed onto the ledge. He unhooked the rope from his belt and coiled it, leaving it at the base of the trees.

"Ready?" he said, facing her.

Jane tried to smile. He rubbed her arm and smiled back.

She followed him past the apple trees and into the shade among tall, mushroom-covered rocks. As they moved farther, the trees dwindled until they were in a maze of boulders. Rowan scanned the surroundings as he led her deeper in, until he stopped.

"The entrance is here somewhere. Wait here a moment."

He glanced up at the sun and all around, as if getting his bearings, before he slipped out of sight between two boulders. Jane didn't move—not that one could get permanently lost in this limited area, but knowing her luck, she'd walk right off the edge if she tried to follow him.

In less than a count of fifty, Rowan reappeared. "This way."

He led her in a zigzagging path between boulders until they entered a narrow channel leading inward. It narrowed so much Rowan had to take his pack off and turn sideways to fit. He examined the space overhead as if he might climb in from above but ultimately dragged his body through. Had Sunshine picked this spot knowing a large adult couldn't enter easily?

The channel widened into a flat courtyard. Rowan stopped.

Sunshine waited on the flat stones ahead. She was as big as Axe and her scales were a brilliant green. Her eyes narrowed as they faced her. Her wings were folded but not tightly, and she crouched on her clawed feet as if about to pounce.

Where was Elle?

Rowan observed Sunshine silently but his hand wrapped around Jane's wrist and held her tightly. Sunshine snorted a gust of hot air across the space. She blinked slowly and turned to look as she lifted one wing. Elle peeked out.

Jane started forward and Rowan's grip tightened and held her beside him.

"Mama!" Elle cried. Sunshine lifted her wing farther and Elle clambered up and ran to Jane.

Rowan released her and she fell to her knees and wrapped her arms around Elle. Elle clung to her, her small face against Jane's neck. Tears wet Jane's cheeks.

"Mama," Elle said. She pulled back. "I missed you."

"I missed you too. I—"

"I'm learning magic. Want to see?"

Jane nodded, wiping her tears. Elle's first thought was about magic? Her own questions could wait.

Elle detached herself and darted back toward the huge green dragon. Jane stood and stepped forward, but Rowan grabbed her again.

"Go slow," he murmured.

Jane forced her shoulders to relax and he released her. They moved into the courtyard. Sunshine kept her gaze on them until they stopped by a boulder with a flat top. Rowan tugged on Jane's sleeve and she sat beside him in the sun.

Sunshine's massive head turned toward Elle, seated cross-legged on the stones a few paces away. Elle's hair was tangled and she had smudges of dirt on her face. Her dress—the one she'd been wearing when Jane had last seen her, lying on the grass and talking to the daffodil—was in one piece, albeit dirty. But her face was glowing. Her green eyes were alight and she watched Sunshine with eager anticipation. And she sat waiting without saying a word. At home, the children were always hanging on Jane's sleeve or asking for something, even Elle. Jane had never seen her quiet and focused like this.

How did Elle stay warm enough with only that dress and her feet bare? Sunshine didn't have blankets. Did Sunshine truly keep her warm at night? Did she sleep under her wing? Maybe they'd been napping all morning as they waited for the sun to warm up the rocks.

Sunshine snorted again and Jane tensed. This time, Rowan put one arm around her shoulders and held her with his other hand. Dread pooled in Jane's gut.

Sunshine exhaled and a thin stream of flame shot from her nostrils toward Elle. Rowan's grip tightened as Jane whimpered. But Elle reached up a hand and . . . the flames disappeared. Elle grinned at her palm. She pressed it against the stone floor with a hiss.

She beamed up at Jane. "Did you see, Mama?"

Jane failed to get a word out so she gave a big fake smile.

Jane stared as the dragon sent stream after stream of fire at Elle, and Elle snatched each one and snuffed it out with her hands. Elle began using both hands, and the puffs of flame grew larger. "She's learned fast," Rowan whispered. He'd loosened his grip as Jane relaxed but kept his arm around her waist.

When the fire finally stopped coming and Sunshine lowered her head to the floor, Elle stood and stretched. She stumbled over to Sunshine and threw herself on the dragon's neck, petting her like she would Mouser. Tears pricked Jane's eyes. She knew where Elle wanted to be. What should she do?

Sunshine turned her snout toward them. Rowan's arm around Jane tensed. He shook his head. He stood abruptly, letting go of Jane and stepping in front of her. Flames teased out of Sunshine's nostrils, a small tumble of them, reaching slowly toward Rowan. Jane tried to see around him but he backed against her. The flames burned out. Sunshine hesitated, huffed, and turned away to rub her face against Elle until the child giggled.

"What did she just do?" Jane asked. Rowan was so close in front of her she had to hang on to him to stand, nudging him forward.

"Nothing." He stared down at his palms.

Jane held on to his arms. It wasn't nothing. Something had transpired between him and the dragon.

He lowered his hands and turned, breaking her hold on him as he stepped back. "I can tell you what Sunshine said about Elle."

Jane frowned at the change of subject but nodded.

"I told her you're Elle's mother," he said quietly, "and you hadn't known about her ability or the workings of fire magic, being a human. And that you were frightened by her arrival and worried about Elle. Sunshine told me Elle called to her, and after so many seasons of silence from the fairies, Sunshine was elated to be called. She also considered Elle young but took her because she was eager to go. She didn't realize no one knew Elle was leaving."

How did the fairies manage this relationship? Did the fairy children tell their elders one day that a dragon was on the way? Why didn't Elle tell her—or did she, and Jane wasn't listening? Elle said so many fanciful things about talking flowers and messages on the wind that if she'd ever mentioned a dragon, it would have gone right over Jane's head.

She was a terrible mother.

And if Elle babbled about dragons and they were real . . . Jane swallowed. Were the daffodils really talking? What about the wind?

"Do flowers talk?"

Rowan's brow wrinkled. "What?"

"Do flowers talk to fairies?"

"Not that I'm aware."

Jane sank back onto the rock seat. At least she didn't have to worry about that. Last moon she'd snapped off a few daffodils to take on a visit to Synne, the village healer; the other flowers probably had nothing nice to say about her.

Rowan loomed beside her, as quiet as a distant mountain. So Elle had asked Sunshine to bring her here. But that knowledge solved only part of her worry. "Can Sunshine communicate with Elle?"

"Sunshine said it's awkward. Elle's words come to her in a babble of thoughts and emotions that she tries her best to sort out."

"That's not so good. Did she share anything else?"

Rowan smiled a little. "She was enthusiastic about being named after the sun's light. She mentioned it several times."

Elle had climbed onto Sunshine completely, as if the dragon's neck were a pony. Jane leaned back. Rowan sank down beside her and they sat in silence, watching.

Elle eventually slid off the dragon's neck and came to Jane's lap.

Jane introduced Rowan but Elle was already propping her little bare feet against his thigh. Elle babbled about all the mushrooms she'd eaten and apples that Sunshine kept stored and dried berries, and about sleeping under Sunshine's wing. She pointed to a cave at the south side of the courtyard where they could go if it rained, and described drinking from pools of rainwater as if she were Mouser. She said something about a bath and how Sunshine wouldn't make her bathe the way she had to at home.

"But I missed you, Mama," Elle said, snuggling under Jane's chin. "I'm glad you're here. It'll be so much better now."

Sunshine watched them across the stone floor. She lay with her wings folded against her back but her eyes remained alert.

Jane met Rowan's gaze. What was she going to do?

Chapter 12

ELLE STAYED ON JANE'S LAP a little longer, digging her toes into Rowan and fiddling with the fabric bracelet at Jane's wrist. She did that sometimes, although she couldn't possibly remember the blanket the strip of fabric had torn from. Soon her attention waned and she slid down and padded back to Sunshine, and they began more practice. Elle had such focus for the task with the fire, doing it over and over as the puffs of flame grew larger.

Unable to sit any longer, Jane left Rowan lying in the sun and drifted around the edges of the courtyard. Sunshine's den had chest-high rock walls around the entire perimeter except at the entrance they'd used. Elle couldn't fall off the edge unless she went back through the entryway. Jane leaned on the wall, enjoying the warm sun. To the southeast, Axe's rocky peak rose up at the edge of a green hillside, clearly below them at this height. From up here she could see over the slope of the hillside, over more forest and far away to a blue horizon where an uneven shape poked up. Was that the castle in Woodglen? She squinted but couldn't make it any clearer.

She drifted along the wall. To the east more tree-covered slopes spread out and to the north she gazed down on the top of the mountain they had climbed on the main trail. The magenta rhododendron flowers dotted the greenery and nothing moved or cried out. Maybe birds avoided Sunshine's peak, whether or not she ate them. Although Axe had been able to communicate with those towhees, but maybe the forest creatures found him less threatening than Sunshine.

Past the mountain to the north was another and another, trailing away in a never-ending ridge of rolling, forested peaks, with gray rock showing on the farthest ones. The entrance to the courtyard was on the west side and the wall rose higher there, blocking out the view.

Jane let the afternoon slip by, not wanting to think about the decisions before her. Finally the sun got low in the sky. Elle gathered a handful of fire mushrooms from a patch on the wall, and Rowan sat up, watching her. Jane joined him.

"What's happening?" she whispered.

"Just watch."

Elle piled the mushrooms in front of Sunshine. She caught some of Sunshine's flame and picked up one of the mushrooms, and it sizzled in her palm. It exploded in a ball of fire that turned to smoke and drifted away. Elle frowned, staring at the charred bits in her hand.

Rowan held back a smile.

Sunshine gently nudged the child aside with her massive snout and when Elle crawled away, the dragon shot out a delicate curl of flame to roast the mushrooms.

Rowan handed Jane a travel biscuit. "I told her we'd eat our biscuits tonight," he said. "I didn't like to use up her supply of mushrooms." They had removed the climbing belts and he packed them into his bag before peeling off his own biscuit.

How long would they be here? She couldn't imagine taking Elle away from Sunshine or leaving Elle here. But that meant she would have to stay, which seemed outlandish—living up here and eating fire mushrooms every day? No doubt if she asked Rowan, she'd learn the mushrooms had all the nutrients a growing child needed. But even if she could stay, what about Rowan? He'd offered to find Elle, not to spend his summer living on a remote peak with her.

He sat close enough his body heat warmed Jane's arm.

"What happens now?" she asked.

"They'll sleep. They practice in the afternoon when it's warm."

"But what about tomorrow?"

He took a deep breath and let it out slowly. "Let's sleep on it and talk in the morning."

He was right. She couldn't do anything but wait a day—if they weren't going to stay, they couldn't climb down from here before dark. She nibbled off a bite of her biscuit. Rowan had devoured his and was already wiping the sticky bits off his fingers with a kerchief. He stood and after a moment of silence as he communicated with Sunshine, he took out one of the hammocks and hung one end on a protrusion of rock. He stretched out the material and tied the other end to a twisting branch of a tree hanging over the courtyard.

Were they going to share a hammock again?

Jane focused on Elle, who was licking her fingers. Skies her child needed a bath, but if Sunshine said she didn't, Jane wasn't about to get into an argument with the dragon about it. Maybe all that dragon fire kept Elle's fingers clean. And they couldn't waste the little water they had up here on bathing.

The sun was down behind the rocks and treetops in the west. Elle leaned on Sunshine's flank with a wing draped over her and her eyelids fell closed.

Sunshine exhaled. Her eyes darted to Jane and back to Rowan. He stood straighter and listened. His brow furrowed. "She says . . . she says we can have hot baths?"

Was Sunshine teasing? Had she known what Jane was thinking? Jane slid off the rock and walked over. "Elle said something about bathing."

Rowan tilted his head and glanced toward the back of the den, where the rocks rose up over Sunshine's cave.

"What is she saying?"

"There's a deep pool of rainwater on the back side of the cave. She uses the water to warm her cave through the night during the winter. She's offering to heat it for us to bathe."

Soaking her weary muscles in a hot bath? Scrubbing off the grime of the past few days? "Yes, please," Jane said, smiling at Sunshine.

Sunshine nudged Elle to sit upright and folded her wing as she rose to her feet. She glanced pointedly at Jane—she didn't have eyebrows but the ridge above her eyes rose—and Jane scurried forward to sit with Elle. With her wings lifting for balance, Sunshine lumbered across the courtyard.

"I'm ready to sleep, Mama." Elle fell against her side.

Her child had never said those words before. Usually getting her to bed took cajoling and patience. If only all the children could have dragon nannies. "It's almost time," Jane said, snugging her arm around Elle. "Sunshine's heating the bath water for me and Rowan."

"You don't have to." Elle yawned. "Sunshine won't make you bathe."

"Unlike you, I like being clean." But Elle was slumping over and didn't reply.

Sunshine lowered her head into her cave and huffed out flames. They curled against the rocks at the back. She paused, inhaled with a woosh, and let out a torrent of fire.

Jane cringed back, gawking at the display. Beside her, Elle didn't budge. Heat seared across the patio in uneven blasts. Sunshine kept gushing fire as a minute ticked past. She huffed out a final gust and her flame disappeared. She put her nose near the rock for a few heartbeats and stepped back.

Sunshine shambled back across the courtyard to lie against one wall. Elle was half-asleep against Jane's side. Jane kissed her child's head and stood, lifting her. Sunshine had her back leg out in an odd position. Jane watched her face for approval as she placed

Elle there. The scales were warm and Sunshine's wing came down, wrapping around Elle and holding her safely. Elle murmured, limp with sleep, and Sunshine's wing covered her.

Jane waited a moment more, watching the place where her child had disappeared. Elle seemed content here. And Elle being here felt *right* somehow, like Elle and Sunshine fit together. At home, Elle played with the children at times, but other times she went off on her own like her mind was somewhere else, drifting in her imagination. Here with the dragon she seemed entirely present.

Sunshine's eyelids drooped closed.

Rowan touched Jane's elbow. "Come," he whispered.

Jane exhaled and turned away. She followed him across the courtyard to the cave. Heat radiated out. A bath would be marvelous, especially with the twilight air turning chill. And Rowan—

Jane paused. Bathing meant getting naked. And *Rowan* would be there.

They'd be naked together in some kind of bath. If he did want her, surely something would happen. If this morning's situation hadn't been his usual one, if he found her attractive, he had to let it show. And if not . . . The night was dark with no moon and only the fading sunset. She could pretend to ignore him and the darkness would hide her blushing. Because she was sure to start blushing at the first glimpse of his long, lean body with—

"Here," he said. He'd been pacing along the outside of the cave, examining the stone. As she moved toward him, he pointed to a cleft in the rock to the right of the cave's entrance. Hidden behind a boulder, a narrow opening led behind the cave and upward.

"There's another stair on the other side," Rowan said. His face was shadowed. "I'll head over there if you don't need anything from me."

Her hopes sank but she wasn't about to tell him she needed him to satisfy all her prurient fantasies. "I'm all set."

"Okay." He moved away and into the rocks opposite her.

Jane stepped into the gap and climbed. She'd assumed they were going to bathe together. And she'd been looking forward to it.

Well, she had a hot bath to enjoy even if she was enjoying it alone. Since he wasn't interested, this way was better. This way she wouldn't be tempted to sneak glances at his broad shoulders, his naked chest, maybe a little lower . . .

Drat. She *was* a lecher. Rowan was probably glad to bathe in peace without her ogling him.

The steps in the rocks led outward to a wall with a view of the deep purple sky. Bright smudges of orange and yellow sunset stained the horizon to her right. She followed the steps around and farther up. Her feet were bare and as she reached the wide, flat stone at the top, it warmed her toes. Tall rocks surrounded her with the ones on the cave side radiating heat. A steaming pool of shimmering purple water reflected the sky overhead. Rowan must have another pool on the other side of the high dome of rock over the cave.

Rainwater running off the top of the dome over Sunshine's cave must fill the pools. At the outer edge of the pool, the rock was only a hand's width over the water's surface, offering a view to the west and south. Rowan had given her the side with the sunset view.

She no longer had her spare underclothes, since she'd left her bag at the bottom of the peak, but maybe she could use the hot rocks to help with laundry. She would rinse all her soiled clothes and lay them to dry while she bathed. She peeled off her shirt, trousers, and underthings and wished she had her socks, but she was naked and she didn't want to go back down to the chilly courtyard to get them.

Hot air off the rocks hit her front side as the cool wind over the mountains nipped at her shoulders and bottom. The first stars were out and she was up so high, as if she were up in the dark sky. Utterly naked. She studied her arms, holding them out and spreading her fingers against the sky. Her bracelet slipped down from her wrist, the one tiny bit of clothing she wore.

Being in a place like this was exactly the kind of thing that happened when you spent time with a fairy, wasn't it? She never could have imagined doing anything like this. Maryanne would *not* approve of her reveling in her nudity with a fairy right across the rocks. Nudity was one step closer to tumbling. But the fairy in question couldn't see her and he wasn't interested anyway. It felt freeing to have the wind caressing her in places it had never touched. And besides, Jane thought with a grin, Maryanne approved of baths in general. Jane could assure her that dragons had all the facilities needed for keeping children clean.

Look at her, lying like a fairy.

Jane bundled her clothing near the water's edge where she'd be able to reach it and stepped into the pool.

Skies it was hot. Her leg sank in and landed on a step, knee deep. She got her other leg in and paused to let her body adjust to the fierce heat. Brief snatches of cold stirred her hair but the intense heat of the pool rose up and chased it away. In the falling darkness and with the tendrils of steam off the water, the far edge of the pool was becoming hard to see.

She slid her foot along the step to its edge and down. This time the water rose to the top of her thighs. She reached back for her pile of clothing and pulled it into the water with her. Sitting on the first step sank her in to her chest. Skies it felt pleasant. Her sore feet and tired legs and stiff back were all softening. She relaxed and scrubbed at her clothes one by one, laying them on the warm rock dome to dry. When she finished with her laundry she slipped her body all the way into the pool.

The water was delightful. It closed over her shoulders as she bobbed farther in. If she stood, the water came to below her shoulders but when she floated it closed up to her chin.

The water wasn't cooling at all. It must keep taking heat from the mass of rock all around it. And how easily Sunshine had heated it in only minutes. Dragon fire was remarkable.

The sky was dark with more stars shining. Steam filled the air—Jane could barely make out the edge of the pool, an arm's length away. It was long and narrow, and she moved along the edge, watching the final orange glow disappear from the horizon. When she peered back toward the entrance, her white linen shirt spread on the rock was a bright blur in the dark. Steam beaded on her upper lip and forehead. Her bangs were plastered to her skin.

She let down her hair and worked the braid out until her locks floated around her. She scrubbed at her face with the water and dunked her head, staying under to let the water seep in toward her scalp. Her lower half had been soaking long enough that when she scrubbed at her skin, the layers of grime sloughed off easily. Jane kept at it until every bit of her skin was rubbed clean.

Was Rowan done bathing? Jane didn't want to hold him up with going to sleep. He must be tired, especially after keeping guard two nights ago and sleeping in the hammock last night.

But the water was splendid. And Rowan could go to sleep without her. He wouldn't mind if she stayed in the bath longer. She waded back to the steps to check the sleeve of her shirt—still damp. Her trousers might not dry tonight, but she could sleep in her underclothes and shirt. Or just her underclothes. She could lie on Rowan in only her underclothes . . .

Desire shivered through her center in spite of the steaming bath. She tried to focus on the water but her mind had other ideas—imagining his arms binding around her, his shirt open to press her breasts against his broad chest (where had her underclothes gone?), spreading her legs to straddle his hips, undoing the buttons on his trousers to feel that bump of his pressing against her . . . right . . . between . . . her legs.

Jane was so flushed with heat she reached for the edge of the pool as a wave of dizziness passed. Rowan was close, simply across the rocks from her in the neighboring pool. He'd *hear* her thinking lascivious thoughts about him! She had to get herself under control before they were face to face, whether they slept in one hammock or two. It wouldn't be fair to lie beside him—or on top of him— with waves of desire rolling off her.

Of course tumbling would probably hurt if he pushed inside her. It always had before. But maybe it wouldn't this time. Maybe this time it would be different.

But hadn't she thought that every time before?

Regardless, she couldn't have him inside her until she was drinking bitter tea again. Maryanne had probably "forgotten" to pack any tea for her intentionally, for this exact reason—to stop her from tumbling Rowan.

But Maryanne equated tumbling with intercourse. Jane could think of many other ways to enjoy it.

She pulled her body to the edge of the pool and leaned her arms on the top of the rocks. The air outside the pool and over the edge of the cliff was cool, even unpleasantly nippy with the sun down. She couldn't leave the water while it felt so sublime—leaving would waste Sunshine's effort to heat it.

And Rowan might be enjoying the hot water as much as she was. He might be drifting in *his* pool, thinking lascivious thoughts about *her*. Except he wouldn't, would he? His behavior was so *appropriate* all the time, so reserved and controlled. He held himself back. He seemed likely to deny himself even a pleasurable daydream. And yet, he might feel attracted to her, given the reaction of his body that morning. He had to know she wouldn't mind if he fantasized about *her*, not after the way she'd thrown herself at him. Was it something about her he didn't like? Did he not want to get involved with a person who already had a child? Or was it too awkward to be with her after what had happened between Larch and her all those winters ago? Larch couldn't still be interfering with her life, ruining things for her, could he?

Jane willed away her frustration and anger at Larch. She pulled her cold arms back into the hot water and pushed off along the edge of the pool. The vast spaces to the west of the mountain were shadowy now that the sky was night dark with only pinpricks of stars. The stars were brighter here than in the village, as bright as they'd been when she was young, growing up in Gold Gulch with no village lights. Here above the trees the sky seemed closer. She held a hand out at arm's length again. She could barely see her fingers, pale white in the starlight.

At the far end of the pool, facing south, the light on the distant forest changed to a pale gold. Jane stared, confused for a moment before she glanced left. A giant golden moon was rising in the east. She crept toward the moon, entranced. Humans always said fairies' skin glowed like moonlight. Larch had hidden this from her until he had her under the spell, but she remembered him having a sort of silvery sheen about him. But Rowan was different—golden like this moon peeking over the treetops. Warm and kind.

Someone cleared his throat behind her.

Jane whipped about. Someone was there, at the far end. It had to be Rowan, of course. But why would he have come to her side of the bath? Had he gotten tired of waiting for her to finish bathing? It was unlike him.

"Rowan? Are you all right?"

"Uh . . ."

Jane peered through the steam at him. He sat on the step at the entrance, slightly off to her right. His chest was above the water, reflecting the stars and moon. And there, a bit to the left, was her white shirt lying on the rock. And the steps she'd come down, even farther to the left.

The pool was one long curve. And she'd drifted around the end to Rowan's side.

Jane might've blushed but in the steaming pool she couldn't tell. Rowan hadn't moved. His eyes were wide. Somehow in the faint

                    Jane Buehler

light and steam she could see his chest expanding and contracting, or maybe she imagined the motion and was feeling her own labored breathing. Rowan was so solid. And skies he looked handsome with his hair wet and spiky and his chest bare. All around him was darkness and silence.

"I'm sorry," she said. "I didn't realize our pools connected. I was watching the moon."

His lips parted slightly and he watched her . . . with longing? This was what she thought every time she liked a man, and every time she was wrong and embarrassed herself.

"I could go back."

He stared at her in silence. What was he thinking? Maybe he didn't want her to go? He hadn't responded with a solid, That would be a good idea.

She'd promised Maryanne she wouldn't do this. Well, technically, she had promised not to fall in love with Rowan. She had not promised she wouldn't tumble him in a hot bath at the top of a mountain in the moonlight. She drifted a little closer.

Rowan swallowed.

"Do you want me to leave?" He wouldn't answer with a lie.

He didn't respond.

She stepped closer until she had to tilt her chin up to see him. "Do you want me to stay?" she whispered.

Still no reply. What if he didn't want her?

"Please tell me, Rowan." Her voice sounded desperate even to her. "You said you wanted me to trust you. You didn't want to keep secrets. But it *feels* like you're keeping a secret. I'm probably wrong. I'm always wrong about this. But it makes me feel crazy that I feel sure there's attraction between us but you keep rejecting me. Don't mislead me. Am I wrong?"

"You're not wrong."

Relief swept through her. She wasn't imagining it. "Do you

want me to go? It's fine if you do. I understand you might not want to do any—"

"I want you to stay."

And suddenly Jane didn't know how to proceed.

As if sensing her helplessness, Rowan slid down a step closer and the water crept up his chest. "You're right. Hiding my feelings is misleading. I'm sorry I did that."

"Why did you hide them? You can tell me if you don't want me. I know I'm not—"

"You're perfect."

"I'm not."

"You are to me."

She wasn't but she wouldn't bother to argue. "What is it then?"

He dropped his head toward the water. "I'm afraid to touch you. I don't want to upset you."

Jane crept closer. "What if it upsets me that you keep away?"

He smiled and shook his head. "I don't deserve you after what I did."

"What if I deserve you?" She wasn't backing down.

His smile faded. "I have nothing to offer you."

"I can think of something." Skies she sounded confident, and her fingers reached for him and brushed against his knee under the water, settling lightly on him.

"I don't deserve you," he said again, this time with a hitch in his voice.

"Couldn't you tumble me anyway?" She bit her lip and gazed into his face, hopeful.

The barest smile curved his lips.

She traced a circle on his knee with her fingertip and teased him with a coy smile. "You wouldn't have to enjoy it or anything." His smile widened.

"I would enjoy every breath of it."

His words trembled over her. She slid her hand onto him, both hands now, holding his knees on either side. "I can't risk getting pregnant," she said quietly.

"I understand."

"And sometimes . . ." She didn't know how to explain that she wanted him so badly while knowing having him inside her might be painful. If she started something with him, she'd eventually have access to bitter tea and her excuse to avoid *that kind* of sex would be gone. And if it hurt . . . She was tired of having sex that hurt. But if she didn't offer him that kind of sex, he might no longer want her. She didn't want to start things by misleading him about what she could give him.

He lifted his arm with a gentle splash and his warm finger tilted her chin up until their eyes met. "I wouldn't do anything without asking you first, tea or not."

"I might disappoint you."

"I have no expectations," he said.

"But—"

"You won't disappoint me if you take care of yourself."

Somehow in that moment she believed him. And maybe they wouldn't even be together in a few days. She might never need to tell him about her issues if this was a one-night tryst inspired by the romantic mountaintop views. Although his words, the way he looked at her . . . Deep down she knew this wasn't only a fling for him. But she couldn't get out the words to tell him about her condition.

His arm dropped back to the water as she gripped his thighs and pushed herself up to perch on his knees, bringing them face to face. Her hair swirled around her and clung to her shoulders. His arms were braced at his sides. Jane curled her fingers around his legs and squeezed. Even in the hot water, Rowan's body felt hotter.

His perfect lips beckoned her, closed now but they would open for her. Tilting forward on her arms, she leaned toward him and kissed him softly. Her body floated away from his, breaking her kiss. He had closed his eyes. She pulled herself down onto his lap and kissed him again and a fire ignited inside her. It happened easily—one touch and two kisses and she ached for more.

He kissed her sweetly, letting her tongue in without ravishing his own tongue all over her mouth the way other men had. The water lapped against her chest in a gentle slap and she kissed him harder, glad when he didn't pull away.

His thighs were hard under her fingers and between her own legs, but in the center where she wanted him to be was only water. The absence built until she was moving sideways without even meaning to, over and off him, slipping her leg between his. In wanton longing she landed on his right leg, pressed him into her body, and sighed into his mouth with relief. She abandoned their kisses to focus on where she straddled his thigh, pulling it up against her and grinding on him with delicious sensations. She was so close it would take nothing for her to finish and she had no self-control. With a buck of her hips, dragging against him back and forth, she whimpered and shuddered, quivering through the waves of release until she went still.

She panted as she let go of his leg, floating up. She opened her eyes to find Rowan watching her. His expression betrayed nothing. His hands remained at his sides.

"Sorry," she whispered, licking her lips. "I got carried away and I've been wanting you for so long." She bit her lower lip.

One of his eyebrows lifted.

She floated back to his lap and closer to his body. He shifted and his hands found her thighs, holding her on. "Do, um . . ." She licked her lips again. "Do you want to keep going?"

He nodded slowly.

This time, with him holding her on his lap, she reached for him and settled her hands on his collarbones. She pulled her body forward to kiss him again. He kissed her back, matching her pace, and his firm hold on her legs started her body tingling again. He remained controlled this whole time while she had lost herself in a hot minute with his leg between hers and was all ready to go at it again. His composure felt like a challenge to her. A challenge to see if she could break it.

She parted from their kiss but leaned her body closer, pressing her breasts against his chest as she kissed his neck.

"Do you ever think about me?" she whispered in his ear. "When you're alone?"

She took his earlobe in her mouth. It tugged against her teeth as he nodded. He breathed harshly through his lips. She sucked on his neck and wiggled her bottom closer until her shins brushed the rock step he sat on.

"What do you think about?"

He drew in a ragged breath.

She slid her hands down his chest and around his body and pulled herself against him and there he was, his erection seated against hers. She rolled her hips, rubbing on him with her own body from her base to her chest as his hands moved to her bottom and pulled her back in for another round. He moved in time with her, pressing into her. She had to slow down or she was going to climax again before he'd had any relief. She slowed, clinging to him.

His arms closed around her, hugging her against his broad chest. He dipped his head.

"Is this what *you* imagine?" he whispered.

Jane gasped as his soft voice rolled down her.

His arms held her fast. "You seem to like having your way with my body," he murmured, and she tried to grind against him but she was too high up, pinned against his chest and unable to satisfy her longing. Even her arms were pinned beneath his. She stopped her struggle because she didn't want him to let her go.

He held her in place with one arm as he pulled her sodden hair back from her neck and kissed her damp skin. His lips moved back to her ear. "I imagine you having your way with me." His arms loosened and his hands smoothed over her back. She was free but she clung to him. His palms traced her sides to her waist. He kissed her ear. "I imagine you tying me to your bed and teasing me until I lose control and beg you."

"I wouldn't!" she whined, but he was kissing her neck again, lifting her up and sliding down beneath her until she straddled his torso and he'd lifted her half out of the water. Cool air shivered down her back and arms and tightened her breasts until his warm mouth closed around the tip of one.

She hung on to the rock behind his head, writhing under his hold as he sucked at her breasts, one after the other, hot in his mouth and cold out of it. But she couldn't find enough of him to rub between her legs to bring her to completion.

"Rowan," she begged, pushing him down but her movement only lifted her higher until he was leaning her back, back onto the surface of the water. She caught the edge of the pool and held on, watching him kiss down her belly as he stood.

His face tilted up and his dark eyes found her. "This?" he asked.

She hooked her leg over his shoulder. "Yes. Please."

Cold gripped her thighs as they came out of the water, his thumbs stroking their backs as he parted them for her, and as the air shivered between her legs, his warm lips covered her, kissing and sucking with the friction she'd been dying for. He held her steady and sucked on her. He didn't let go as she squirmed in pleasure. His tongue pressed against her between his lips. Water sloshed over her belly and she twisted in his hands until he sucked again, harder this time.

Her body warmed hotter from her chest out as her heartrate accelerated. Her knees bent over him, kicking as his tongue explored until she moaned and his mouth pulled at her aching center with a deep sucking kiss that never let up. She stifled a cry as she shook, splashing and kicking until she was done.

Her shaky legs slid off his shoulders. She sank down into the water with her fingers on the wall the only thing that held her head above the surface. Rowan was beside her. He reached up and smoothed her wet bangs off her forehead.

Jane peeked up at him. "Do you really want me to tie you up?"

His eyes crinkled. "I might like imagining that more than I'd actually like it happening."

Jane sagged. "That's a relief because I'm terrible with knots. The children always have to go to Maryanne with their shoelaces."

"I'd be embarrassed if you needed Maryanne to untie me from your bed," he said seriously.

But he was teasing.

"Are you all right?" he asked.

"Me?"

"Was that too much, or . . . ?"

"That was amazing! But what about you?"

"I'm enjoying this."

"But you should have more attention. I keep losing track of you and pleasing myself. I'm being selfish."

He smiled then. "I don't mind."

"I want to push you over the top too."

Still he hesitated. He was maddening. She stepped up to him and wrapped her arms around him, and her legs and her whole body, like some kind of octopus until she was hanging on him in the water. He was still hard, pressed into her lower belly. She grinned up at him. "Stop denying yourself, Rowan. You'll make me doubt my appeal."

"We can't have that." He didn't lose control. But his hands were caressing her shoulder blades.

She squinted. "Do you always want someone else in charge?"

"Not always." He traced a circle on her back.

She let go of him and made her own circle on his belly under the water, through a trail of hair that would be dark, matching the locks on his head. She zigzagged a finger down it.

"I like teasing you," she whispered.

He leaned down. "I think you've teased me enough," he whispered back.

He caught her hands, and she inhaled sharply at the change in him as he held her fast and loomed over her. He stalked forward, taking her with him until her back met the wall. He pinned her hands up against it, protecting them from the hard stone with his own, his thumbs rubbing the insides of her wrists as he bent to her neck, sucking on her and biting, and if she'd been able to speak, she'd have begged him only to do it harder. Her body was limp, able only to submit to his ministrations. He turned her to face the wall, pinning her with his body and sucking on her neck from behind. Her heartbeat raced and she couldn't stop her hips from tilting, rubbing her backside on him.

He flattened her hands on the top of the stone, one then the other, then one of his own holding hers down. Her body was caught between the rocks and his chest, but his arm slid across her stomach, taking the rough scrape of the stone off her skin. "Okay?" he asked.

She panted in and out before she could reply. "Yes."

He dipped his head to kiss below her ear. "Tell me if you ever want me to stop." He pressed his erection against the cleft of her bottom, not poking but nestling into her. His hips swiveled up and back, sliding his length along her and against his own foreskin. It felt . . . new. It was kind of strange but it didn't hurt her at all. And from the sound of Rowan's pants, it must feel good to him. She entwined her fingers with his and closed his fist over hers, holding his hand tightly in front of her face.

He slid down and pushed against her bottom again, up and back. She pressed into him to give him more friction and he responded by pinning her hips to the wall with his motion. His rhythm grew faster until he was bucking behind her and his shaft had worked its way in between her butt cheeks so it rubbed right against her, and she started to want him again. She clenched his fist to stop herself from interrupting his rhythm.

He untangled his hand from hers and hoisted her into his arms, one hand across her chest, the other latched between her legs and oh, she had been right, his hands, those fingers there, were marvelous. But his motions didn't tend to her needs this time. He pulled her body down as he thrust upward, and then the fingers between her legs pushed her back up as he rubbed the other way, ignoring her squirming and trembling for more. He only bucked against her harder, taking her body up and down across him in his pulsing need until he gasped and shuddered.

He went still after his climax. He kept holding her against his chest with her legs dangling. Was it selfish to sate herself against him one more time?

He'd said he didn't mind her being selfish.

She reached down between her legs, nudged his hand away, and caught what remained of his erection in her hand. She positioned it between her thighs. He was stiff enough that she could press his length against her folds. Using his body was better than using only her hand.

He caught on and held her belly to keep her in place against him. Her legs splayed out as she held his penis and rode him with a forward and back rhythm, twitching like she was the eager pony, then pausing for a long slow glide. His skin felt incredible against her. She rolled her hips, rubbing him everywhere she could, before resuming her cadence atop him.

"Oh!" she softly cried.

Her body shook and she held on as her orgasm crescendoed and faded. She rolled over him one last time before letting him go. Her legs drifted closed and her toes grazed the floor of the pool.

Rowan's arms snaked farther around her until he held all of her tight against him. He rested his forehead in the crook of her neck. When Jane opened her eyes, the moon was before them, its gold fading to silver as it climbed over the forest.

Chapter 13

Jane leaned back against Rowan's chest. The water in the pool wasn't as hot as it had been. Or maybe she was used to it.

"I've never done *that* before," she whispered. "It felt good to you?"

"Very good," he murmured.

"The way you pressed against me—it makes me think of a sausage between the halves of a bun."

Rowan snorted. "A sausage? That's the ground up animal bits in a casing, right?"

"But the shape—"

"I know the shape," he said, kissing her neck. His kiss turned into a nibble. "The fairies call that position an eggplant sandwich."

Now Jane snorted. Eggplant sandwich? Like anyone ate a whole eggplant that way. But the fairies had a name for the position . . . as if using it were common enough to be named. She'd never have thought a man would be satisfied by merely squeezing his erection between her butt cheeks like that. Of course, her main experience was with a man whose sole purpose had been to get her pregnant, so he had focused on the usual form of tumbling.

It was the usual form, wasn't it? Maryanne loved gabbing about all the ways she and Wells went at it, and while they seemed to like variety (beds, floors, kitchen tables, bent over an anvil in the tin smithy), their tumbling always seemed to involve Wells eventually sticking his penis into Maryanne's vagina. And Maryanne liked it that way, at least according to her gabbing. But did all women?

Another thing about Rowan—who'd stopped kissing her neck and seemed content leaning against her while holding her in his arms and watching the moon—was he let her be in charge sometimes. And he seemed to like her being in charge.

Larch had always called her over to him, like he was the skies' gift to womankind. And . . . well, she felt embarrassed thinking it, but with him tumbling was kind of the *same* every time. But again, maybe that was because he'd been trying to get her pregnant, not offer her an inspiring sex life. And she'd been so besotted with him—she'd been gratified simply having his attention and everything had felt wonderful all the time. Even her usual pain had been muted. Dratted fairy love spell. Only afterward could she look back and see Larch hadn't been very original in his techniques.

No eggplant sandwiches with Larch.

Jane relaxed and rested her head back against Rowan. The moon had faded to a silvery white as it crept up the sky. Rowan's chin brushed her cheek.

"Are your fingers prune-y?" she asked.

"Are they what?"

"Prune-y. Wrinkly like prunes."

"What are prunes?"

"What are *prunes*?" She twisted to stare at him. "Dried plums. Don't fairies eat prunes?"

"Of course we do. We call them dried plums."

"'We call them dried plums,'" Jane mimicked him, but she smiled and kissed his cheek to show she was teasing.

"What do you call those dried cherries you put on the oats?" he asked.

"Dried cherries."

"I asked, What do you call them?"

"Dried cherries are just dried cherries."

Rowan turned to gape at her. "Well *that* makes sense."

Jane couldn't stop smiling.

"What other lucky dried fruits get special human names?"

"Um, dried grapes are raisins. Figs stay figs though. Same with apples and apricots. I think it's only dried plums and grapes."

"Huh."

It was kind of strange when she thought about it.

He shifted her in his arms to examine his fingertips. "They look prune-y."

"I think all of me is prune-y."

He bent to whisper in her ear. "Want me to check?"

Jane laughed and swatted him away as she turned from the view of the moon.

"Do you want to dry off?" he asked.

"Yes, please."

He stepped back and followed as she waded around the curve to her side of the pool. Her clothes spread on the rock were dry, even her trousers.

"You don't have towels in that pack of yours, do you?" Jane asked. The night air had been cold when she'd lifted her arm from the water to check her laundry.

"No, just the blanket."

"We need to keep that dry so we can sleep under it."

"Wait a moment." Rowan climbed up the steps—she forced herself not to ogle his backside as it emerged in the moonlight—and vaulted himself up on the rock beside her clothes. "The rock is warm," he said. "Come lie up here."

She climbed up the tall steps and out of the water. The walls around the entrance to the pool radiated a faint heat as she gathered up her clothing to create more space for them to lie down. Rowan pulled her up beside him, and she crawled toward the center. The rocks grew hotter beneath her palms. Sunshine had heated the rock in the center of her cave, so it made sense the center of the dome would be hottest.

Jane lowered her belly down and stretched out on the warm rocks, hiding beneath the cold night air. Rowan lay beside her. He turned his face toward her. The pale light lit his cheekbone and the tip of his nose.

"Was it rude?" she asked.

"What?"

"Tumbling in Sunshine's pool."

"Rude how?"

"Her rainwater was all clean before we went in. And now it's . . . not."

"Bathing would have dirtied it."

"I know. But she invited us to bathe."

"Maybe she invited us to tumble and I didn't tell you."

Jane lifted her head. "Did she?"

Rowan grinned.

"She did not."

"How do you think dragons make their sex mushrooms?"

"Their *what*?"

"Like the fire mushrooms but with an extra ingredient."

"Rowan!"

He kept smiling at her. He'd lain on his front too and he rested his head on his folded arms. His long hair fell away from his eyes. "She'll blast enough heat from below to evaporate the water after we're gone, and the pores in the rock will fill with fire mushroom spores. But our tumbling will fertilize them and turn them into extra nutritious sex mushrooms."

"That can't be true."

Rowan's grin widened. "It's not."

"I thought fairies couldn't lie."

"I don't think it counts if it's a lie that stupid."

Jane's front was getting toasty. She hitched herself up and onto her back. Her front protested but it was dry and the cold was less biting than it had been. The ends of her hair had dried against the rock, but her head was damp. She lay back, turning her face again to Rowan.

"Do you think she's had other visitors?"

"Sunshine? Not likely. Why?"

"No reason."

"Are you wondering how many couples have tumbled here before us?"

Jane's face heated.

"She actually will empty the pool before the next rainfall. That's how they keep the rainwater fresh for drinking. Axe told me that once. One blast of dragon fire can clean anything."

Jane watched him. If he'd slipped up in mentioning his time with Axe, he didn't show it. But she didn't want to risk making the moment awkward by trying to find out more.

They were silent for a few beats.

"I don't know what to do about Elle," Jane said at last. "I don't want to take her away from Sunshine."

"Then don't."

"You think it would be all right to let her live up here for several moons?"

"I do. I know this idea is new to you. But working with dragons is something the fairies have done for ages."

His assurances calmed her. This must be what it would be like having a partner in life, a partner who cared about her welfare, too. Getting an opinion she could trust, making decisions together.

"I don't think I could leave though," she said.

"We don't have to leave."

"You would stay with me?"

"I can hardly return to Woods Rest without you. Maryanne would have my head."

"But what would you do up here?"

"You mean aside from getting naked with you every night?"

Jane's heart thumped. No bitter tea. A whole summer of his touches without having to worry about pain. "But what if it doesn't rain?"

He convulsed with a laugh into the crook of his elbow, hiding his face.

"Don't laugh. This pool could get dangerous."

Rowan looked up smiling with his eyes shining. When he smiled it was like the sun after a quarter-moon of rainstorms. "I would lay you down on the grass under the apple trees and shake the branches to watch the petals drift onto your bare skin before making love to you."

Jane's lips parted but she had no words. That was the most romantic thing she'd ever heard.

"Although with the way you squirm," he continued, "we'd kill the grass in no time."

She shoved at his arm.

"But there's always the hammocks. We could hang one out among the trees."

Jane frowned. "A hammock doesn't seem to allow much variety."

Rowan smirked. "It does if you know how to hang it."

"What do you mean?"

Rowan rested his chin on his arms again. "Fairy hammocks have loops in a few places that allow you to hang them a few ways—for sleeping, for sitting. For tumbling in various positions." He didn't even smirk as he said it, as if such a thing were commonplace.

"The fairies make sex hammocks."

"You sound unenthused. We don't have to use it."

"No, I would try it." Jane stared overhead at the stars. Her brow furrowed. The fairies invented things. They thought of things—like a hammock you could hang to make sex better. They seemed to always know more about everything than humans did. Maybe a fairy healer could help her. Maybe they would know what caused the tightness in her body that made intercourse painful. "The fairies know a lot about sex," she said at last.

"We got bored all those winters underground. We had a lot of new inventions. Silver lining, I suppose."

She turned her face back to him. "New sex inventions?"

He grinned. "Maybe."

"Like what?"

"Oh I don't know."

"You do too. You're such a tease."

"One of the inventors made something all the fairies were talking about. Everyone wanted one. Especially everyone with a vagina."

"Rowan! Tell me."

He hitched himself closer across the rock, lowering his voice. "Do you know what a dildo is?"

"Of course! Humans have . . . those."

"Why don't you want to say the word?"

"I don't not want to."

He lifted his eyebrows.

"Fine. Dildo." She couldn't meet his gaze. "My brothers used to make jokes, that's all."

"Did you ever have one?"

"No."

"It's nothing to be embarrassed about."

"I know. I just . . . never had one."

He bit his lip a moment before continuing. "One of the fairy inventors made a vibrating dildo."

"A vibrating . . . ?" Words failed her. It vibrated? How?

"She calls it a wand. Apparently the vibrations feel quite nice."

Jane frowned. Vibrations—like when a cart rumbled down the lane and the house shook? "I don't understand. It just shakes around down there?"

"Not exactly. She made it with hummingbird wings. And mag-ic."

"*Hummingbird* wings? How could you hurt a—"

"No one hurt a hummingbird." He shook his head, smiling.

"Then how did she invent it?"

"Maple—she's the inventor—Maple said she had the bird perch on the tip and flutter a bit and she captured the motion."

Jane pieced together the information. Hummingbirds were dizzyingly fast. Way faster than her hand.

"For a while she had a backlog of orders," Rowan went on. "She got permission to visit the gardens, and she'd sit by the flowers waiting for hummingbirds to come by so she could ask for help. She traded them honey water in exchange for their time. They seemed happy with the trade."

Was he kidding her again? He didn't have a gleam in his eye—he wasn't even watching her. As if vibrating fairy dildos were real. They were going to have to discuss this again when they got home.

Rowan traced a finger over the rocks. "Now that we're talking about sex," he said, and his eyes darted up to her and away, "I don't think I can resist touching you when you're lying beside me like that."

Jane folded her arms behind her head and arched her back. "Like what?"

Rowan groaned.

"Go on then," she said, biting her lip to hide her grin.

He leaned up on one elbow and reached out to touch her chin lightly with his fingertips, followed by her lips. Heat off his hand warmed the base of her neck a moment before he touched her there. He trailed his fingers down her center in a line, feather soft, over the gentle slope of her belly and . . . back up.

Now Jane groaned.

"Shall I stop?"

"No! Just don't be such a tease."

His fingers were on the way back down again. "Can I kiss you?"

"Yes."

"Close your eyes."

She studied Rowan's face one more moment before closing them. His fingers reached her belly. They stopped.

His body scuffed across the rock as he moved closer. He brushed aside her hair before cradling her head, nudging her own arms aside. She wanted to reach for him but she didn't want to interrupt whatever he was about to do so she closed her hands and left them beside her head. His fingers splayed across her belly before smoothing back up to rest his warm palm between her breasts, and he dropped kisses on her eyelashes and across her cheeks.

"You look beautiful in moonlight," he whispered.

His hair brushed her face as he nuzzled to kiss her neck and she risked a peek. Her body was silvery in the darkness, and the view of his tanned fingers pressed between the swell of her breasts made her crave his touch. He traced his lips over her skin, along her collarbone and kissing up her neck. She closed her eyes again.

His lips pressed against hers as he danced his fingers across her breast. She arched up seeking more of his hand and his lips, with a kiss back just as he pulled his face away. He came in again, staying this time with a gentle force while his fingers landed and stayed on her breast, circling slowly and slowly pushing harder. It was too lovely, the never-ending kissing and the torment of her breast, but when she tried to move toward him the hand cradling her head fisted in her hair to stop her.

"I could touch you," she whined against his lips.

He breathed into her ear. "Wait your turn. I can only focus on one thing at a time."

"You're—"

He cut her off with another kiss and she gave herself up to his attentions. For a while, he kept kissing her lips, his hand resting on her breast. Her body responded, wanting him more and more the longer he denied her any other touches. Was it a game to drive her mad? Rowan didn't seem to play games. But he might like to tease her.

"Why are you only kissing me?" she murmured between kisses.

"I like kissing you. Do you want me to stop?"

"I like it too." Her mind was a haze of desires, half of them pushing her to climb on top of him and the other half too lazy to move.

"Do you want more?"

"Mmm."

He bit her neck. Even with it done gently, her eyes flew open and her body arched. The stars wheeled above her. His fingers landed between her legs. She arched again, trying to get them closer. His body had the top of her torso pinned. He ran his fingers lightly over her, then harder, stroking between her legs until she settled back.

"You like this?" His strokes turned to slow swirls. "Tell me what you like."

"I like that."

His skin pressed against her side was hot from lying on the rock. Already she wanted his fingers to go harder. But it wouldn't take long for her to finish so she enjoyed his soft stroking a little longer. His kisses slowed until he rested his cheek against her collarbone. As if he were focused on the hand kneading between her legs.

Her body's yearning grew until she reached for his hand in her hair. She wrapped her fingers over his, clutched his hand, and arched up against his pressure between her legs. He responded with a faster cadence. Not harder, just faster, like the hummingbird wings he'd teased her about but skies it worked. The quivery motion triggered her so fast she barely realized it was coming before her desire peaked and spilled out in a spasm of moans and Rowans and futile attempts to press against his hand, which kept vibrating on her and keeping her peak going until she couldn't take any more and clamped his hand against her.

He lay across her as she went still, catching her breath. She kept hold of his hand between her legs, not ready to let go of the solid pressure against her. He was moving against her hip, nudging and snuggling closer. Skies the rock beneath her bottom was hot, and she was sooo sleepy. Her body had begun to melt limply onto the rock. When he quieted, she gave him back his hand. His head was below hers and she stroked his hair. She couldn't fall asleep until he'd had another turn.

"My turn to touch you?" she asked in a tiny voice.

Rowan moved but kept his head down as he rolled off her and sat up. "Um. I'm sorry. I couldn't wait." Was he actually blushing? She couldn't tell in the moonlight. "Just, uh, watch out right there on the rock when you move."

Jane blinked up at him. So that's what that snuggling had been about—Rowan had been humping her side. She grinned. "Next time you go first," she said, reaching out to touch his hip.

He kept his face averted but a bashful smile graced his lips.

"I'm done drying off I think," she said with a yawn.

"Get dressed and we can go to sleep."

Jane slowly sat up and pulled on her underclothes as Rowan climbed over the rock to where he'd left his things. In the end, she put on all her clothes because the night would only get colder as it grew later. When she descended the steps around to the courtyard, Rowan was waiting. Sunshine's head rested on the ground with her small forepaws curled beside it. Her eyes were closed but Jane would bet she knew they were there—and probably everything else about their evening. Elle was out of sight, her presence given away only by Sunshine's slightly unfolded left wing.

The dragon and the cave radiated heat but the lone hammock Rowan had hung was on the far side of the courtyard. The temperature dropped as they padded over to it, and the faint smells of smoke and singed mushroom faded into cold mountain air.

Did he want to share again? They needed to share the blanket for warmth. And she wanted to share because she liked snuggling against him. And he seemed to like her, too, not only the kissing and touching but talking with her and teasing her. And after what he'd said about making love in the grass and the hammocks and whatnot . . .

Maybe she was wrong. She was usually wrong about these things. Maybe their activities in the pool were a one-time tryst. But she didn't think she was wrong this time.

"Do you want to share again?" Jane asked.

And Rowan nodded.

He spread his blanket in the hammock as he had done before. This time he'd secured the hammock on a rock and branch instead of using the slug glue, so it wouldn't fall in the morning. She climbed in after him and lay back. His arm went around her immediately, and when she shifted, trying to maneuver her way onto him, he shifted too and pulled her all the way on so her head rested on his chest. He pulled the blanket over her and stroked her back beneath it, and he was warm and lovely and even her feet were warm, snugged against his calves.

Falling asleep was much easier after three—no, four—orgasms. She woke once when Rowan turned onto his side. He muttered an apology and pulled her against his broad chest. And much later, Sunshine moved outside. Her wings beat the air once, twice. Rowan shifted again.

"Stay here," he said, and slipped out of her arms, wrapping the warm blanket around her. She drifted back to sleep.

Chapter 14

JANE WOKE ALONE IN THE shadowy hammock. Hints of light came through the weave so the sun must be rising. Without Rowan's heat and even with the blanket wrapped around her, the cold morning air seeped in.

Jane closed her eyes and pulled the blanket tighter. Her body felt leagues different than it had yesterday. Her muscles still ached but the long soak in the steaming water had done wonders. Not to mention all the tension she'd released with what happened after. Skies above, making love with Rowan had been amazing. He'd been so attentive. And so generous. And so . . . sweet. He'd probably glare at her for calling him that, but he had a streak of kindness and charm hidden beneath his daunting exterior.

Unbidden, Maryanne popped into Jane's mind. Drat. She had utterly failed in her promise to Maryanne. Or had she? She hadn't fallen in love with Rowan. They'd tumbled once, for skies' sake. Or twice—but both times in one night which maybe counted only once? This attraction between them might not last long enough to turn into love. It was like Maryanne had said—they were out in a forest and sleeping side by side under the stars, so their situation seemed romantic and exciting. Although it was hard to imagine that excitement fading.

But Rowan hadn't wanted her at first. And while he might have changed his mind about wanting her—or at least given in to her begging—his mind could change right back once they returned home. Maybe that would even be for the best. Of all the partners she'd imagined finding, none had ever been a fairy. If she and Rowan became mates, she might have to see Larch again. Rowan might want to live with the fairies, and Jane would never bring Elle back to the place where she'd been trapped for two winters.

She'd have to see what happened today.

Everything was silent. Maybe Rowan was making tea and oats. They had no wood for a fire up here. Would Sunshine heat the water? Jane held herself motionless and listened. Elle must be keeping warm beneath Sunshine's wing because she wasn't babbling or poking at Jane to get up, and Sunshine wasn't moving around in the courtyard, her tail dragging over the stones. Rowan was always silent. But shouldn't there be *some* kind of noise?

Jane peeked out through the top of the hammock.

The courtyard was empty.

She twisted, scanning the far side and down to Sunshine's cave. Dread crept across her chest, sticking to her ribcage, but she ignored it. The others were here somewhere.

She sat up and swung her feet to the ground, shivering as the air found her. Rowan's pack was against the wall nearby. She inhaled a calming breath and relaxed her shoulders. He was here, and Sunshine must've gone for a flight or to get something she needed. And Elle could be with Rowan or—Jane swallowed—with Sunshine. But Elle was safe.

The sun was over the treetops in the east and warming the stone all around her. A soft wind blew and a hawk cried somewhere nearby.

"Rowan?" She said his name quietly, unable to bring herself to shout even though no one was in the courtyard. Nothing happened. "Rowan!" she called more loudly. Nothing moved or changed. The dread ebbed up her throat.

Jane wrapped the blanket around her and stood. She crossed to Sunshine's cave and peered under the rocks but it had no hidden spaces inside. Quickly she climbed up to check both sides of the pool simply to rule it out. The rocks were cold and the water was placid and clear, without any curls of steam rising off the surface.

She hurried down the steps and over to the narrow entrance on the far side of the courtyard. She called again as she wound through the maze of rocks. Rowan and Elle might be hidden among the boulders, but she kept calling and no one replied. She cleared the pine trees and came toward the edge. The apple boughs swayed in the breeze and a few petals drifted down. Rowan's rope looped around one trunk and trailed across the rock to the edge of the cliff and off. The neat coil of rope he'd made was gone.

Jane crept to the edge and peered over. The rope hung off the side of the cliff with one end tied to the iron loop fastened below and the other swinging in the air. As if someone had gone down using the rope. Nothing stirred. She couldn't see any of the other ledges or ropes they'd used on their climb, but with no voices or sounds of movement, she sensed she was all alone on the peak.

It was happening again. Jane closed her eyes and tried not to panic, but the same thing was happening, just like last time. Just like last time she lost Elle.

She'd woken in the cabin in the forest alone. Where was Cedric? And where was Bluebell? She went to the door, listening to the silence among the trees. She called and called, circled the cabin as her fear grew, and ventured in among the trees in case they'd been injured. What if an animal had taken Bluebell? Had Cedric gone after to rescue her? Or had Bluebell gotten sick and he'd taken her to a healer in a nearby village?

Jane had waited and waited and no one returned. She found no hint of what had happened to them. She waited until she grew hungry and the food was all gone. But even after she left the cabin, she kept believing in Cedric. They'd find their way back to each other. She could gather more supplies and return to the cabin to continue waiting. Or he would search for her in the nearest villages.

And then she had learned the truth: that Cedric was a fairy named Larch who had stolen her baby. That he hadn't ever loved her. He'd put a spell on her. He'd tricked her and used her in the worst way so he could procure a child for his queen. And she'd not once suspected him.

And it was happening again. Rowan had climbed down the peak and Elle was missing. And Jane had not suspected him once, not since he had confessed to her in the hayloft. And now he was gone and Elle was gone with him.

But Rowan had left his pack. He must be coming back. And he wasn't Larch—he wouldn't kidnap her child. He had helped Jane find Elle! He wouldn't have brought Jane all this way to find Elle only to steal her away the next day. Would he? The old story *wasn't* happening again.

But she had never once doubted "Cedric" either.

Jane shook her head. Fabricating possibilities was no use. She needed more facts. She needed a plan.

She turned away from the edge of the cliff and startled. The fire mushrooms that had covered the rocky wall behind the apple trees and the nearest boulders were ruined, torn off in great slashes. Piles of them littered the ground. The pool of water beneath the trees was cloudy with dirt.

Jane slowly shook her head, trying to make sense of the mess. Rowan wouldn't hurt the mushrooms, for skies' sake. Sunshine needed the supply of them. Who would have done this? Did someone else want Sunshine to leave? Had they climbed up her peak last night, or flown to it? Had the dragon fled with Elle because they'd been in danger?

Frowning, Jane returned to the courtyard, hunting her way through the boulders until she found the correct path. All of the mushrooms on the outermost rocks had been destroyed, but once she was behind a row of boulders they were fine. She emerged in the courtyard, dropped down beside Rowan's pack, and pulled it open. The climbing belts were on top—both of them. If he'd needed to climb down, why hadn't he used one? He'd used the belt when he'd dropped down each cliff, but maybe he could do it without the belt, too.

The oats were in his bag, and the packet of travel biscuits, as well as his knife, his fire kit, and the tin dishes and utensils. She pulled out the second hammock, a few kerchiefs, the container of slug glue, a toothbrush, and a few small pouches that smelled pungent like herbs. Down at the bottom were more iron loops, spring-clips, rope, and the heavy hammer. Their two drinking gourds were beside her shoes. He hadn't taken anything—except his coat. His coat had been draped over the courtyard wall last night and now it was gone.

Jane sat back, staring at the opposite wall as her mind spun. What was going on? Had Sunshine left with Elle for some reason and Rowan had gone after her? But Rowan would have woken Jane to tell her where he was going. He wouldn't have abandoned her on top of this peak.

Would he?

No. Something must have happened and he'd had to leave quickly.

Wait—Sunshine's wings had flapped in the nighttime, hadn't they? Jane had been so tired—warm and listless and unable to function, and Rowan had woken, too, and told her to stay put as he left the hammock. But why would Sunshine be flapping her wings in the middle of the night when she was supposed to be keeping Elle warm beneath them? That must have been when she flew away. Was that when Rowan left as well?

Had Rowan and Sunshine planned something? Had they left together, leaving Jane alone on the mountain? And why? For the fire magic? Elle clearly had magical ability. Nothing Rowan had done had seemed odd but Jane was such a poor judge of character. She'd been tricked before. She'd been just as enamored with Larch—and he'd taken Elle from her.

It couldn't be happening again. It couldn't.

Elle would be okay. Sunshine clearly cared for her. Wherever they had taken her, Sunshine would care for her until Jane could find her.

And Rowan stealing Elle made no sense. If he had wanted to, he could have traveled here to find her without Jane stumbling along behind him, twisting her ankle and slowing him down. Why had he agreed to let her come? Why had he come to her house to offer his help in the first place?

Maybe he'd wanted to seduce her—like Maryanne had warned her. Maybe Rowan resented Larch. Maybe seducing her was an act of revenge. But Larch didn't care what happened to her. Unless he did. What if Larch secretly missed her, and Rowan had made it sound like he didn't to thwart Larch?

What if . . .

A sick sensation overwhelmed Jane. What if Larch had sent Rowan? What if he'd found out about Elle's ability and decided to take her back? Rowan had done Larch's bidding before. Could he still be working for him?

She would go mad trying to sort through the possibilities. Only one thing was clear: If something was going on between Sunshine, Rowan, and/or Larch, she had completely fallen for it. She was such a fool. She would never learn not to trust the wrong people.

And another certainty: She was alone on top of a pillar of rocks. Maybe Rowan or Sunshine was planning to return, but if they didn't she needed to get down on her own. She could sit here and wait and see what happened, or she could start climbing down.

Last time she had waited. And waited and waited, and no one had come for her. And she'd had food supplies and a clear spring for water. All she had now was a bag of oats, raw mushrooms, and pools of dirty water.

And she couldn't manage a night on a ledge halfway down the peak, slug glue or not. The morning sun was low in the sky. If she started now, she might reach the bottom by sunset. She'd be slow but she could use the ropes and the iron pieces already in place.

Half the time climbing up the peak had been spent waiting as Rowan installed the safety ropes.

If instead she waited to see if someone returned, and no one did, she'd have to wait a whole day before setting out. She couldn't handle sitting up here all that time if no one returned. She'd rather start climbing and have to come back up if she were wrong.

She resisted the urge to crawl back into the hammock and do nothing. She had to get down from here. The only way to do it was to climb. She would go have a look over the ledge. Maybe the climb wouldn't be that bad. She had come up it, after all.

The blanket had slipped off her shoulders. She pushed it aside and crouched by Rowan's pack. She unloaded the hammer and all the iron loops except one from the pack. She wasn't strong enough to use them, but she'd keep one just in case it might be useful.

She buckled on the smaller climbing belt and left Rowan's with the hammer. She packed the extra rope and spring-clips, the knife, the glue, and the travel biscuits but left the cookware and oats to avoid their weight. The heavy drinking gourds felt full. She packed a few kerchiefs, wrapping one around the knife. She left the hammocks so the bag wouldn't get heavier—she would get to the forest by nightfall and whatever happened then, she could get by without a hammock.

Taking his blanket would weigh her down. But she might end up spending the night out somewhere and who knew if her own blanket was still at the bottom of the peak. She folded Rowan's and tucked it into the pack. The blanket was cold, the same as the pools and rocks where she'd lain naked with Rowan last night. Best not to think of that.

Standing, she swung Rowan's pack onto her back. Skies, it weighed a bit, more than her own satchel for sure but less than the weight he had carried. His pack had two straps, one for each arm. When she had it in place, it sagged in back but the straps stayed on her shoulders.

She eyed her shoes, tucked beneath the hammock. She had

blisters on the backs of her heels and being barefoot yesterday had been a blessing. Rowan had climbed the rocks barefoot and it seemed easier to find the cracks and avoid slipping with her toes instead of shoes. But would she want the shoes when she was back on the forest floor? She picked them up, bounced them in her hand to assess the weight, and returned them to the ground. She could berate herself later if she missed them.

With a final scan of the courtyard, Jane walked to the gap in the rocks. She was cold but Rowan's coat was gone and she wouldn't have worn it to climb anyway. Soon enough she'd be warm. She strode through the boulders and trees and slowed only as she neared the edge. She peeked over.

It was a vertical drop. The wall was sheer rock—what in the skies had she held on to when she'd climbed up that?

Black skies, she did not want to climb down that rock on her own. But every moment she delayed was a moment lost. She didn't want to be halfway down when darkness came. If she made it to the forest, she could shelter in the trees overnight and climb down the trail tomorrow.

At least she'd have the safety rope tied on. She grasped the loose side of the rope and pulled it up. The metal spring-clip dangled off the end. She clipped it to her belt. If she fell, it would stop her from dashing her head on the ledge below or plunging over the edge to her death. And she'd be able to pull the rope down after her if the lower ones were missing. But Rowan had left the ropes in place as they climbed up, instead of removing them as he had done at Axe's, so they should still be there.

Rowan had descended the cliff faces by lowering himself down and slowly letting out the rope—he'd done it with only one arm on the rope so he must not have been holding his full weight. Descending that way would be faster. But he'd used a special knot and she had no idea how to tie it, and it would be foolish to assume she could invent such a thing and use it without practicing. So, she'd be climbing.

     Jane Buehler

She scanned over the top of the peak one last time. She should eat some mushrooms while they were available. She bypassed the ones on the ground, found a clump, and peeled a few off. They were spongy and cold but she'd need the energy. She drank from her gourd and braided her hair tightly.

She returned to the ledge and got down on her hands and knees, ignoring the wind chilling her through her clothes. She checked the rope one last time, reasoning through the process of climbing down and how the rope would catch to stop a fall, and how she'd unclip and move on at the bottom.

She crawled backward off the top. She wedged her toes into a crack a few hands' lengths down, clinging to the top with her fingers. This was trickier than going up had been. But at least if she fell, she'd end up closer to her target.

She couldn't see anything below her. She eased herself out until she could see below her feet. Some of the bumps she vaguely remembered, but she had climbed so much in the past few days, the cliff faces had become a blur. She found a lower toehold, moved off the top, and hung flat against the wall. She found another handhold and lowered herself down.

Moving down the wall went slowly but her mind focused on finding the next handhold or crack for her toes. A few times she got stuck and hung on the rock, searching with her toes or a palm the way she'd seen Rowan do the first time he'd scaled each wall. She avoided looking down as much as she could. One move after another, on and on, until her toes bumped the ledge. She was down. She'd made it to the first ledge.

One climb done.

Her scraped hands ached. She shook them out and flexed her toes as she scanned the trees below and the wide valley. The sun was behind the peak but the peak's shadow to the west was shrinking, showing that the sun was considerably higher than when she'd left the top.

Jane undid the spring-clip from her belt and let it hang as she turned to check the next rope. It dangled loose through the loop in the rock, but when she pulled it up the end was empty. She opened the pack and got out a new spring-clip and held the two rope ends side by side. She had to tie the new clip to the empty rope, which meant she had to copy the knot Rowan had used.

The hanging rope ended at her midsection. She found a crack wide enough to wedge the clip into so she could work with both her hands while referring to it. She fumbled with the new rope and clip, threading them in and out, tying knots that twisted in on themselves or fell apart when she pulled on them. She had to stop or she'd scream in frustration.

She sat and had a drink from her gourd and tried not to notice the ever-shrinking shadow on the forest far below. She took a few deep inhales of cool air.

She stood again and traced the line of the knotted rope up and over the metal and around. She took the bare rope and followed the same path with it and this time she ended with a knot. She held the two clips side by side, turning them up and around. The knots appeared the same from every angle. She clipped the rope to her belt and tugged on it a few times and the knot stayed solid.

One by one she descended from one ledge to the next. Each time, the rope they'd used when climbing up waited for her and she tied on a new spring-clip. The shadow of the peak shrank to nothing and the sun appeared overhead. Now she could watch directly as it marked out the time she had left before darkness.

She reached the ledge where she and Rowan had sheltered two nights before but no sign of their presence remained. She ran her fingers over the wall but the dried slug glue must have peeled off and blown away. The sun was firmly in the west.

She didn't have any clips left but she'd tied the knot so many times she could do it without a model to compare. She untied the clip from the previous rope and retied it on the next one as the sun crept closer to the horizon. Her stomach gurgled with hunger as she departed but she kept on. She had only a few cliffs left, from what she remembered. If she hurried, she—

Her foot slipped and she clung on with her hands, panicked. She was too heavy. Her fingers were slipping. Her toes scrabbled against the cliff and one toe hooked into a crevice and held her up. Her other foot searched for the crack she'd been standing in and found it.

She hung stationary a moment as she calmed. She wedged her toes in farther and regained her balance. She couldn't become sloppy or she'd fall.

She resumed the climb, careful all the way down to the next resting point. This time she paused for water and a travel biscuit. She shouldn't dawdle—if she stopped too long, she might think about how her muscles ached even worse than the first time she had done this. She might think about how she was on a narrow ledge on the side of a cliff and only luck was getting her down it. But she needed to rest and eat.

The next descent brought her to the ledge that would take her around to the north side of the peak. Only one climb to go. This was the first face they had climbed, where Rowan had removed the rope. She could pull the previous rope loose from the top loop and take it with her . . . but if she needed to go back *up* she'd have to do it with no safety rope. And she had an extra coil of rope in the pack. She left the rope hanging and proceeded around to the north.

Down below her was the narrow trail around the edge of the mountain and the place where they'd stopped and climbed out on the rocks. The afternoon sun slanted in from the west, illuminating rhododendron leaves higher up on the slope. Her satchel lay under the bush where she'd left it . . . but her blanket, coat, and scarf were strewn on the ground beside it. Had Rowan searched it? He knew it had only her clothes and a little food. Maybe an animal had gone after the apple rings? A few broken branches lay beside it.

She located the loop in the rock ledge and startled. A rope hung from the loop—and it wasn't a fairy rope. It was dull and fraying, and the knot was huge and bulging with knobs of bristling fiber as if whoever had tied it didn't know how to tie a proper knot so they kept adding new knots on top of each other, hoping it would hold. Rowan never would have tied a knot that messy.

Someone else had definitely been here.

Jane scanned the forest below but nothing stirred except the leaves in the breeze. She swallowed and knelt by the iron loop. She wanted to untie the ugly knot and use the fairy rope, but untying that mess could take her an extra hour and the sun was already low.

Down below, the rope trailed across the ledge. It was too long. She pulled it up and threaded it through her clip, guessing how much she needed to pass it through so she'd stop short of the ledge if she fell. Once it was tied, she lowered the clip to check the length. She clipped herself on and began the final descent. As she climbed down, she moved into shade and a brisk wind nipped at her right side.

Finally, finally her toes touched down on the first ledge. She wobbled there a moment, hardly believing she had done it. The sky was deepening and the wind picking up. She unclipped the rope from her belt one last time and lowered the clip to hang against the cliff.

She followed the ledge around to the western side of the peak and caught the last orange glow on the rocks. As she picked her way down the field of boulders, using her arms and legs, the rocks were warm from the afternoon in the sun. Moving downward was harder than upward. Half the time she was sitting and hoisting herself from one seat to the next. She tried turning herself around and moving down backward but the light was fading faster and she couldn't see well enough to find places to step. Loose scree slid beneath her toes. Go carefully, she reminded herself. She didn't want another twisted ankle this close to the bottom. Rowan wasn't here to carry her.

Rowan. Her insides clenched at his absence—at how she missed him and how he might have betrayed her the same way Larch had all those seasons ago. She might never find Elle again. But she'd never have found Elle the first time without Rowan's help. She couldn't let her exhaustion dictate her thoughts. She didn't yet know what had happened or why the others had left her.

She stepped onto a wide, flat rock, almost at the bottom of the boulder field, and glanced up to see the last bit of the orange sun dip beneath the horizon, the light catching in the cloud that hovered around one of the volcanoes. Just a few hops and she—

Her foot slid on loose stones at the base of the boulder. The momentum of her final hop down carried her skidding across the space, angled slightly downhill. She crashed to the ground, banging her hip as she scrabbled for anything to hang on to, but she was sliding too fast with more stones rolling under her, bearing her like an offering to the ravine below the peak. Her foot kicked open air and she went over the side.

She was going to die. And no one would ever know what happened to her.

She fell. Her arm smacked against a sapling, wrenching her shoulder as her hip knocked into rock. She spread her arms, flailing for a hold. The next sapling snapped against her wrist but slipped out of her fingers before she could grab it. Her knee buckled into a twisted tree and she reached for the tree and caught it as her body flew past. Her weight yanked on the branches but the tree bent and held.

Jane hung from the tree, panting. The cliff face pressed against her shoulder, a steep slide into dark treetops, but a few paces below her dangling feet the face ended and she couldn't see what the rocks did next, before the bottom of the ravine. Above her head, the surface was sheer with only a few protrusions of rock and a handful of stunted bushes and trees. She'd never get up that, and at this point, the ground was closer.

She clung to the tree branches and carefully slid her toes along the rock. It was smooth and warm, and she found nothing she could edge her toes into to take some of her weight off the little tree. After a moment she gave up and struggled to pull herself higher. Her wrist panged but she ignored it. Rowan's pack still hung off her shoulders. She let go of the branches with her right hand and slipped the pack off her shoulder before hefting herself into the branches until her right shoulder was over the tree's main trunk. A loose bit of rock fell from the roots and bounced away.

Clinging to the pack, she moved it around to the front of her body. She caught the top flap with her teeth and lifted it, flipping it open. Thanks the stars, the rope was on the top.

Very slowly, she lifted the end of the rope in her mouth, pulling it from the pack and leaning until she could grasp it in her fingers. She worked it through the branches to her other hand and wove it down and back up around the tree trunk. She had to let go of the branches to tie it, leaning on her shoulder over the tree. She tied a simple knot but when she tugged on it, it began to pull free, so she tied a second loop. She pulled on the rope and the two knots slid up against the tree trunk and held.

She didn't know how long the rope was, or how far down she had to go. Should she find the other end and tie it to her belt? That way if she fell it would catch her . . . but the rope might snarl or she might end up dangling at the end of it, unable to let go. And the longer she took, the more chance the little tree's roots would give out.

Hooking her shoulder firmly over the tree, she pulled the pack out of the branches. The rope spooled out as the pack moved. She shook the pack sideways and the bundle of rope fell and tumbled away down the rock and out of sight. Thank the skies Rowan knew how to bundle a rope and she wasn't stuck working out knots.

She hugged the pack between her chest and the tree and felt inside for the kerchiefs. She clinked the knife handle against the iron piece and pushed aside a gourd before her fingers grazed the soft woven material. Tugging at it, she pulled out a kerchief and wound it around her right hand. She wrapped her left hand next.

Could she hold her own weight? She carried Elle and she kneaded bread dough and pounded stakes for the tomato plants in the garden, but she weighed considerably more than Elle. But she didn't have a choice. She had to try or she'd hang on to the tree until she weakened and fell. No one was coming to save her.

And if she fell . . . maybe no one would ever know what had happened to her. But at least Elle would have Sunshine to care for her.

Jane swung the pack back to her shoulder and it caught on a branch and slid down her arm. She reached for it and her grip on the tree slipped. Hissing, she focused on the tree limbs and caught herself as the pack slipped off her hand and fell, banging once on the sheer rock as a gourd rolled out and both objects disappeared past the edge.

Drat. Well, nothing left in the pack would have helped her get down. Maybe she was better without it.

She had to start moving. She gripped the rope with her left hand, tensing her arm muscles and pulling it taut as she wrapped it once around the kerchief covering her hand and eased her right shoulder off the tree. The rope tightened and held, squeezing her fingers painfully, and the tree shook but stayed firmly rooted in the crack in the cliff.

With one last glance at the knot holding her up, Jane let go of the tree. She worked the rope off her hand until she could slide down it, flexing her hands to grip again as she fell faster. The rope cut into her palms even with the kerchiefs wrapped around them. She caught herself and the rope dug in, stopping her momentum with a jerk to her left shoulder. She started again, letting herself slide farther, jolting and slipping her way down. Her knee banged the rock and her arms ached but she had to keep going. Her sleeve caught and with a r-i-i-i-p the fabric tore as she fell past.

Her toes worked against the rock to slow her descent until they cleared the edge and dangled into space. As she left the cliff face, she risked a glance down in the fading light of sunset. The rope dangled below her and caught in the top branch of a tree.

She held fast with her right hand, unlooped her left hand, and grasped the rope lower, then repeated the motion on the right, hand over hand as she spun in the air, free of the cliff face. She could do this motion, over and over, and—

Her body dropped a hand's length and caught. The whole rope had dropped. The knot or the tree must be giving out. Jane unwrapped both her hands and loosened her grip, sliding down the rope even as it tore through a kerchief and bit into her hand. Down down down, gripping and letting go to slow herself in jerks, and all at once she was falling with the rope still in her hands. Twigs scraped her legs and she crashed against a branch, was knocked sideways, and fell into another branch before she caught herself and cried out at the pain in her wrist.

She hung in the branches of a tree, panting, as her heart thundered in her ears. The fragrant scent of pine filled her nostrils and a soft brush of pine needles tickled her cheek. A mess of rope was tangled in the greenery all around her. She moved her neck and her braid caught, and now her wrist throbbed in dull pain. Only dim light came through the branches above.

The ground was twenty paces below and the pine branches spiraled out ready to catch her. She ached so badly and her arms were so wobbly that she was tempted to let go and hope for the best. But she was so close now. She grabbed the rope nearest her face and pulled downward and it caught and held. She used it to lower herself until her toes brushed a bough and she stood, let go of the rope, and squatted past the smaller limbs to hold the bough at her feet. She lowered herself again, her body swinging down as sap stuck to her fingers and her feet rested on a larger branch. After a few more branches, her toes touched the earth.

Jane collapsed onto the ground. She lay back and breathed in the moss and pine needles and peered upward at the snatches of twilit sky beyond the tree. She had made it down from Sunshine's peak—down farther than planned but down nonetheless. Her wrist began to ache, not with the dull throb she'd felt earlier but with a sharp, relentless pain. She wiggled it and the pain shot up her arm.

The kerchief from her left hand was gone and the one on her right was in tatters. She slowly sat up and unwound the remnants before scanning the forest around her. The forest floor beneath the tall pines was clear of underbrush and ten paces away lay Rowan's pack. She scanned again and spotted a gourd.

Holding up her injured wrist like Mouser might, she crawled across the ground to the pack. It was almost empty—the other gourd was gone and the blanket too, maybe caught up in the tree branches over her head. Down at the bottom of the pack she found the flat iron piece with the looped end and the walnut shell that held the slug glue.

She pressed the flat body of the iron piece against her wrist to hold it straight and tried to tie it on with the tattered kerchief but the worn fabric snapped in two the moment she pulled it tight. She could tear a strip from her shirt—it had already ripped—but the knife had fallen out of the pack and she didn't have the strength left to tear fabric. She'd have to move and simply be careful of her wrist, before it got any darker.

Wait. The darkness—the sun was down. That meant . . .

Jane scooped up the walnut shell and pried it open. She poked a finger in and it squished into the slug glue, strange and slimy. It didn't seem sticky at all but what did she have to lose? The rest of her was covered with dirt and sap and probably bruises. What was a little slug slime?

She scooped a fingerful out and smeared it along the inside of her wrist, wincing at the contact. When she had a coating, she again pressed the flat of the iron piece against her skin. It slid a smidge in the glue and then it stuck.

Jane slowly let go, expecting the iron to slide off her wrist but it didn't budge. Did the glue have to dry? Rowan had smeared it on to hang the hammock that time and she'd tried to tug it off just moments later. She counted to ten and another ten to be sure and pulled at the loop in the iron. It was stuck fast to her skin, holding her wrist straight—at least until sunrise.

She closed the walnut and returned it to the pack before reaching for the one gourd that remained. After a long drink, she donned the lightened pack and wobbled to her feet.

By now the sky was barely lighter than the dark forest but the beige rock of Sunshine's peak gleamed brighter through the treetops. The forest floor sloped away but if she followed it uphill and kept the peak on her right side, she should end up back where she and Rowan had started.

She hefted herself up a few steps and clung to a tree as dizziness seized her. The way was almost as steep as the rock she had slid down but soft with moss and roots. She leaned forward and curled her fingers over a root, and began to climb on all fours.

As she worked her way up, she rose past the branches of one tree only to pass the base of the next. Her muscles ached like she'd spent a quarter-moon digging up potatoes and hauling them to market without a wagon but she stood on solid ground with saplings and roots and branches to cling to, and that was a comfort. She climbed and climbed and tried not to think about how everything hurt, and finally the branches cleared and she crawled out of the trees.

Stars filled the sky with only the barest smudge of twilight at the western horizon. The moon wasn't up yet but her eyes had adjusted to the darkness. In the starlight, she located Sunshine's peak a short way off, and the treacherous slope of boulders where she had tumbled off the edge. She climbed toward the shadowy base of the peak and her feet landed on the hard-packed dirt as she made her way behind the peak toward the place where she and Rowan had first emerged from the forest. She could find a place to sleep under the trees . . . but her mind wasn't the least bit tired. Her pulse pounded from the exertion. Her thoughts spun with what to do next.

She stepped onto the ledge they had followed around the edge of the mountain and located her bag and the blanket that had tumbled out. Her crackers and pecans were gone but the napkin of dried apples was wedged into a corner in the bottom. She donned her coat and scarf and ate a handful of the apples. She packed the rest but left her bag since she had Rowan's to carry.

She climbed back along the lip of the mountain, back along the chasm where the birds had guided them, and stepped away from the edge and into the dark forest. The wind had faded as darkness came and here it only rustled softly in the branches, and the deep earthy scent of the ground permeated the air. She peered into the trees. All was still, the birds and daytime critters tucked into their branches and hollows for the night. She could make out only the vague shapes of rocks and bushes, but this part of the walk had been easy. She and Rowan had been talking as they walked side by side over flat, even ground. He'd been easy to talk to even then, before they'd . . . She swallowed. Before they'd been naked together and kissed and touched for hours, and he'd been so lovely to do it with.

She crept into the silent forest. Her steps landed on solid ground, and she moved more confidently. She couldn't see the sky but she sensed the uphill slope to her left and stayed on level ground, hoping she walked north. She walked quickly over the flat terrain and passed the large rhododendron grove. Her wrist ached but the stiff piece of iron held it straight and avoided sharp pains. The darkness grew so complete she slowed to a careful pace until the way lightened a smidge. She hurried on.

Jane stepped out of the trees at the top of the trail and stared out at the wide sky. Even without a breeze the air was cold here. The bushes around her glowed faint in the starlight, as did the treetops spreading below. The woodlands and mountains to the west were so vast. What if they'd taken Elle out there? Even Rose and an army of fairies wouldn't be able to find them.

She turned from the view and trudged down the trail and into the tunnel of rhododendron bushes. Without trees above, the starlight filtered down to her. Her steps grew heavier as tiredness caught up with her. Maybe she'd have to stop but as long as she could see enough to walk she would keep going. She watched for the fairy markers and soon found one on a thin sapling. She'd have to stop soon, but she'd lie awake the whole night as Elle was carried farther and farther away.

She continued to the next marker, this one daubed on a rough tree trunk. She could barely see it this time, now that a tree towered overhead. Should she stop? The moon should be up now but it must be behind a slope of the mountain and the starlight was faint here under the leafy canopy. As she neared, she reached out to touch the marker, pausing to run her fingers over the hard bumps of sap. They rolled down in beads as if the sap had slowly dripped after whatever fairy painted it on the bark, until it hardened in place. She leaned on the tree and closed her eyes. She didn't want to stop moving. She needed to get home, to find Elle. If only she could see the markers in the dark.

The hardened sap warmed under her fingertips. Jane yanked her fingers back with a sharp inhale. The marker had begun to glow with an eerie light, like the last of the orange sunlight but the light emanated from within the sap. It grew brighter until it was so bright she couldn't make out the bark around it. Carefully she touched it and it pulsed a little brighter.

She stepped back, staring in wonder at the beacon. A second orange glow appeared ahead and to the left. And a third glowed far down the trail. The markers were lighting the trail. Maybe they came on at night. Rowan hadn't mentioned that.

Jane started toward the next orange marker. She had to watch every step in the darkness but she could see her feet as she headed for the glowing light. Her eyes adjusted to the darkness and she avoided looking directly at the beacons to keep the glare out of her eyes. Eventually she could pick her way along at a steady pace. The glowing markers continued to appear, but when she glanced back, they faded behind her as if they lit only when she was near. How could they tell? She'd never heard of the fairies making anything so complicated—at least not until Rowan had told her about the magic hummingbird orgasm wand. Maybe he'd been making that up. He had said he could lie about things if they were stupid enough no one would believe them. No one, except someone as gullible as her, apparently.

Time passed but she had no sense of how long except she'd passed dozens of the markers, maybe even a hundred. Moonlight appeared in patches on the ground, so the moon must have cleared the tops of the trees. The markers swung to the right and led across a flat, hard section of trail before dropping in among a series of boulders. An owl hooted and night creatures cheeped, occasionally rustling in the leaves.

The rhododendron bushes gave way to more saplings and the trail grew rockier. The moon had risen just in time—without its light she'd have twisted another ankle for sure. On and on she went.

The trail turned to packed dirt. Pale moonlight shone down on a post in the ground ahead. It couldn't be the mine already. But it was! She'd reached the iron mine, which meant the trail would be wider. And also . . . Jane shuddered. That flat place she'd crossed— that had been the sheer rock with the drop off the edge. And she'd walked right past it without holding on to the bushes or anything. Thank the skies she hadn't slipped or stumbled.

She approached the signpost and stopped. Could the miners help her? If she kept walking, she'd have to get past the two campsites before reaching the crossroads at the bottom. She'd have to rest eventually. That could take her two days. One of the miners could surely get down the mountain faster if they were willing to help. Or they might let her take one of the mules used to climb down the steep path, if they had a mule at the mine. And they'd have food and water. She didn't know if she could find the springs under the trees where Rowan had refilled their gourds.

However many days ago, Rowan hadn't wanted to go near the mine. He'd said it was too quiet and that he worried for the dragons' safety. Were humans truly a danger to dragons, though? Now that she'd seen Sunshine spewing fire, Jane couldn't imagine how a human could touch her. But a chill went down her spine as she peered down the dark trail. Without the comforting lights of the trail markers, the trail to the mine seemed menacing.

But the miners might help her. Maybe they'd even seen Sunshine flying away and knew what direction she'd taken Elle.

She would go carefully. In the middle of the night everyone should be asleep. She could poke around and see how the place looked and if anything seemed off, she'd leave and sleep in the woods.

She stepped onto the side trail. If only it had comforting glowing markers to encourage her along. She walked slowly into the darker forest, and when she looked back, the markers had all gone out.

Chapter 15

JANE PACED CAREFULLY ALONG THE shadowy trail toward the mine camp. Even if Rowan hadn't mentioned the suspicious quiet of the location, she wouldn't have known what to expect. Did the miners dig holes to find iron ore or chip it off a rocky cliffside? Master Smith might know.

A group of people lived and worked at the mine from the spring thaw through the summer and into the autumn. When the snows came, they retreated to the villages at the base of the mountains—many to Woods Rest. Maryanne had had a fling with a lanky miner named Roy one winter. Finding Roy in his undershorts in the kitchen had been a bit embarrassing, but he'd been pleasant enough. And less of a slob than Wells. But he'd headed off to Nor Bay, so he wouldn't be at the mine camp tonight. Maybe she would recognize other miners from around the village last winter.

She kept her steps light and her breathing quiet. The carpet of pine needles aided her stealthy approach. If anything moved ahead, she could step off the trail into the trees and crouch in the darkness to stay hidden until she saw who, or what, it was. But nothing would move—at this hour, everyone would be asleep.

The night had been quiet before, but now not even a hint of wind stirred the trees. Even the night animals had gone silent as if they'd given up on hunting as midnight passed. The chill air seeped through her clothing. She held the straps of the pack in her fists. Gradually she made out shapes ahead—only more trees, but they had a yellow glow about them. The trail opened into a cleared space and moonlight slanted down on a small wooden structure with a bright lantern hanging on the corner, shining onto the surrounding trees. The shack would shelter a few people and not much else. She paused but no sounds came.

As she crept forward, misgivings stirred in her chest. No one would intentionally leave a flame burning unattended in the middle of forest like this. Had the lantern been left by accident? The small window revealed only an empty space. She came level with the shack and peered into the open doorway on the side. A stool stood in the center of the single room. A shelf edged along one wall and a ledger lay face down on the floor. Jane reached in the doorway to lift the book, releasing a musty smell. Its pages had creased badly while it lay sprawled open. Tallies of numbers with dates covered the pages, ending halfway down the right side. They ended with a date a few quarter-moons ago. She flattened the parchment, closed the book, and placed it on the stool.

Beyond the shack, rows of wheelbarrows waited in the shadows. They were filled with rocks, with piles of rocks on the ground behind them. The rocks glittered in the moonlight. This must be the iron ore on its way from the mine to the trail. Was this the ore Master Smith was waiting for?

A few of the rock piles had long, lumpy sacks draped over them, and more sacks littered the ground. Rowan had said the miners used mules to bring the ore down to where the trail widened into the wagon road. They must load it on the mules in these sacks, then move it off the mules into wagons like the abandoned one they'd passed on the way up. The wagons took the ore down to the ironworks. Or maybe the mules helped the wagons cart the ore down.

A door hinge creaked in the darkness out beyond the wheelbarrows.

Jane darted into the shack and crouched inside. Opposite the window facing the way she had come, a second glassless window faced out toward the camp. She crawled into the shadows at the far end of the shack, held on to the window frame, and lifted herself up to peek out.

A second light shone out in the darkness, moving her way. Beyond the throng of wheelbarrows and nestled among saplings she could now see a larger wooden building, faintly illuminated. Dark woods towered on the left side of the other building. To its right lay more open space, and a sheen of moonlight suggested a broad roof of yet another building slightly downhill from the first. Footsteps crunched on gravelly dirt. Someone carrying a lantern moved into view up the slope. They neared the closer building and moved out of sight. Yellow light brightened. Voices sounded momentarily—aggressive, deep voices. It went dark as a door banged shut.

Nothing else moved. Jane took a slow breath and let it out. She squinted as she scanned across the other building. Was lamplight glowing on the trees at the left side? It was, as if the building had a window there.

Before she could consider what would happen if they spotted her, she darted from the shack and past the wheelbarrows of iron ore into the shadow of the building the person had entered. She skirted along the wall to the back and climbed into the undergrowth. Light did indeed shine out a window on this back side facing the forest.

She crawled under the window. Glass blocked the sounds from inside but muffled voices were speaking. The glass was grimy and smudged with dirt. Hooking her fingers onto the wood below the glass, she raised herself up slowly to peek in.

A handful of people formed a ring in a bare room. They stood facing in, one holding up a lantern, and one person sat in a chair right in the middle with his back to her and with all eyes on him. They were all men and they were all scowling.

Panic filled her as she clung to the window ledge. A rumpled coat lay on the floor. As the lantern moved, its light glinted off an object sticking out of the pocket—the handle of a dagger. And a pile of something orange lay scattered alongside. She swallowed with difficulty. The pile of something orange . . . it was fire mushrooms. And the dagger—it had tumbled out of Rowan's pack two days ago and startled her. She'd forgotten all about it.

The man in the middle—his hands were bound behind him. His coat was off. She couldn't tell his height but his shoulders were broad and his hair was dark. It was Rowan they all watched.

Had they caught him escaping down the mountain? Why would they stop him and restrain him? Or had they been at Sunshine's peak? That made more sense. Someone had been there and destroyed all the fire mushrooms. And Sunshine had flown away when they came. But why would they take Rowan captive?

She had to hear what they were saying. They might see her if she pressed closer to the glass, but they had only the two lanterns in the center of the room. The edges of the room were dim. And the men all seemed focused on Rowan. As long as she didn't draw their attention, they shouldn't regard the dirty back window.

She stood to the side of the window and carefully cupped her hand against the glass, pressing on it to avoid rattling it. Once her hand was firmly in place, she added her other hand and rested her ear between them.

" . . . nothing there . . ."

The voices were fuzzy but words came through.

" . . . go back. Might find something in the light."

"You think we missed seeing a dragon?"

"He said she fled when he arrived."

"Why should we listen to him?"

"She might return. We'd be waiting."

"There's no gold even if she comes back. We searched."

"But we could harvest her scales."

"There's no magic in dragon scales." Jane tensed. Rowan's clear voice rolled through her and tears pricked her eyes.

"You'd hardly tell us if there was," a man said. "Why were you up there waiting for her?"

"I told you," Rowan replied. "I'm a visitor from the south. I'm interested in the medicinal properties of fire mushrooms."

"You're traveling in the mountains without any supplies?"

"Sounds like a load of dung."

Jane's head spun. The men were after Sunshine. They wanted to harvest her scales—exactly what Rowan had worried about. Humans fantasized about dragons with hoards of gold and magical scales. Did they not understand how dangerous Sunshine was?

Somehow the miners had learned about Sunshine. They'd found her location. Jane closed her eyes, cursing as she remembered with dismay her bag at the base of the cliff. She'd given away Sunshine's location.

These men must've climbed up using Rowan's ropes. Maybe they'd even started climbing the same day that she and Rowan reached the top. Maybe their own arrival had distracted Sunshine and prevented her from noticing the intruders. And these men had been coming closer and closer as she and Rowan made love under the stars. She shuddered.

Sunshine had been asleep when Jane and Rowan returned to the courtyard to lie in the hammock. But her wings had beaten in the night—she'd heard them approaching and taken Elle to safety. Jane warmed in gratitude, in spite of the fact that Sunshine had abandoned her and Rowan.

And Rowan had gotten up and never come back. He must have heard Sunshine leave—he must have gone to investigate. He would have wondered why the dragon was leaving in the middle of the night. Jane should have wondered too, but she'd been tired and Rowan had told her to sleep. And if he encountered this group of men invading Sunshine's den, what would he do? Would he fight? She couldn't imagine Rowan pushing someone off the cliff's edge without giving them a chance, but once the men surrounded him, he wouldn't have been able to fight them all—how many had been up there?

She'd imagined Rowan abandoning her, stealing Elle, using Jane for vengeance against Larch, even working together with Larch. How could she have thought those things? He hadn't betrayed her. He'd protected her. He'd kept the men away from the hidden entrance to the courtyard, so they would leave without finding her. And they'd taken him with them.

A chair scuffled as a man in back stood. He stepped toward Rowan and punched his jaw, and Jane winced as the man yelled something about Rowan not telling them everything. Rowan's head hung to the side, his long hair hiding his face from view as he slumped in the chair.

Rowan would never betray a dragon. But even if he did crack and tell them the truth, Sunshine was gone and she wouldn't return while any threat remained. Sunshine had escaped and surely she'd taken Elle with her—wherever they were, they'd be safe.

But nothing Rowan could say would appease the miners, not when they wanted gold and dragon scales. Were they even miners? The one in the center was older than the others with graying hair and a lined face, and the rest were men about her age. They could be miners but none of them looked familiar.

She had to rescue Rowan and get them both out of here.

Jane sank to the ground. With all those men she'd have to wait. She pressed her forehead into her knees and willed the men to leave. It was the middle of the night. They must have been climbing and walking all last night and into the daytime. They'd have to sleep. How long had Rowan been tied here? What else had they done to him?

The door on the far side of the building banged again. Jane froze and listened.

"... been dragging this out. He knows something."

"We'll make him talk."

"That climb was harrowing, sir. The men need a rest."

"Fine. Rest till morning and then I want answers."

The footsteps faded. Jane stood and peeked inside. Rowan remained in the middle of the room with two of the men. One leaned on the doorframe, picking his fingernails clean with a knife. His head was shaved and his shoulders filled the doorway. The other sat slumped on the floor, carving something into the floorboards. He was shorter and wiry, but he kept stabbing at the floorboards as if he liked hurting things. Only two of them, but she couldn't fight those men, especially not when they were armed. She had to get Rowan out, but how?

The mine had a crew of dozens. She'd met whole families who spent the season here, with children and grandparents. They couldn't all be in on a plot to steal riches from a dragon, or to hold Rowan captive until he helped them do it. Where was the rest of the mining crew—sleeping? Did they not know their comrades were holding Rowan prisoner?

Maybe she could find someone to help her.

Jane left Rowan's pack tucked behind the building and crept around the far side. The waning moon was high overhead and lit the way brightly. The road leading farther into the mine camp was empty and no voices sounded from the men who had left.

She stole out and through the trees until the wide track bent, and the guard in the doorway was out of her sight. She moved toward the track but kept to the shadowy edge under the trees and continuously scanned for movement. The roof she'd glimpsed earlier was on a large, flat building, probably the bunkhouse given its size. A light inside went dark. The next building down with its large chimney and a few wooden tables under a covered porch must be the mess hall. Other structures loomed in the shadows of the trees surrounding the camp. At the bottom of the hill she passed a building padlocked with a heavy chain through the handles of the doors.

The road split. From the shelter of the trees, Jane studied each direction. To the right, the night sky gleamed on cleared ground and the land dropped off with no buildings. Empty wheelbarrows leaned on a fence by an open gate halfway down the path. Maybe that direction was the pit where the workers dug out the ore.

To the left were more structures, so she crept in that direction. The trees opened into a moonlit yard. A large stone structure with a chimney towered over one side, iron tools leaning or hanging on hooks at the side of a hearth-like opening. It had a roof built over it with the chimney poking through. The hearth had only cold ashes in it, but a row of cast iron pots and kettles lined the shelf at the base of the chimney above it. Wooden boxes were stacked under a lean-to beside the chimney structure, and opposite the chimney the ground rose in a strange domed shape. The chimney was similar to the furnace at the ironworks. Perhaps the miners could process ore here at the mine instead of sending it down the mountain. Maybe they had extracted the iron right here at one time and cast items like the pots decorating the chimney.

She circled the clearing, creeping behind the structures, but the forest enclosed it with no roads or trails leading out. The clearing was a dead end.

Movement flickered behind the chimney and she stopped dead. She peered into the shadows. Something had definitely moved. It happened again and an animal snuffled. Beyond the clearing, a ramshackle rail fence lined the trees and a large animal stood behind it, watching her. It had tall ears. It must be one of the mules the miners used.

She slowly let out her breath. When she had calmed, she walked back to the split of the road. The night was eerily silent. No crickets or birds called, and the wind remained absent.

Should she check out the mine pit? The continuous fence blocking the way suggested she should keep out—she didn't want to slip off the edge of any more scarps. But she hadn't missed anything on—

A voice murmured somewhere nearby. Jane strained to hear. Where had it come from? It hadn't been at all like the men's voices from earlier. She was too far from the bunkhouse to hear anyone there.

Someone sniffled and the voice murmured again. Jane turned to the sound. The building with the chain on the door was behind her. It had no windows, only solid plank walls over a stone foundation, with a stone chimney built into the wall. She tiptoed toward the building, pausing every few steps to listen. The voice kept speaking in soothing tones, like someone calming a frightened child. Jane started around the building and the voice faded. She turned the other direction, and the voice returned as she neared the chimney.

The chimney had a grate in the side for sweeping out the ashes. She knelt beside it and listened.

"It'll be okay." A woman's voice. And someone sniffled again.

This building had people inside. And the chain on the door made it clear they were trapped. Who were they? Given what she'd seen of the people on the outside, helping the people trapped inside seemed a safe step.

"Hello?" she called quietly.

The voices stopped.

"Hello?" Jane called again.

"Who's there?"

"I'm, uh, my name is Jane. Can I help you?"

The woman hissed a few names and boards creaked with movement. "Jane," she said clearly. "We're locked in. Can you get the door open?"

"It's chained shut. I don't know where the key is."

"Could you break the lock?"

"I don't think so. The chain is massive. And I'm . . . not."

"Jane." A man's voice this time. "Down the path behind you is the furnace. It has a tall chimney. Can you see it?"

"I saw it."

"There are tools beside it. Iron tools with long handles. If you slipped one through the chain on the door, you'd gain leverage to help you break it."

She doubted she'd have enough leverage. But Rowan's words from days ago came back to her: It doesn't take much strength if you know how to hold the hammer.

"I'll try," Jane said.

She ran three steps back toward the furnace yard but caught herself and slowed, moving into the shadows. She couldn't get careless. The two men guarding Rowan were awake and not far off, and others might be awake. She circled the clearing and came under the roof of the furnace.

All the tools were iron—tongs and shovels and other, mysterious implements. One bar leaning in a cluster was the longest. She gently lifted it, wincing at the pressure on her hurt wrist. But the bar was so heavy it didn't budge. She heaved with more force and the bar came up. It grated against the other tools and caught, and all the tools slid sideways with a loud grating noise. Jane grabbed the whole bundle in her arms and cut off the noise with one final clank. Her heart hammered as she nudged the tools upright and held them in place as she maneuvered the one with the extra-long handle out of the bunch. Skies it weighed more than a sack of grain. She worked it sideways until it leaned alone on the side of the furnace and she could stabilize the other tools and let them go.

The bar was solid iron, three fingers thick and as tall as she was. One end flattened and curved ninety degrees into a sideways bar—maybe to pull ashes from the furnace?—while the other end tapered. She hefted it up in both hands and lugged it back to the locked door.

The chain through the door handles was pulled tight. She hoisted the bar over her head and fit the tapered end in between the lengths of chain. The fit was too tight, but by wiggling back and forth she shifted the chain enough to allow the end in. She shoved it down. It made a horrible scraping noise that echoed through the camp. Jane froze, staring in horror over her shoulder and up the hill, but nothing happened. She slid the bar in farther, little by little so the noise of it was only small squeaks, wedging it down until about half the bar was on the lower side of the chain.

Jane closed her eyes. She could do this. She had to free these people and ask them to help her save Rowan.

She pulled the bent end of the tool toward her, straining against the chain. The bar moved out and stopped at a narrow angle with the door. She increased her force, pulling with everything she had and the bar gave a little. It was working! She checked the chain and frowned. The chain was as tight as ever. The bar had moved because the bottom end had dug into the wood of the door.

Could she split the door in two instead of breaking the chain?

Probably not. She braced herself with a foot against the door and jerked on the tool as hard as she could, pulling and pulling. It moved farther into the old wood and stopped, and the chain groaned and bent a smidge. Two links had warped slightly. Jane let off the pressure.

Her strength wasn't enough and now the tool was lodged farther in the wood. It might get completely stuck. She needed something hard and flat to protect the old door and brace the iron bar against.

What if she flipped the tool around so the wide implement pressed against the door? That would spread out the force instead of concentrating it the way the tapered end did. She hadn't been able to fit the wide end through the chain before but the chain had loosened a little. She carefully withdrew the tool, little by little until it was free, and rotated it halfway around. It took work to slide the bent end through the chain, but she got it through and repositioned the tool.

She set the tool in place, braced with her foot again, took a deep breath, and pulled. Something cracked. She screwed her face up and focused on the bar and kept pulling. The bar jerked forward and stopped.

A link of the chain was cracked on one side.

It had worked! She leaned the tool on the door and grabbed the broken link with shaking hands. It held the chain together but by turning it she slipped it loose from one side. She carefully unthreaded the chain from the door handles and lowered it quietly to the grass before moving the tool aside and opening the latch on the door. The door swung open.

People inside clustered in the dark, vague shapes in the bare light from the doorway. Anticipation ruffled through them as voices murmured. A man with a deep voice—perhaps the one who had encouraged her—came out first and whispered at those behind him to be silent, and the murmurs died. They squinted as they came out, people of all ages, in a stumbling stream.

The first man turned to Jane. He had shaggy hair and an uneven beard. He towered over her, leaning close, and his face was serious but not threatening. "Who are you?" he asked quietly. "You're in danger here."

"I know," Jane whispered. "My . . . friend and I were on the mountain, and the miners captured him. They think he knows where to find gold but he doesn't. They've beaten him and tied him up, and I need to help him."

The last of the people exited the building. They stayed together near the door. They numbered twenty or so, and the moonlight showed their bedraggled state. A mine must be a dirty place, but the people themselves were dirty, with unkempt hair and bags under their eyes. All the men had beards as if no one had shaved in a moon. A few children hung on adults and one man lay unconscious on the ground with another tending him.

"What happened here?" Jane asked.

"A mutiny. Some of the miners got ahold of weapons and poisoned the crew chief. They locked the rest of us in."

"Why would they do that?"

"They were criminals. They were sent here as their punishment to work. They staged an uprising in Cliffside last moon."

"I heard about that." Kitty had been in Cliffside when it happened.

"Do you know where they are?" the man asked.

Jane scanned the mine camp. "Two of them are guarding Rowan in the small building at the top of the hill. The rest went to sleep, I think. I saw a light on over there." She pointed to the bunkhouse. "They said they'd be back for Rowan in the morning. Please, can you help me free him?"

"Yes. Did you see any guns?"

"Only daggers."

The man scanned the crowd, gesturing a few times, and a handful of people moved forward. He glanced down at her. "I'm Os, by the way. And you're Jane, right?" Without waiting for an answer he addressed those who'd gathered around him. "There were at least three guns in camp they might have found. And they have daggers. If we can surprise them all at once, we might stop them without anyone being hurt."

He began assigning tasks. A burly couple headed to the furnace to retrieve iron tools to carry as weapons, and a woman moved through the crowd with her chin up, consulting on who would volunteer to fight, while another woman gathered the youngsters and some of the adults—maybe the non-fighters, given how timid some of them looked.

"Myra," Os whispered loudly, "take the—"

"Take the others to safety," said the woman, whose hair was tied up in a kerchief. Turning, she let out an exasperated sigh. Even in the faint light, Jane could tell she had the deeper brown skin of a far northerner.

Os looked down and crossed his arms over his chest. "Yes."

Myra waited.

"Please," Os added, and his lips pressed tight.

Myra smirked in his direction before turning back to the people around her and motioning them to follow her. They moved into the shadows of the forest, carrying the injured man.

As they moved away, Os lifted his chin. Ten people remained, all of them muscular with determined frowns on their faces and all focused on him.

"I'll go to the bunkhouse with six of you," Os said, "and you three follow Jane to the meeting room." He pointed and three people separated off, including the burly couple who had gone for weapons. They both had longish hair, with the woman's braided into pigtails that fell over her bulging arms. Everyone remaining carried an iron tool. "Warin, you stay out here and keep watch in case anything goes amiss."

Os turned to Jane and her three companions. "We'll listen for you and move in as soon as you do," he said. "But try to subdue them quietly in any case."

"No war cries," the burly man said, brandishing the iron bar Jane had used to break the lock open, and he grinned.

Os grinned back. "Right. No war cries, Derek. Go on now."

The three fighters assigned to Jane turned to her. "Would you like a weapon?" Derek asked.

"I don't think I'd know what to do with it."

"Here," said the woman with pigtails, and she handed over a narrow iron rod with bristles fastened to the end to make a broom. "Take this. We'll take care of the fighting, but if you need to defend yourself, you'll have something to whack with."

Jane gripped her broom and followed the three into the shadows and up the hillside. She pointed them through the woods the way she had come and whispered a description of what she had seen through the window. She clenched her trembling hands as they neared. Thank the skies the miners could handle a fight. She clutched the iron broom handle as they took the lead.

They emerged along the side of the building, and Jane hung back as the others moved in with no hesitation. All together they rounded the corner and leapt out of Jane's sight as the guard shouted. Jane darted after them.

Two of the miners had the first guard in their arms already. They twisted his wrist and his dagger clattered to the ground as the guard from inside appeared in the doorway. The third miner held up the iron bar and grinned as the guard scowled and held up his dagger. The guard moved forward out of the doorway to meet the miner. The fight would be over in a heartbeat but the moment the doorway cleared, Jane charged toward it. She had to free Rowan.

She reached the doorframe but faltered at the sight of Rowan. They'd gagged him since she'd watched through the window. Both his eyes were blackened and blood stained his lip and chin below the gag. His eyes were brown. They widened and he struggled against the ropes binding him.

A hand grabbed her hair and dragged her backward. A knife came at her face.

Jane thrust the iron broom handle up and the knife skidded off it. She kept the handle in front of her face as the knife danced back and forth. The grip on her hair yanked and shook her. She grabbed the arm holding the knife, pulled it toward her, and bit it as hard as she could.

Her attacker jerked and loosened his grip on her hair, and she dropped to her knees as someone behind him pulled him backward. She crawled to Rowan.

His ankles were bound to the legs of the chair. She dropped the broom and knelt before him to work the gag from between his cracked lips.

"My dagger," he rasped.

Jane scurried to the items strewn on the floor beside him and snatched the blade from his coat pocket. It was tiny compared to the daggers the guards carried. The doorway had cleared and shouts sounded outside. She crawled behind Rowan's chair.

The rope around his wrists was stiff. She slid the blade between his arms and down and sawed at the top rope. Once it was embedded in the rope, the dagger couldn't slip sideways and cut him so she worked it faster. Little by little the first rope gave until it snapped free. More people were shouting. She loosened the remaining coils of rope as Rowan wriggled his hands free.

"Give me the dagger." He used one swift stroke to free each of his legs. He stood and swayed a moment. Jane clambered to her feet and caught him in her arms, and together they stumbled to the door.

The two men who'd guarded Rowan lay unmoving on the ground. The three miners who'd helped her stood out in the road and watched down the hill. Jane and Rowan staggered out and stopped beside them.

Outside the bunkhouse, two groups faced off in the moonlight. Os and his team of seven faced uphill and opposite them were four men—pointing guns.

"We can come from behind," Derek whispered, panting.

"Wait," Rowan said in a hoarse voice.

All three turned to him.

"Wait a moment. No one needs to risk anything."

A shadow flickered across the moonlit ground, running along the path and over the two groups of fighters before veering off over the bunkhouse. Jane looked up. The treetops stirred in the wake. Wings beat in the air and everyone turned, even those at gunpoint. The shadow reappeared below the people, larger and growing as something swooped down onto them. Flames burst into life and people shrieked. Some scrambled out of the way, but the four men with the guns were silhouetted against the brilliant fire. Jane ducked her head against Rowan's shoulder so she wouldn't see what happened.

Derek cursed and footsteps pounded away from them. Rowan's arm came behind her waist. He tucked her head under his chin before closing his other arm around her shoulders. "Hang on," he said and his arms clenched her like the climbing belt, like he was buckling himself around her, clasping her tightly.

Claws closed around them and with a sickening lurch, her feet jerked off the ground as a dragon carried them up into the night.

Chapter 16

JANE AND ROWAN HURTLED THROUGH the night sky. And all that was holding them up was the flapping of dragon wings.

Jane kept her face against Rowan's chest. If she opened her eyes and saw the moonlit ground a half-league below, she might swoon and Rowan would be stuck holding her limp body. Not that it would change anything. The dragon's claws were locked tight around them. Rowan couldn't drop her if he wanted to.

Which he didn't. She could tell because he kept kissing the top of her head and retightening his grip around her body. Rowan hadn't betrayed her—all the hurt and anger of that morning had gone.

Instead she felt ashamed. Ashamed not because she had trusted the wrong person but because she had betrayed him. At the first moment of something appearing to be wrong, she had lost faith in him and assumed the worst. She'd thought she'd been wrong to trust him, but this time, she'd been wrong *not* to trust him. And that felt a whole lot worse. All the more reason to keep her face hidden.

"It won't be much longer," Rowan said in her ear. His calm voice cut through the roar of the wind as they flew. The icy air stung the tips of her ears, but if she turned her head to warm them, her nose would be exposed. Rowan was warm somehow and keeping her from freezing. And he smelled comforting in the bracing gusts of air.

She didn't know if he would hear her or if the wind would carry her voice away. "Where are we going?"

"Woods Rest."

"Who's carrying us?"

"Axe."

So Axe had come for them. How had he known they needed him?

"Do you want to see the sunrise?" Rowan asked.

She gripped Rowan's sides tighter—his sides were the farthest she could reach her arms around him, given how tightly Axe held them. "Is it worth it?"

"We may never get to do this again."

Get to do this. Like he was enjoying it. Was he? She held on and opened her eyes, turning her face away from Rowan's chest.

She blinked in the unexpected light. Treetops spread endlessly below them under a pale dawn sky. The ground was flat—they were no longer in the mountains. Axe held them sideways, which she'd suspected from the way the forces pulled at her. But she hadn't been sure because she hadn't opened her eyes once since he'd snatched them off the ground and flown away.

His massive wings beat the air above them. Through the spaces between his claws she located the horizon, where the sky was lightening as the sun neared. The pink dawn shimmered on a flat plain—it must be the ocean.

Her vision spun and her stomach grew a little woozy. She closed her eyes until it passed and reopened them. She hadn't fainted. And the view of the ocean glimmering pink and golden at the edge was beautiful.

"I can see the end of the woods by the village," Rowan said.

Jane glanced aside but the dizziness returned. She kept her eyes on the horizon as it brightened until at last the edge of the sun sparkled above the water.

"Just in time," Rowan said.

Axe's wings spread and he coasted down, and the top of the

sun disappeared again behind the flat horizon, which disappeared behind the trees. They coasted over the last of the forest and above the fields intersected by the road to Woods Rest that they'd traveled on in the back of the wagon of cabbages. Axe circled and Jane closed her eyes again. The sick feeling in her gut told her they were dropping fast. His wings beat at the air, slowing them. His claws loosened suddenly, and she squeaked and dug her fingers into Rowan. Rowan kept hold of her as she dropped onto poking grasses and cold soil.

She'd stopped moving. She was on the ground. But Rowan didn't let her go. He lay half on top of her and if anything, he held her tighter. The ground shook and footsteps swished through the grasses. Something moved against her back—something solid. Axe settled down behind her. And his scales warmed.

Jane peeked out from Rowan's chest but all she could see aside from his shirt was the predawn sky. Grasses prickled under her but Rowan's arm was under her head. Axe huffed and exhaled, his body relaxing behind her, and he stretched his wing over them. It blocked the sky and wrapped around Rowan, and the whistling of wind in the grasses faded.

Jane saw his bruises again. "Are you hurt?" she whispered.

"Nothing that won't heal."

Tears leaked sideways from her eyes and she began to shake. It was all too much—from Elle being taken to learning dragons existed and climbing into the mountains to find her, then falling for Rowan only to think he'd abandoned her and realizing she'd been wrong. And then Rowan being a prisoner. And the men beating him—had Axe killed them last night? How could he not have with that burst of flames? She wanted to think they deserved it for all the people they'd threatened and harmed. And they would have hurt Rowan worse in the morning! But she kept rehearing the shrieks as Axe had flown down to rescue them—or to rescue Rowan, at least—and instead of relief or gratitude she felt sick.

Would Sunshine do something like that to protect Elle?

Jane sobbed into Rowan's chest, and he held her silently. When she could catch her breath, she turned her face up to him but he didn't loosen his grip.

"I thought you'd left me. I thought you'd left and I didn't know why so I thought the worst of you. I'm so sorry." She broke down again.

Rowan rubbed her back. "I would never willingly leave you."

"I'm sorry," she blubbered again.

"I'm to blame."

"No—"

"I should have known something was wrong," Rowan said. "We could have hidden until the intruders left."

"But—"

"Instead I got caught. I left you up there all alone."

"What happened?"

He stroked her hair and kissed her head again. "I heard Sunshine take off," he murmured against her. "I should've been more careful. She wouldn't fly away with Elle in the night for no reason. But I went out to investigate. When I stepped out of her den, the miners were climbing over the edge of the cliff. I couldn't think. I wanted to keep them from finding you."

"And you did."

"But I left you to get down on your own. What if you'd fallen?" He kissed her forehead but wouldn't meet her gaze.

"I didn't fall. Well, not too much. Just once."

His arms tightened.

"Mostly I used the belt and the ropes."

"I'm sorry, Jane."

She was the one who'd wronged him, and he kept blaming himself.

"Did they really think she had gold?" she asked.

"Gold and magical scales they could sell." Rowan's voice went hard and flat.

"How did they find her?"

"From what I gathered, one of them saw her flying simply by chance. They'd been planning their mutiny ever since they arrived at the mine. They'd been there only a moon or so, working as punishment for something."

"They staged a rebellion in Cliffside. Kitty was there."

"When they saw Sunshine they thought they'd use her 'riches' to escape the continent. So they turned on the leaders at the mine, and once they were free they spread into the forest to find Sunshine. One of them knew about fire mushrooms, and they used those to narrow their search. When they found our ropes, they suspected she was at the top. And the ropes made it easier for them to hoist each other up."

"My bag," Jane said. "The ropes were hidden. The bag I left on the ground gave her away."

"It doesn't matter now." He couldn't say she was wrong.

"You told them you were studying fire mushrooms."

His hold on her loosened. "How did you know?"

"I heard you at the mine camp. I was at the back window. They had you . . ." She couldn't finish. He squeezed her.

"I told them I was a naturalist. They were still searching for Sunshine, so I figured she'd flown away to the east without them seeing her and wouldn't be back. I said I hadn't seen a dragon, but they didn't believe me."

"How did you say all that without lying?"

"Fairies can tell a direct lie, you know."

"They can?"

"It's uncomfortable but it can be done."

"So you lied?"

"Not really. I believe I said, 'I study nature. I'm interested in fire mushrooms. I haven't seen a dragon today. And so on.'"

"Clever."

"They snooped around for a while, but in the dark they never found the entrance to her courtyard. When they gave up, they forced me to climb down and marched me back to their camp to try to make me talk."

"They hurt you." All her guilt at doubting him returned.

"How did you get down so quickly? Did you use the ropes to lower yourself?"

"Hardly. I didn't think I should try that without knowing how you set the ropes."

"I can show you."

"Why?" She frowned. "We're not doing that climb again, are we?"

"I suppose not."

"I climbed down the way I went up. I started down as soon as I woke and found you gone. I made it to the trail but I couldn't follow it. But the fairies' markers started glowing."

"Glowing?" He pushed off her and gazed into her face at last. His beautiful green eyes were ringed with hideous, swollen purple skin.

"I touched one of the markers and wished I could see them in the dark and it started to glow orange, and the next one after it glowed, and the next, all along the trail."

He blinked and his lips parted but he said nothing.

"I thought they were meant to do that. Aren't they?"

"I don't know," he said slowly. "Sometimes . . . sometimes magic does unusual things." He shifted his weight to the arm under her head and brushed her bangs off her face. "Are you warm?"

Against her back, Axe's flank was like a rock in the sunshine, and the air under his wing had warmed. "Very. Is this how Sunshine keeps Elle warm at night?"

"Yes. We should go to the village. Axe thinks Sunshine took Elle back."

Jane envisioned Sunshine swooping over the village square and torching the shops and the peacekeepers. "Would Sunshine . . . hurt people?"

"I don't think so. Elle would never tell her to. And her first instinct would be to take Elle and escape, not to fight."

"She wouldn't light Woods Rest on fire."

"No."

"When you called to Axe, did you tell him—"

"No." Rowan stared off above her head. "I . . . I'm not sure exactly what I communicated. I panicked when I saw you in trouble."

"Why didn't you call him to help you sooner?"

"I tried. At first I didn't want to because I didn't want him to get hurt. But I needed to get free to go back for you, or to send him to get you, so I tried to reach him. But it didn't work."

"But then Axe came," Jane said.

"When I saw you in the doorway and the guard with the dagger grabbed you, I was terrified. I think I called to him again without realizing it."

"And it worked that time?"

"Yes."

"He came quickly."

"He wasn't far away, as the bird flies."

"Or the dragon."

"The moment I realized he had come I tried to stop him," Rowan said. "I tried to show him the miners were friends. He didn't hurt any of them. Only those four men."

Thank the skies no more of the miners had been hurt. She'd have to alert the peacekeepers to send help up the mountain. And she could tell Master Smith why the ore had been delayed. Hopefully the miners would recover and they'd be able to return to work soon.

"Can you sit up?" Rowan asked and at last he let her go. With his arm around her back, he helped her up to lean against Axe's flank.

Rowan crouched by her side. His tangled hair hung in his face and a bloodstain trailed across his linen shirt, but when he touched her face he was calm, like nothing else existed. "Stay here a moment. I'm going to speak with Axe." He crept away and ducked out from under the dragon's wing.

The crushed grasses around her hands had thin heads of grain on their stalks. Jane leaned her head back. Axe's wing branched around her.

They'd be home in a short while. And if Sunshine had brought Elle back, this whole ordeal would be over. She had to figure out how Elle could continue training with the dragon safely.

Would Rowan leave? He didn't seem eager to be done with her. After they'd tumbled each other in Sunshine's pool, he had offered to stay with her all summer. Maybe he would continue to help her figure things out. Of course, now they were home, he didn't need to guide her or protect her. But he wanted to be with her—and she wanted that, too.

Sunshine's pool . . . Jane closed her eyes. She had told herself she wasn't breaking her promise to Maryanne if all she shared with Rowan was a tumble, but that had never been all it was, had it? She liked him so, so much. She'd been heartbroken when she suspected he'd betrayed her—and not only because she was left behind. She'd been sorry to lose him. And she'd felt desperate when the miners planned to hurt him again. Now that Elle was, she hoped, home safely, if Rowan left the village, she'd hate being without him.

Her affection for him wasn't just because he'd been amazing—really, really amazing—at touching her, at making her feel desired and beautiful. Over the past few days, she'd gotten used to being around him and talking with him. He didn't say much but when he spoke, he knew about things. He knew how to brew tea from foraged herbs and how to tie useful knots. He could take care of things and manage things, and having someone to share tasks with was such a relief after all her seasons of trying to run her household while her daydreams wandered hither and thither. And it might be buried deep, but Rowan had a sense of humor. And he was kind and caring, toward both her and Elle.

And she wanted to take care of *him*. He seemed to carry some pain she couldn't figure out, something from his past and related to Axe. She'd bet her last coin it had to do with fire magic.

Now, thinking back about the time she'd spent with Larch, the way they'd been together was hollow and insignificant. Larch had been perfection to her, like an ideal she would never find again. But her perception had shifted leagues away from that. She'd told Rowan nothing could compare to how the love potion had made her feel. It wasn't true at all. Just talking to Rowan or hiking through the forest with him felt more full and real than anything she'd experienced in her time under the influence of the love potion.

Axe's wing lifted and harsh sunlight hit her face. As his wing contracted over her head, Jane scrambled to stand to avoid being shut under it as it folded against his body. The hot air he had trapped drifted away in an instant, but the chill morning air wasn't bad after the cold of the sky and after being warmed so thoroughly. She took a moment to steady herself on her feet. Wind ruffled across the heads of grain surrounding them. The road was a few paces off.

The iron splint fell from her wrist and clanged on the ground. Jane lightly touched her wrist. It was swollen and it still hurt. Thin wisps of dried slue glue sloughed off. She retrieved Rowan's iron piece and slid it into her pocket.

Rowan stood by Axe's snout with his hand resting on the scales of the dragon's head. Jane exhaled, stretched her shoulders back, and limped over to join them. Skies, her feet hurt.

Rowan stepped away from Axe. She said goodbye to the dragon, and they backed away farther as Axe lumbered to his feet. He stepped forward with his front feet and leaned into them, stretching his back the way Mouser did, and lifted his hind legs one after the other to stretch them. Heat wafted off him but he seemed to have stopped radiating it the way he had when purposely warming them. He took a few deceptively calm steps forward as his wings came out and with a mighty flap he lifted off. He swept forward with another flap and cleared the trees, climbing in a wide circle over their heads once before he flew off toward the mountains. They watched in silence until he was gone.

"Come on," Rowan said quietly and turned to the village.

Jane followed as he trudged across the field. The spring wheat was up to her thighs and thick enough that she pushed it aside to wade through it. She stumbled on the uneven clods of dirt and Rowan caught her elbow. He was always ready to catch her.

They pushed through to the edge of the wheat and onto the strip of grass alongside the dirt road leading to the village. Opposite were rows of new green plants and a rooster called from the nearest cottage. The sun was clearing the trees and pink light illuminated the fields.

The road was deserted. It was early—but shouldn't someone be out in the fields early on such a clear spring morning?

Rowan let go of her arm and started along the road. Even a glimpse of his profile made her wince at the ugly bruises. He hadn't had a moment to wipe the blood from his face, although he ran a hand over his stubbled chin as they walked, as if he suspected what a mess his face was. His clothes were stained and torn, as if the miners had dropped him off the cliffs, and his toes were caked with mud. Being marched as a captive was probably unforgiving on bare feet.

Of course, she must be a sight too. Her clothes were disheveled with the ripped sleeve hanging off her arm and her once-braided hair had gone so frizzy with loose ends poking out, she dreaded brushing it out. Her bangs were snarled with bits of twigs and leaves. And her own bare feet were so sore she'd started limping in a futile attempt to ease the pain. She'd been awake for . . . was it only one day? Rowan had been awake longer than she had. As soon as they found Sunshine and Elle, Jane was going to insist he go to bed. Or take a hot bath. Maryanne wouldn't want him in their house, but she would have to make one exception to her anti-fairy rules. Or they could go to Rowan's place, but where did he live? She'd never asked him.

She hobbled beside him as they neared the first cottage. A thin trickle of smoke curled from the chimney, but no one moved inside the open front window. The road remained empty as they passed more cottages on the outskirts of the village and even when the village square appeared ahead. No one moved about in the opening between the buildings, as if the square was vacant. The day was young but not *that* young. Was something wrong? Were all the villagers hiding from Sunshine? She limped a little faster, and Rowan kept pace without comment.

They passed the bakery and entered an empty village square. Jane slowed. The sign at the general store was flipped to CLOSED, and the shades were drawn at the milliner's shop. The scent of fresh bread wafted from the bakery, but no one lingered in the front of the shop. Down the lane to their left, no clangs of hammer on iron rang out from the smithies.

Voices buzzed somewhere. Jane glanced at Rowan. He met her gaze but his face was relaxed. Sunshine didn't worry him. Jane continued into the square and a few paces in, the view opened down the lane to her house. A crowd filled the road.

If Sunshine had arrived with Elle last night and she was here, word must have gotten out and the villagers wanted a glimpse of her. Maybe she had landed in the backyard. If she was lying down, she'd be behind the cottages and trees.

Jane and Rowan reached the edge of the crowd. Heads turned to see them. One by one the villagers stopped talking and stepped back to let them through. Master Smith nodded to her, and Jocelin from the grocery, and Gilbert, the carpenter's lad. She knew everyone's names, but they goggled at her like she was a mythical creature who'd crawled out of the village pond.

A sea of faces watched her, and the crowd parted as they walked through. And as the villagers ahead stepped apart, the hole left by their parting revealed a cluster of horses tethered to the low branches of a maple tree alongside the road, nibbling on the new grass by their hooves. Canvas tents covered the front yard of her house and a group of people filled the front walk.

Not local people. They wore matching dark-green tunics with tight britches on their legs and their skin shone in the morning sunlight. And they were barefoot.

They were fairies. And in the center of them, watching her, was Larch.

Chapter 17

JANE STOPPED AND STARED AT Larch. He didn't seem real. After how many times she'd imagined him coming here to Woods Rest to find her, seeing him standing in the road in front of her house felt strange.

He was still handsome. His jaw was more square than she'd remembered and his shoulders broader. In her memory he'd shifted to look more like his brother Dustan, Rose's mate, whom Jane had seen a few times in the past turn of the seasons. The last time she'd seen Larch was two autumns gone by. They had been at the cabin. He'd been tucking her and Bluebell under a blanket to sleep.

The memories came and she let them in: Waking alone. Confused. Fearful. What had happened? What had driven him away and forced him to take their baby? Why hadn't he woken her? Calling his name under the trees. Lingering around the cabin, waiting, hoping. Believing in him even as she left, hungry and dirty and exhausted.

Larch had taken their baby from her arms and brought her to his monstrous mother to use as a servant. Jane's well of anger simmered, and for once she didn't try to stop it. She wanted to hit him. If he smiled at her, she wouldn't be able to stop herself. He wasn't smiling but he was looking her way—why was he looking at her? He should be looking at the ground. Or kneeling on it.

Her breathing was harsh and the longer she watched him the more she wanted to hit him, or hit *anything*. She could forge a hundred door hooks for Maryanne with the rage building inside her.

Dimly she noted Rowan by her side but a step away. As if Rowan had stepped back the way she did when Mouser faced off with the neighbor's cat: if someone touched Mouser then, he'd turn his claws on them in his frenzy. The fairies around Larch stepped back as well, as she moved forward.

"What are you doing here?" she hissed.

She stopped a few paces in front of him. The sight of him after all these winters was difficult enough for her to manage. She didn't want to smell him or remember how she had thought she loved him.

But he stepped forward and she winced. He stopped.

"We received your message," he said evenly. "I wanted to help with the dragon. I know I wronged you in the past and I hoped to make amends."

Jane narrowed her eyes. "Rose told *you* to come?"

Larch shifted on his feet. "I wanted to come."

"What *exactly* did Rose say?"

"She said, 'You should help.'"

Jane glared at Larch, grinding her teeth. Her voice came out a snarl. "Black skies, Larch, stop with your crap. Tell me the truth."

At last he had the grace to drop his gaze to the ground. "A bluebird brought the message. Rose asked me to translate."

"And what did you tell her the message said?"

He inhaled. "A dragon was spotted to the north and the villagers might need help."

Jane shook her head. Of course he hadn't told Rose she was involved or Rose *never* would have agreed to his coming without speaking with her first. Well he was here. Could she simply send him home? "We don't need your help."

Larch's mouth set in a hard line. He kept his head down but lifted his gaze to her. Those longing green eyes used to make her do anything for him.

"She's my daughter too, Jane."

Heat flooded Jane. No words came when she opened her mouth

to shout at him. She stepped into his space and shoved at him. Her push didn't move him much but the retinue he'd brought scurried farther back, leaving him alone in front of her.

"How dare you!" Jane cried. "How dare you say that to me!"

Larch lifted his hands as if to placate her—as if she were the one who was out of line.

"No," she said. "You don't get to manipulate me any longer. Tell me what you want with her."

Larch exhaled and lowered his arms. His shoulders dropped but he held her gaze as if he had some power here. "I want to help train Bluebell. She can't possibly communicate well with a dragon—I could translate."

"She's been doing fine without you." Jane pressed her lips shut before she blurted out that Rowan could act as her translator.

"She should come to the fairies' enclave in the forest."

Jane's hands curled into tight fists. "You want her to return to the place where you *imprisoned* her?"

Larch flinched but he kept his chin up. "It's not safe here. What if the dragon sets the fields ablaze? The villagers won't like having a dragon here all summer."

"And the woods are better?"

"There's a rocky place in the woods near our home where they could practice without the risk."

Jane frowned but she couldn't think of a rebuttal. Having Sunshine in the village was never going to work. They'd have to go somewhere. But *there*?

"It would be faster to learn there," Larch hurried on. "There's an elder fire magic user who could help train Bluebell. She wouldn't have to be gone more than a season."

"Gone? She's not going anywhere without me."

He dipped his chin in assent.

"Why do you want to help? Don't lie to me."

He frowned. "I'd like to do something right. The fairies are out of fire powder. I'd like to help."

Jane sensed Rowan coming to stand beside her. "It's a little late for you to be helping with that." His voice was quiet.

Larch's eyes winced the tiniest bit before he smoothed his features and faced Rowan. "I've made mistakes. I want to fix them."

Jane closed her eyes and shook her head. She couldn't make a decision about what was best for Elle amid the stew of rage and memories and the exhaustion of the past few days. "I'm going to see Elle." She stole one glance at Rowan before turning away, but he was watching Larch and his blank expression gave away nothing.

She marched toward the house and the few villagers on the grass stepped aside as she stomped by. Drat. They'd all been listening to her and Larch fight. The entire village would gossip about her. Not that they hadn't already been gossiping about her, what with the dragon kidnapping her child and her public departure with Rowan. And to think she'd been worried people would notice her flirting with the new apprentice blacksmith.

Jane trudged between the tents pinned on the grass and up the porch steps. Mouser was absent, but with the crowd in the road and the horses—and the dragon out back—his disappearance was unsurprising.

Jane tugged open the door, and Jacob's wailing hit her ears. She went in and the door banged shut behind her.

The front rooms were empty except for Mouser, whose paws stuck out from behind a basket of wool in a corner. She walked down the hallway to the kitchen. Maryanne leaned on the table, bouncing the screaming toddler on her hip. Wells sat in a chair beside her.

"Skies, you're a mess," Maryanne said. She had circles under her eyes.

Wells smirked from his seat and leaned back on two chair legs. A plate with crumbs sat before him.

"What's wrong with Jacob?" Jane asked, reaching out to touch the boy's cheeks. Tears streamed down his face as he struggled and reached over Maryanne's shoulder.

"He wants to pet the dragon." Maryanne turned to the window.

Sunshine lay on the grass at the back of the garden, right at the spot where she must have snatched up Elle however many days ago. With her head down on the grass and her tail straight out behind her, she stretched from the stone wall to the shed. The sun was over the treetops, and Jane shaded her eyes from the morning light beaming in the window. Elle sat on the grass leaning on Sunshine's neck.

"Has Elle been out there all night?" Jane asked, slipping the baby from Maryanne's arms. He quieted, staring up at Jane and whacking his little fists into her face.

Maryanne nodded.

"When did they arrive?"

"They were out there when the sun rose yesterday morning."

"Um," Jane said, "where are the rest of the children?"

As if she'd heard Jane, Sunshine lifted her wing slightly. The other four children were asleep on the ground beside her. The wing tucked back around them.

"They would not leave its side." Maryanne glared at Jane as if this were her fault before exhaling. She wilted back against the table. "I think they were scared the villagers would try to kill it."

"Her name's Sunshine."

"*Sunshine?*"

"Apparently the dragons let the children make up a name for them. Have . . . have you been out there?"

Panic came into Maryanne's eyes. "They got out the door before I could stop them. Elle was out there and refused to come in, and the others wanted to see her, and they barged past me and it turned into this impasse. They spent all day climbing on its tail—her tail—and running up and down the grass beside her. She hasn't moved once."

"Have they eaten?"

"I gave up on trying to call them in and left sandwiches on the back stoop. I thought for sure once they got cold they'd come in to sleep."

Jane laughed, bouncing Jacob to keep him quiet. "You won't get them inside that way. The dragons are like furnaces. They were probably warmer out there."

Maryanne stood and stretched. With one last glance outside she crossed her arms and focused on Jane. "Did you find her den? Why did she return here?"

"We found her den. But it would take a quarter-moon to tell you about it so it'll have to wait." Jacob struggled and she flipped him around in her arms, wincing as pain shot up her wrist, and carefully turning him away from the windows. "I don't know what to do. When did the fairies arrive?"

"I sent the message as soon as the post carrier came through— the day after you left. Two days later they rode into town. Rose must've sent them right away. They made a camp on the grass but they haven't done anything useful."

"That figures, since Larch seems to be in charge out there."

Maryanne's eyes widened. "*Larch* is out there?"

"Rose can't have gotten the whole message. She never would have sent Larch."

"I'm glad I didn't let them in the house."

"He says he wants to help Elle learn from Sunshine at a safe place in the woods. It would be safer to house a dragon there and she would learn faster." Her voice rose. "As if he has any right to help after what he did! I don't trust him. I don't know if it's actually about Elle or about her abilities. Or about his ego."

"Does Elle have to learn at all?"

"You didn't see her, Maryanne. She was so happy with Sunshine and so proud of herself. Sunshine was shooting little flames at her and she was catching them out of the air."

Maryanne grimaced.

"Sunshine is careful. And protective. I think it might be wrong not to let her learn." Rowan popped into Jane's head, along with her suspicions that he possessed fire magic.

"If she goes," Maryanne said, "you'll have to go with her. You can't send her off with Larch."

"I know. Maryanne, come outside with me and meet Sunshine."

Maryanne slowly exhaled through pursed lips before nodding. She turned to Wells.

He leaned farther back in his chair. "I'm fine right here."

Maryanne rolled her eyes as she followed Jane and Jacob to the door.

Jane walked across the grass slowly for Maryanne's sake. Elle spotted them and waved. Jacob stopped all his squirming but watched Sunshine so eagerly, Jane was sure he was poised to re-sume his wailing if they changed direction. As they approached Sunshine's head, one large green eye opened and she expelled a gust of hot air. Maryanne was shaking beside Jane, who moved close so Jacob's reaching hands could touch Sunshine.

"Gently," she said. Sunshine didn't have any fur he could tug on or ears to pull, but it seemed safer if Jacob didn't start grabbing or hitting her. Sunshine's eye shifted to Jane and she blinked and snorted again, but lightly. Jacob patted her and her eyelid drifted shut.

Jane carried Jacob along Sunshine's neck. "Go check on the children," she told Maryanne as they reached Elle and Jane sat. Elle grinned at Jacob as Jane leaned back against the warm wall of dragon scales. Jacob crawled over her shoulder to keep touching the dragon.

Maryanne watched a moment before exhaling and whispering, "Okay." She licked her lips, wiped her hands on her dress, and moved slowly down the yard, staring at Sunshine's clawed front foot as she circled far around it. She ducked her head under the tent of Sunshine's wing.

"How are you?" Jane asked her daughter.

"I'm okay. Sorry we left. Sunshine said we had to."

"You can talk to her?"

"A little."

"Do you want to go back to her mountain?"

Elle's smile faded. "Not if you're sad."

"I want you to learn to use your magic."

"Why are you sad?"

"This happened very fast. I thought you'd be at home with me until you were much older."

"*Mama*," Elle said, exasperated, "I'm not leaving for *good*."

"I might have a new place for you to learn fire magic. We could go together."

"Will Rowan be there?"

Jane's heart skipped a beat. "You like Rowan?"

"He makes you happy. And he saved me in the pond."

Jane startled. "You remember that? That was Rowan?"

Elle grinned.

"He might be there. I need to talk to him."

"I want magic if you can come."

What was the best thing to do? Elle had to learn. A rocky location away from any fields and villages would be a much safer place to have a dragon spouting fire all summer. And the fairies would no doubt have a plan to feed Sunshine—right? The fairies must know all about dragons, given their history together. Jane didn't even know what Sunshine ate, other than fire mushrooms.

But was living with the fairies the only option? And if they did go there, could they go without Larch being involved? He was acting like this was all about him. But he wasn't actually in charge, was he?

Jane wanted nothing to do with him, whether he was Elle's father or not. But what was best for Elle? She wouldn't remember his role in any of the things that had happened to her as a baby. Was it important to introduce him to Elle simply because he was her father? And did he truly want to make amends and be a stable part of her life?

If he did, why had he shown up only now? He hadn't cared to come see her until Elle's unique magic had been revealed.

Rowan would give her sound advice. He wouldn't lie to her about the fairies' intentions, and she could trust him to suggest what was best for Elle. He might know this location in the woods, and he might have opinions on Larch's motivations.

She'd left him out front only minutes ago but already she missed having him beside her. His steady presence had become comforting, and after being torn apart, finding him again at the mine and being in his arms had felt so right. She wanted to be back in the mountains, only the two of them, and of course with Sunshine and Elle. But she could go talk to him and see what he thought about Larch's proposal. Maybe if they went to the fairies' enclave, he would come, too.

She turned to Elle. "Will you stay here and make sure nothing catches on fire?"

"Mama! Sunshine's careful."

"Watch Jacob, okay?" Jane set Jacob on the ground and he crawled right back to Sunshine's side. Maryanne was out of sight. Hopefully she'd come around to Sunshine when she saw how protective the dragon was of the children.

Jane pushed herself up with her good hand and headed around the side of the house. Each time she stopped moving she forgot how sore she was, but her bare feet flinched with each step, her arms and legs and shoulders ached, and the scrapes on her hands stung when she ran her fingers over them. She straightened and proceeded slowly, trying to hobble as little as possible.

Around the front of the house, the crowd of villagers had dwindled. Her arrival must have been the peak of the event, and they'd given up on seeing the dragon take off. Some of the fairies were packing up their tents. Larch stood in the lane, frowning at the peonies dropping petals on the front walk. A tremor of nerves ran through her—Rowan was gone.

Jane approached one of the fairies on the lawn but before she could speak, Larch strode toward them.

"Where's Rowan?" Jane asked the other fairy, a tall woman with silvery skin and straight dark hair that fell to her shoulders.

"He left," Larch said.

"He *left*?" Rowan wouldn't have left without saying goodbye to her.

"I sent him home."

Jane scanned the roadway back toward the village but only a few villagers lingered.

"He rode on Charger. He's gone."

Jane frowned. Did Larch still exert control over Rowan? "What do you mean, you sent him home? Where?"

"Back to the caverns in the forest."

Jane furrowed her brow and glared at him. "Why?"

"He was supposed to watch over you and Bluebell. Clearly he failed to keep you safe."

Jane glowered. Rowan had found Elle in the mountains. He couldn't have stopped the dragon from coming to take her in the first place. And what did Larch have to do with it regardless? "He wouldn't leave without reason."

Larch sniffed and his lips flattened. "I wanted him here to watch over you. I've sent him home."

"*You* sent him here?"

"I suppose he left me out of his story."

Jane's insides churned in confusion—her heart dropping at yet another betrayal, her gut telling her not to doubt Rowan, and her chest struggling to keep her breathing steady. Had Rowan changed his mind about her? That seemed unlikely. But he'd been quiet as they'd returned to the village, unlike how he had been in the mountains—relaxed and smiling when they'd been climbing, and loving and passionate when they'd held each other. Maybe being out in the forest was easier for him. With their rescue mission over, maybe something had changed. After all, he had spoken that one time as if he wouldn't be staying at the smithy in Woods Rest.

But Rowan wouldn't leave her. He'd told her he never would. Something more was going on here, something between Larch and Rowan that Larch had used to get rid of him. And Jane wasn't going to tolerate Larch messing up her life again.

She wouldn't give up on Rowan until she had a chance to speak with him. Especially not based on something a liar like Larch said. She trusted Rowan. Her instincts told her to trust him and find out what was going on. And maybe she'd be wrong again, but she'd rather trust someone and risk being hurt than be a mistrustful person who assumed the worst of people. If someone broke her trust, it made only them a bad person. It didn't make her one.

The trouble was, she didn't know how to get to the place in the forest where the fairies lived. Even if she knew where it was, finding it could be tricky for a human. She could go to Woodglen and ask Ladi's fairy friend for help, but that would take days. She wanted to go after Rowan right now and catch him before he even made it back to their caverns.

And she had to get Elle's situation sorted out before the villagers changed their minds about having a dragon in their midst. Or before Sunshine accidentally torched the fields.

Larch had no business knowing anything about her and Rowan. And Larch wouldn't take her to see Rowan even if she begged.

But Rose would.

Chapter 18

ROSE WOULD KNOW HOW TO find Rowan. Rose would help Jane, she was sure of it.

Jane lifted her chin. "I'd like to meet the elder fairy who uses fire magic and see this place where Elle can apprentice with Sunshine. *Before* I bring Elle back through the forest to the place where you *imprisoned* her for two winters. And I want to talk to Rose."

Larch's eyes narrowed but after a moment, his chin dipped once and he turned away. "Very well."

Larch stood with his arms crossed and didn't move. Jane stepped beside him. "We'll be leaving soon?"

Instead of answering, he dropped his arms and tilted his head side to side as if working the cricks out of his neck.

She had had enough of him. What was his role here—was he even in charge? She turned back to the first fairy she'd approached, the tall one. "I'm going back with you to make plans for Elle to learn fire magic. I can leave now and I'd like to get started. Can we leave soon?"

The fairy swallowed and glanced past her to Larch.

"That's fine," Larch said without turning toward them.

The fairy blinked at Jane. "The tents are packed. We need to get the horses ready." Her words were rushed and breathless. She peered at Jane with big green eyes. "Um, do you have your things ready? Ma'am?" Maybe she wasn't used to speaking with humans.

Jane held out her hand. "I'm Jane," she said. "I'm a friend of Rose, your queen. Thank you for bringing me to see her."

"Aster." Aster reached a tentative hand to hers.

Didn't fairies use handshakes? It seemed very human all of a sudden. Jane didn't know much about fairy habits or culture. Her time with Larch had been focused on one thing, and besides, she hadn't known he was a fairy back then. And afterward she had dwelled on the romance of having a fairy lover and that hadn't been based in any reality. And eventually she hadn't wanted to think about fairies at all.

Jane shook Aster's hand gently. "I'll get my things and be ready soon." Hopefully Maryanne had another bag Jane could take since her first had been left in the mountains.

Inside, Maryanne had returned to the kitchen, where she sliced the remains of a hunk of half-stale bread. She must not have baked today, with all the excitement of having a dragon in the backyard. A kettle heated on the stove and two cups of herbs sat on the table, waiting for the hot water. Wells had disappeared.

"I'm going to go talk to Rose," Jane said, "and find out about this place where Elle could have her apprenticeship. It might be safer than having Sunshine spewing fire in the backyard."

"Rose will know what to do."

"I lost the satchel in the mountains. I mean, I know where it is but it would take three days to get to it."

Maryanne raised her eyebrows. "You did have an adventure, didn't you? Can you tell me the highlights? How much time do we have?"

"The fairies are getting ready to go."

"Give me some idea of what happened."

"Um, Rowan and I visited a dragon he knows, who told us where Sunshine's den was. It was all the way at the crest of the mountain and up a rocky peak—we had to scale cliffs but Rowan knew how to do it. And we found Elle and met Sunshine, but before I could decide what to do—"

"Wait, wait. Go back to 'a dragon he knows.' Rowan knows a dragon?"

"He won't talk about it. But I think he must possess the same kind of magic as Elle. He'd been to see this dragon before and . . . they seemed sad together. Like they missed each other or something."

"Like he was Rowan's Sunshine?"

"Yes, exactly."

"So why did Sunshine bring Elle home if you were there?"

"There was an uprising at the iron mine. The men who tried to take over Cliffside this spring—remember Kitty told us? They were sent to work at the mine and they mutinied." Jane recounted what had come next, up to their return to Woods Rest, although she left out all the parts about sleeping on top of Rowan and tumbling and all the distress of thinking Rowan had abandoned her. Maryanne's eyes widened at the part about soaring through the air in Axe's claws. She clutched her chest until they were safely on the ground.

"Rowan found Elle," Maryanne said at the end of the tale. "And he kept you safe."

"Yes."

"He was true to his word."

"Maryanne? About that promise . . ."

Maryanne sighed. "You've fallen for him, haven't you?"

"I think I might be headed that way."

Maryanne finished buttering the slices of bread. "I knew it would happen. Luckily you're back so you can have bitter tea again. In fact . . ." She reached for the kettle.

"Bitter tea isn't strictly necessary yet. We didn't—"

"But you will."

"How do you know? He might not want to."

Maryanne rolled her eyes, the kettle in her hand. "He climbed a mountain to rescue your daughter and got beaten in the bargain."

"Maybe that's changed his mind. He's gone home already without saying goodbye. Larch said he was only here on his orders."

Maryanne scoffed. "And when has *Larch* been someone you

should trust?" She poured the water into the teacups and handed one to Jane.

Jane inhaled the familiar, slightly acrid scent. "I'm sorry to leave you with a dragon in the backyard. I'll try to figure out a plan quickly."

"Rose will know what's best. I'll go find another satchel."

Jane had a burning sip of tea and left it on the table to cool. Upstairs, she shed her torn and grubby clothing and washed in the basin. She had only the one pair of trousers so she put on a dress, which wasn't ideal for riding on horseback but she couldn't worry about it. She found a kerchief and tied the iron piece to her injured wrist as a splint, using her teeth to pull the knot tight. The slug glue would have been easier, but it was in Rowan's pack at the iron mine, and besides, the sun was well up by now.

She packed a few things in the new satchel Maryanne procured from some corner of the house. After she'd eaten a slice of bread and drunk her bitter tea, she said goodbye to the children and left them having a picnic beside Sunshine. Maryanne was coming out the back door to join them as Jane left.

The fairies had loaded their saddlebags and mounted their horses. They waited in the road in a loose company with Larch out in front. Was he in charge? Or did he act like he was and the others went along with it?

Of course they had no horse for Jane. No way was she riding behind Larch. She walked to the back of the group to the large horse bearing Aster. "May I ride with you?"

Aster swallowed and surveyed the other fairies on their own mounts, but before a beat passed she licked her lips and turned back. She leaned to slide off her horse, landing in front of Jane. "Would you prefer to ride alone? I can go with—"

"I've never ridden a horse alone before."

"Oh. Okay." Aster knelt on the ground and patted her knee. "Step up here and pull yourself onto his back. I'm sorry we don't use the . . . the human tools. You can hold his mane if you need to."

Human tools? Stirrups, she meant. And saddles and bridles and all that. The fairies rode on the bare backs of the horses or on a blanket. Of course they could communicate with their horses without pulling on their heads and poking a heel into them.

Jane sent out a silent apology to the horse, in case the horse could sense it, and stepped up. She pushed with a hand flat on the horse's back and hoisted herself up, and as she pulled a leg over his rump, her dress rode up her thighs. She wobbled as the horse stepped sideways. Her heart thumped in panic, and she grabbed the mane. Aster caught her elbow, steadying her.

Once Jane settled, she pulled her dress down as far as she could, and Aster easily vaulted herself up and over the horse to sit in front of Jane. The other riders moved forward immediately.

"I don't mind if you hold on," Aster said quietly. As the horse's movement rocked Jane, she gripped the fabric of Aster's tunic. "Let me know if you need anything." Jane was starting to like Aster. She seemed about the same age as Jane. And she acted more confident without Larch in her face.

The lingering villagers in the lane in front of the house watched the riders pass. The line of horses had to walk through the village square, where more people stepped out on their porches. Jane ducked her head and watched Aster's back until they were out of the village and heading south on the Forest Road, across the fields toward the forest.

The route they followed led to Woodglen. The fairies lived in a place west of the road, hidden in the forest. Fairies knew how to find it but no clear road led there, as far as she knew. She would have to see how they traveled today to reach it.

She had been through the forest to Woodglen a few times in the past seasons, but she had never left the path. The thought of stepping off the human roadway gave her chills. After Larch had abandoned her in his cabin and she'd given up hope of him returning, she'd stumbled through the trees trying to find her way out. She hadn't had any idea where Larch had taken her. But since they'd never left the woods from the time he had seduced her in Gold Gulch, she'd guessed they were west of the main road that traversed the continent from Nor Bay to Sar Bay. She had walked east and eventually come out on the Forest Road, where a farmer gave her a ride to the nearest village. In Woods Rest, Ladi and Kitty had taken her in and explained what had happened to her.

Somewhere along the road today, they would pass the place where she'd emerged all those seasons ago. She wouldn't recognize it—she never had on past trips this way. But the idea of leaving the road and moving into the trees made her shudder.

The horses ahead trotted more quickly. "Okay?" Aster asked before stepping up their pace.

"Yes. Are you able to talk?" Jane asked.

"Um, yes?"

"I didn't know if you need to focus on the horse to communicate with him."

"Oh. No, we're good for a while. He knows to follow the road."

"Is this group of fairies part of a guard unit?"

Aster shook her head. "We're one of the groups that forages for herbs and things. We're most familiar with the mountain region, so we came with Larch because we thought we might have to find the dragon."

"Have you met dragons before?"

"Oh, no. No one's seen a dragon in twenty winters or more. Except . . ."

Aster's shoulders tensed. Jane waited, hoping Aster would continue.

"I'm not sure if you want to hear about Larch," Aster confessed.

"Oh." Did everyone know her history? Still, it was thoughtful of Aster. "I don't mind. Especially if you tell me bad things about him."

Aster laughed.

"If you're allowed to," Jane added. "If he's your leader, I understand you not wanting to gossip about him."

Aster's shoulders relaxed. "He acts like he's in charge, doesn't he? But he's not. It's easier to ignore him if we go along with what he says. Assuming it's nothing objectionable."

"Is he still a prince?"

"Well . . . that's a bit murky. We're all clear Rose is our queen, and people call Broadleaf a prince—you know Broadleaf is Dustan's fairy name? But he's Rose's life-mate so it makes sense he's still a prince. The two oldest brothers, Beech and Sycamore, disappeared after the revolution. They were a nasty pair. So it's just Larch and their little sister Snowdrop who don't have a clear role, and Snowdrop couldn't care less about having a title."

"What about the former queen?" Jane asked, and she couldn't stop her hands from trembling.

"She's confined," Aster said softly. "You won't have to see her."

Jane took a moment to calm herself. "Aster," she asked quietly. "Do you know Rowan?"

"Not well."

"He helped me find Elle."

"I heard."

"I was surprised he left today. We spent so much time together. It seems strange he left without saying goodbye."

Aster hesitated. "Rowan is well thought of, but he keeps to himself. He never comes to gatherings. And he lives in the caverns, even in the summertime when all of the fairies move to their homes in the trees."

"I think he has history with Larch," Jane said, "and with the dragons. He knows a dragon from many seasons ago. And Larch seems to have power over him. What were you going to say before?"

"I've heard gossip," Aster said. "I'm not sure how much of it is true."

"Tell me?"

Their horse slowed for a few paces and they dropped farther back behind the other riders.

"I said no one had seen a dragon," Aster said, "except for one time. Ten winters ago, rumors spread that a dragon had come to the forest. Most of us were imprisoned in the caverns, so no one knew who had seen it or how the rumor even started. But two winters later, Rowan disappeared. He used to hang around with us—a bunch of us who were twelve or thirteen winters old—so we noticed he was gone. None of us said anything to the older fairies. We didn't want the queen to find out. She terrified us and the littlest things would set her off."

And Larch had given her their infant daughter. Jane shuddered.

"Anyway, a quarter-moon passed and Larch disappeared, too, and then they returned together and Rowan was different. We never saw him much after that, except sometimes he'd be with Larch. And Larch became a bit of a minion of the queen, although he was never as bad as Sycamore and Beech. Something happened between Rowan and Larch but Rowan has never spoken of it."

"Do you know why Rowan came to Woods Rest?"

Aster shook her head. "I didn't even realize he had. Like I said, he kept on living in the caverns. I never saw him around the enclave."

Jane sat back. A dragon came to visit the fairies and shortly after, Rowan disappeared? And then Larch, too? Aster's story convinced Jane: Rowan should be using fire magic but something had gone wrong. And she'd bet ten gold coins Larch had messed it up for him.

Rowan had a gift he couldn't use, for whatever reason. And his relationship with Axe made her ache although she didn't understand it. Elle would never struggle the way Rowan had. Jane had already seen a change in her daughter in the way she focused when practicing her magic with Sunshine. Elle needed to learn to use her magic or she'd suffer the way Rowan still suffered. And if Elle didn't learn, Sunshine might become as depressed as Axe.

And what about Rowan? Was it too late or could his situation be fixed?

Why had Elle been born with this rare magical ability? Certainly not because of her parents, given who they were—a human and a fairy so incapable he'd needed his friend's help to seduce her. Were fairies born with their magical abilities, or did the abilities come about later? Maybe Jane's fascination with blacksmithing, and—apparently—blacksmiths, had led to Elle's ability with fire.

Or maybe something about Elle herself had caused the magic. Rowan had said sometimes magic did unusual things. The markers on the trees had illuminated to guide Jane through the forest—as if they had known she needed their help. And Rose had had an experience last spring where she'd been in trouble and prayed for help, and a flock of birds had been able to understand her thoughts and come to her rescue. Maybe something about Elle's harsh early life had led the magic to her.

As Jane and Aster had talked, the group had trotted along the road across the meadows. Jane stifled a yawn as they passed under the trees at the forest's edge. The sun was well up and the pale young leaves filtered the light reaching the road. The drumming of the horses' hooves drowned out any sounds of the wind or forest creatures, but squirrels scavenged the last of the fall nuts under the leafy litter on the forest floor. If Jane watched closely, she spotted birds and insects, and they even passed a deer grazing beside the road. The animals ignored the noisy horses. Maybe they understood the fairies wouldn't bother them.

After a long stretch of riding along the road, the pace slowed. At the head of the line, Larch's mount stepped aside and stopped and the rest of the line filed past him. He spotted Aster and Jane, and Jane stiffened. If he tried to rejoin the line behind them, she would absolutely protest. The thought of having him at her back made her twitch in discomfort. But he turned again to the front and rejoined the line a few horses ahead of them.

The new leader veered off the road and headfirst into a bush . . . and disappeared.

"It's an illusion," Aster said quietly over her shoulder.

Jane had clenched her hands on Aster's sides without realizing it. She let go.

"We'll pass right through it," Aster continued. "I can see the trail."

"All I see is a prickly-looking bush."

"If you close your eyes, you won't feel a thing."

"What if I don't?"

"I'm not sure what you'll feel," Aster said, "but it shouldn't hurt you."

The turning point neared. Panic thrummed through her, but as the spiked branches approached, she decided: eyes open. She winced and shrank behind Aster as their horse turned face-first into the thorny bush. The branches shimmered around the horse and the horse kept walking as if nothing were there. Jane entered the bush and thorns scraped over her hair and tugged at her dress, pulling her backward. Her hands held firm on Aster's sides and her body didn't actually move back. The branches slid off her and she was through.

She exhaled and slumped in her seat.

"What happened?" Aster asked with a note of concern.

"I could feel the thorns pulling me off the horse. It only let up when we got through."

"Ugh."

"Is this part more illusion?" Jane asked as they plodded between bushes and over the leaf litter of last autumn. "I can't see a trail at all."

Aster laughed. "No. You're seeing everything. Humans like to pound out a trail anyone can follow but fairies try to destroy as little vegetation as possible."

At one time Jane might have bristled at the implication that the fairy method was better than the human one, but she was starting to agree. She studied the row of horses ahead. "How are you following it? Aside from following the horse in front of you."

"Sometimes I can see the faint track across the forest floor. And sometimes there are markers on the trees or small stacks of stones that show the way."

"Rowan and I followed markers on the mountain trail. They glowed at night."

"I'm glad Rowan knew how to light them."

"Actually," Jane said, and for some reason she blushed, "it was me. I was alone that night and they lit up for me."

"Did they!"

Three horses ahead of them, Larch's head jerked slightly sideways.

"Why were you alone on the trail at night?" Aster asked, lowering her voice. "Where was Rowan?"

Should she whisper to annoy Larch? Her adventure with Rowan was none of his dratted business. But he'd accused Rowan of failing when Rowan hadn't failed her at all, and she wanted Larch to know it.

"Rowan knew exactly where to find Elle," Jane said a little louder than she needed to. "But it took us all day to reach Sunshine's den. And in the middle of the night, a group of men from the nearby iron mine came after Sunshine. It was bad luck we happened to be there. Sunshine escaped with Elle, and Rowan led the men away to protect me. I came down the trail alone."

"Stars!" Aster said. "How did you both make it back to Woods Rest?"

"We rescued the rest of the miners—there'd been a mutiny— and Axe gave us a ride back. He's another dragon that Rowan knows."

Larch definitely flinched that time.

"You flew with a dragon?" Aster said, turning in her seat with wide eyes.

"Mm-hm." Jane grinned.

The line of horses straightened and up front, the leader picked up their speed again. Aster told Jane she had to focus on navigating this section, so Jane was left with only her thoughts for company. She daydreamed of Rowan for a while and tried not to worry about what would happen when she found him. The sun moved up the sky, shifting the dappled shade to smaller and smaller shadows, and she found herself yawning again. She couldn't nod off or Aster would have to tie her to the horse.

Ahead of her, the back of Larch's head bobbed in time with his horse's strides. He'd been so charming when she'd first known him. She must be a completely different person now because she couldn't recapture her admiration for him at all, even when she tried to recall how she had felt. Larch seemed bossy and arrogant and honestly a bit tiresome. Had he changed as well? Or had he always been this way and she'd been too naive and enamored with him to see it?

What had his mother's downfall been like for him? He hadn't left with his older brothers. Was he trying to be a better person? Maybe Rose and Dustan were a positive influence on him.

Larch lifted his face up toward the branches. Jane followed his gaze. A pair of wrens flitted from branch to branch as if they were traveling with the horses. Larch shook his head and lowered his gaze. The horses pranced on and when Jane checked, the birds had disappeared.

The ground before the horses' hooves flattened into a dirt track that even Jane could see, and the horses' pace slowed until they walked sedately among large trunks. Jane gazed all around her, but she couldn't see any of the fairies' famed treehouses. A barn loomed up ahead and as they came out into the cleared grass beside it, most of the riders halted and prepared to dismount.

Larch turned. "This way." He followed the track past the barn and when it split, he turned to the right. Only Aster continued after him.

"Where are we heading, Larch?" Aster asked, frowning.

"To the forge. Jane wants to see it."

Beyond the barn was a long meadow and farther on the track dove under the trees again. Jane controlled her impatience. They could see the forge, as he called it, and then she'd ask Aster to take her to Rose—

"Halt," a familiar voice called out, and hope swelled in Jane's chest.

Someone dropped from the trees onto the path ahead, landing in a crouch. They straightened up, blocking the way, and looked up. Jane smiled and Rose grinned back.

Chapter 19

ROSE STOOD IN THE TRAIL blocking the horses' way and the two horses immediately stopped. A few heartbeats passed with Larch facing Rose—Jane imagined him glaring at Rose but she couldn't see his face—and Aster seemed to be waiting for orders, although Jane wasn't sure who would give them.

"Larch," Rose said at last. She said his name fondly but it still sounded like a reprimand.

Larch's shoulders were tensed up against his neck and his horse stepped side to side. His name hung in the air between Rose and him.

Rose rested her hands on her hips. Her dark hair hung to her chin and her pale skin had tanned on her nose and cheeks. She wore a tunic like Aster's, only a lighter green, and her legs had a dark green coating on them that Jane couldn't make sense of, like they'd been painted instead of clothed. Something fluttered overhead. Two wrens perched on a branch, watching the scene.

"'A dragon was spotted to the north'?" Rose said in a low voice, and arched an eyebrow at him. She huffed up her chest in an impressive imitation of Larch. "'I just want to help the humans'?"

If only Jane could see Larch's face! Watching Rose chide him like an errant child made her uncommonly cheerful. Or maybe the joy came from seeing Rose again.

The two birds swooped down. They passed so close to Larch's face that he flinched away before they disappeared into the forest.

"You may have renounced your evil ways," Rose continued,

"but you still have to respect other people's boundaries." Jane's lips parted. Was Rose joking? Talking to him like that?

Larch's shoulders slumped.

"Holly is working over in the orchard," Rose said. "He would love your help with the pruning. He mentioned you this morning and what a help you've been." Rose's voice was kind, and she was giving Larch an escape. She stepped aside, and his horse moved forward. He didn't look back. Jane sagged in relief as he disappeared among the trees.

Rose turned to her and Aster. "Are you able to dismount, Jane?"

Aster slid easily off the horse's back and helped Jane down after her. She turned to Rose. "Do you need anything else, your high— I mean, Rose?"

"No. Thank you for going on this expedition, Aster. Thanks to your whole team. Azalea sent a message to me when she realized where the dragon was." Rose turned to Jane. "Larch never should have gone anywhere near Woods Rest. I'm sorry, Jane."

"It's all right. I think maybe it did me good to see him. In my memories he was a lot more handsome and charming."

Aster took her leave with a shy smile to Jane and a small bow to Rose. She walked back toward the barn with the horse ambling after her down the path.

"I can't get them to stop bowing and calling me 'your highness,'" Rose said as Aster moved out of sight. She shook her head and turned to Jane, and a moment later they were hugging tightly.

"I've missed you," Jane said.

"Is Elle home safely?" Rose released her and stepped back.

"Yes. I left her and her dragon, Sunshine, in the backyard. I needed to see you."

"I want to hear everything. It's been so long. Liza has gone?"

Jane quickly filled Rose in on her life over the past few moons. Rose knew the bigger news, like about Liza's courtship and Kitty's move to Cliffside just in time for the failed rebellion, but soon Jane was pouring out the entire tale of her futile attempts to court the village apprentices, followed by Rowan's latest appearance and the arrival of the dragon.

Rose closed her eyes and shook her head. "*That's* where Rowan has been? I've completely failed to keep you free of fairies."

"He was careful to hide his identity. We had no idea any of them—him—the apprentices, I mean—were fairies until the dragon came. And he knew how to find Elle." Jane sketched out the rest of the rescue. Rose's expression ranged from horror to awe. "He was wonderful," Jane concluded and, of course, she blushed.

Rose's eyes gleamed. "It sounds like it." Her look only made Jane squirm, but with a smile. "Where is Rowan now?" Rose asked.

"He's not here?" Panic welled up within her. If Rowan hadn't returned here, Jane had no idea where to find him. "He left ahead of us. Larch said he was returning to the fairy caverns."

Rose took her hand. "He might be here. We can check. I was watching the trail for your arrival but not for Rowan's."

"How did you know we were arriving?"

"The birds alerted me."

Jane's eyes widened. "You can speak with them?"

"No, no. Dustan sent them to watch the trail. When they came back chirping and flying in circles around me, I could have guessed your party was arriving—even if Dustan hadn't mumbled something about it being you."

"Where is he?"

"Still in bed." She said it tenderly and her cheeks colored a faint pink.

Jane bit her lip as a smile stretched across her face.

"He likes to be up all night and sleep half the day," Rose continued. "I can't sleep once the sun is up."

"As long as you have a few hours that overlap," Jane said, and Rose grinned.

"What do you need?" Rose asked. "What do you want to do?"

Jane exhaled. "I want Elle to be Sunshine's apprentice, but I don't know how to manage it. It's too dangerous to have her learn in Woods Rest, where she's surrounded by flammable fields and trees. We could return to Sunshine's den in the mountains, but after what happened, Sunshine might not think it's safe there. And I don't particularly want to live on top of a rocky peak all summer eating mushrooms and being idle all day—don't even ask me about the dangers of peeing off the side of a cliff."

"Yikes."

"Larch said there's a place in the woods near here where Elle could train. He called it a forge. We were heading there."

"I know where he means. I can show you."

"But I'm nervous about bringing Elle anywhere near this place. And . . . "

Rose waited.

"I wasn't sure if we could bring her here without Larch being involved. He seemed keen to participate, but I don't know if I'll ever be able to forgive him for what he did to her, and I don't trust him with her. But is that wrong? He is her father."

"I'm not a mother," Rose said, "so I'm probably not the best person to advise you. But I trust your intuition for what's right for her. And you can use any space we have without his interference. We'll send him on an errand to Norland if we need to."

"I want to ask Rowan what he thinks. He knew so many things about the dragons, and he seems to know Larch well. I would trust his advice."

"Let's see if we can find him. I know where he stays."

Rose led Jane along the trail back toward the barn. It was wide enough for them to walk side by side. All Jane's exhaustion had fled with the prospect of seeing Rowan again.

"We'll have to go into the caverns," Rose said.

Jane repressed a shudder. "I understand."

"There's an entrance near the barn, but we can go a ways through the forest and enter closer to Rowan's chambers."

"Thank you."

The trees opened into the sunny meadow. Aster's group was no longer present, and several of the horses now grazed out in the tall grass. They passed the barn and the turn leading to the Forest Road and continued into thicker forest.

"Why are your legs green?" Jane asked.

Rose looked down and paused to stretch out a leg. Her calf was coated with color but it stopped abruptly above her ankle. It looked a bit like fabric but it molded to Rose's leg. "Oh, these? They're so comfortable I forgot I had them on. One of the fairy inventors made them. They use wool and a special fiber from a nettle plant to make them so they stretch over your legs. And magic of course."

"Of course."

Rose pinched the material on her thigh and pulled, and it separated from her leg and snapped back when she let go. "They're marvelously comfortable. This is the first pair. They asked me to try them out. I'm completely in favor of them. As soon as we have more, I'll send you some, if you like."

"Yes, please. What are they called?"

"Nothing yet. Do you have any ideas?"

"Thigh huggers?"

"That sounds like sex," Rose said with a snicker.

"Leggers?"

"Ooo, that's good. I'll pass that one on."

"You're wearing a tunic like Aster's."

Rose touched the light green shirt. "Mine is the color of the forestry team. I finished my training last moon." Her eyes lit up when she said it.

"Oh, Rose, that's wonderful." When Rose had become the fairy queen, she'd had a role to play in stabilizing their society and bridging the gap with the humans. But she'd always wanted to contribute more, and she'd loved learning to climb trees.

"We don't have to wear the uniform," Rose continued, "but I love mine."

"You should be proud." Rose had found her calling. Maybe when Jane returned to Woods Rest, eventually, she would as well.

As they walked, voices drifted down from the treetops where the fairies' treehouses hid among the branches. Rose turned into a clearing and led Jane across to an open expanse of gardens where fairies knelt in the rows, weeding around seedlings and harvesting leaves of lettuce from tiny plants. In the warm spring morning, insects droned and a peaceful breeze stirred the trees surrounding the open land.

Rose skirted the edge of the garden and moved into a row of apple trees just forming fruit. No one was under the trees. A large pecan tree towered at the end of the row along with several smaller trees with tiny yellow flowers, and a wall of rocks and boulders rambled along in back.

"Is this the orchard?" Jane asked.

"No—there's a lot more fruit trees on the far side." Her eyes scanned Jane's worried face. "That's where I sent Larch."

Rose stopped by a tall boulder. "You don't need to worry about his mother, either. She's in the fairy prison which keeps her in with magic. No one could get her out even if they wanted to—unless she truly repented for her actions."

"Okay." Jane licked her lips.

"Are you sure you're comfortable with this?" Rose asked. "I could go down by myself and find Rowan." She pointed.

Behind the boulder was a large opening into the ground. Steps led down into darkness.

Jane peered down the steps. "There's no magic hiding the way in?"

"Not here, and I can get you through the barrier inside."

Jane didn't want to wait a moment longer than she had to, to see Rowan again. "I'll go."

Rose started down the steps. "I've gotten used to being in the caverns, but I can remember how it felt the first time I came here." She meant the time she'd come to rescue Elle and the other children. Jane's ankles chilled as she moved out of the sunlight and she shuddered again.

At the bottom of the steps, a neat tunnel led away from the entrance. A lamp flickered farther on, creating a dim glow. Jane glanced all around as they continued—the tunnel had no cobwebs or dead leaves or other litter. "Why does Rowan live down here?" Jane asked.

"I don't know. I've met him only a few times in the past turn of the seasons. He's never spoken much." Rose stopped at a wall barring the way forward. "This is an illusion. Take my hand and close your eyes."

Jane did, and as Rose led her forward, she felt nothing as she stepped through the wall. She opened her eyes and turned to the wall behind her. She reached out and touched solid rock.

Her pulse thudded harder. "Am I trapped?"

"No. If you need to get out on your own, close your eyes and you'll walk right through it."

Inside the caverns, more lanterns glowed along the passageway. The place was deserted and silent as a tomb, except for once when the scritch of a broom sounded and they came upon a blond fairy sweeping the floor. Rose greeted her with a smile. They passed one alcove and then another, until they became regular along the way. Some had closed wooden doors while others opened into dark rooms. A few tunnels led off in different directions, but they continued straight.

"Maryanne wanted me to get your approval," Jane said, "to spend time with Rowan." Her face heated. It sounded silly when she said it aloud. "That's why she sent you a message. She didn't trust him, but I didn't want to wait to go after Elle."

Rose glanced sideways. "It seems like you know him better than I do."

She did. She valued Rose's opinion but she didn't think she needed it in this case. "You know how Maryanne is about trusting fairies."

"I wish she knew more of them."

"Unfortunately, the ones we first met were not trustworthy."

"Speaking of, I can't believe Larch lying about Maryanne's message that way. I've never seen more creative half-truths than the ones that fairy comes up with. He says he wants to make amends for his past but—" Rose cut herself off. "I'm sorry. I wasn't thinking, bringing that up."

"It's all right. I truly think I might be past it."

They turned a corner.

"It's not far," Rose said. "Like I said, I don't know Rowan well, but I've never heard anything bad about him. He came to speak with me before he left here for Woods Rest, although he wasn't up front about where he was headed. I suspected he wanted someone to know he was leaving so we wouldn't worry once we saw he was gone. I thought maybe he didn't have anyone else to tell."

Jane's insides panged at how alone Rowan was in the world.

"I've never seen him use magic," Rose continued. "You said he hid his appearance?"

"Yes. He said he has only a little ability. But Rowan made the potion Larch used on me," Jane added quietly. She didn't want Rose to hear any rumors and think Rowan had continued to mislead her. Rose's lips parted and Jane hurried on. "He told me right away when I found out who he was. He said he owed Larch a big favor, and Larch wasn't skilled at magic so Rowan made a love potion for him. He doesn't make potions anymore. I think he feels awful for helping Larch."

"Why did Rowan return here instead of staying with you?"

"I don't know. After I confronted Larch, I was so furious I stormed into the house. When I returned, Rowan had gone. I want to know what Larch said to him that made him leave without saying goodbye."

"Well hopefully you can ask him." She stopped at a door in a shallow recess. "I think this one is his. Are you ready?"

Jane crossed her fingers and nodded. She stood to the side of the door with Rose in front of her.

Rose knocked. Jane held her breath. Someone moved behind the door.

The door opened. Rowan stood inside with his chest bare. Oh skies, Jane had missed him. She tore her gaze away from his chest. He wore clean trousers and his face was bruised but the blood was gone, leaving only a cut across his lip. His hair was damp.

Rose scrunched her brow, staring at his face.

Rowan's green eyes were fixed on Rose and spots of color bloomed in his cheeks as his hand moved to the cut on his lips. "Forgive me, your— Rose. I didn't expect it to be you or I wouldn't have answered in this state."

"Who did you expect?" Rose asked.

"I thought I'd imagined the knock. No one visits me."

"Well someone's come to visit you now," Rose said, and she stepped aside, pulled Jane in front of the doorway, and gently pushed her forward.

Chapter 20

JANE STUMBLED THROUGH THE DOORWAY and into Rowan's arms. Maybe landing her in his arms had been Rose's plan, and if Jane was honest, she didn't mind. Rose knew her too well.

Rowan righted her and let her go as the door snicked shut behind her. Jane's face was hot and color stained Rowan's cheeks. She risked another glance up at him as he looked away and rubbed the back of his neck.

He tilted his chin down at his bare torso. "I could—"

"No, you don't have—"

"What?"

"I mean, don't put on a shirt for me." Now she sounded like she wanted him to stay half-naked. Not that she minded, but . . . Jane collected herself. "I mean, whatever you want to do is fine."

Rowan settled for crossing one arm over his stomach and the other bent vertically across the first, with his fist against his heart. A short, fat candle burned behind him and lit his skin with a steady light.

The room was small but not cramped, with a table on one side with the candle and a cot on the other. Jane shivered but it couldn't be colder here than it had been in the tunnels. A shelf on the back wall held a stack of folded clothes.

"You didn't say goodbye," Jane blurted out. "I worried about you. Why did you leave?"

He stared at the floor. "Elle's home safe. You don't need me anymore."

"It wasn't all about Elle. I know you know that. Why did you leave?"

He exhaled. "I'm no good for you. Someone else could offer you more than I ever could."

Jane gaped at him. He sounded like . . . she didn't even know what. Like someone else's words were coming from his lips. Where was the kind, confident man who'd guided her through the mountains?

Jane frowned as ideas clicked into place. "What did Larch say to you?"

"He sent me home."

"He told me you only came to Woods Rest because he sent you."

Rowan finally looked up.

"But I know that's not true even if he thinks it is. That's not what you told me."

"It's not true," Rowan said.

"So if Larch got that wrong, maybe he got a few other things wrong. What did he say to you?"

He rubbed at the back of his neck. "He said . . ."

"What?"

"Now that you want me to repeat it, I worry it's not nice."

"Now you *have* to tell me."

Rowan's brow wrinkled, his eyes pleading.

"I don't give two figs what Larch thinks about anything."

He dropped his gaze. "He said, Jane wants sex and romance— not you."

"Skies, can't I have all three?"

Rowan's face cracked into a smile.

"It's not true," Jane said. "Maybe Larch thinks it is, but it's not. I'd rather have you to walk with and talk to than all the tumbling in the world."

Rowan dropped his arms to his sides. "I know Larch has done terrible things," Rowan said, "and I'm done with him. But he helped me once. He risked his safety to help me. I know he must care about me."

Did he though? From what Jane had seen, Larch did what was best for himself. Seeing Rowan hedging around the truth and making excuses for Larch made her want to hit something. She clenched her fists at her sides.

"Larch said words to make you think you're not good enough for me."

"I'm not good enough for anyone. I'm ashamed of my past. I'm lousy at magic and I've failed at every craft and trade I've tried." His arms came up again, crossing in front of him.

Jane couldn't help herself. She took hold of the fist beneath his chin and wrapped her hands around it, pulling it away. "You *are* good at something. You never had the opportunity to learn how to use it properly. Axe was supposed to be your mentor, wasn't he?"

Rowan nodded.

"And he still wants to teach you, doesn't he?"

"It's too late," Rowan said, and he took back his hand and crossed his arms over his chest. "You have to learn fire magic when you're young."

"How do you know?"

"All the other wielders of fire magic learned when they were children."

"But has an adult ever tried?"

"I can't bear to fail Axe again," Rowan said. "I've already failed him so many times."

"You don't think he'd rather have you try to learn?"

"I can't do the magic. I *have* tried."

"What do you mean? Help me understand."

"I tried to learn on my own. I practiced pulling the heat from lamps and hearthstones. I don't even know if that counts as fire magic, but I could do it and I tricked myself into thinking I was learning. I wanted to learn so badly. But when I tried with a flame, all I did was burn my fingers." He held up his hands and she understood: those marks crisscrossing his fingers were scars from fire.

"But no one expects you to learn on your own. That's why you apprentice with a dragon."

Rowan's shoulders sagged. He wouldn't meet her gaze. She was never going to convince him with her words. He'd keep going in circles with excuses because he was so sure he couldn't learn.

She studied what she could see of his face—his hair falling to hide his eyelashes, his straight nose and curved lips. The cut on his lips pained her but didn't make him any less perfect. He was the most capable person she'd ever met, and it killed her that he couldn't see his own value. And it made no sense they wouldn't be together when he made her so happy, and she wanted to bring him the same joy.

She would want him even if he took up the trade of a tinsmith and bashed candlestick holders to pieces every day. But he seemed to yearn for something—for a craft—and it must be his fire magic. It was in his skin, and he couldn't help but want to use it.

Deep inside, she believed he could learn to use his magic. Because he could do anything. And Axe wouldn't be waiting on Rowan if it were impossible for him to learn the magic as an adult. But she needed Rowan to believe it was possible, too.

Jane tugged at the fabric tied around her wrist, the cloth ripped from Elle's first blanket. It was so old and brittle that as soon as she pulled on one loop, the tension snapped it in two. She loosened the rest and slipped it over her knuckles and off. The length of fabric unwound until it hung a few hands' widths below her hand.

She stepped past Rowan and held the end over the candle. The flame caught it immediately, devouring the bottom and licking up the fabric toward her hand.

She turned to Rowan. His gaze darted to her hand and he gasped.

"Jane, drop it!"

She held the flaming ribbon higher and glared at him. The

flames were climbing eagerly and the heat on her hand grew worse and worse, but she was *not* going to drop it until the last possible moment. Because she needed Rowan to believe in himself. The heat hurt, and she had to bite her lip to stop herself from whimpering. She barely saw Rowan's face shift as his horror changed to resolve.

He stepped toward her and wrapped both of his hands around the fire and in a blink it was gone. The intense heat disappeared. The charred fabric hung from her grip. Not a wisp of smoke appeared.

Rowan examined his bare hands. He wrapped them together as if each was inspecting the other, as if they might not be real.

He looked up with wide eyes, then glanced at the burnt ribbon and his face hardened. "Don't you ever do that again." His voice hitched at the end as his anger collapsed and he reached for her.

Jane lifted her chin. "Don't you ever doubt yourself again."

Chapter 21

OWAN TOOK JANE'S HAND AND she winced.

He stopped rubbing her fingers. "Did the flames burn you?"

"My fingers smart a little when you rub them."

He enclosed the sore fingers gently between his palms and concentrated on them. A few beats passed. His hands were cool, cold really, and the heat and burn of her fingers eased.

"What are you doing?" she asked.

"Drawing out the heat. It should ease the pain."

A memory flickered through her head. "That's how you cooled the poultice on my ankle. It warmed as soon as you stopped holding it."

"Yes."

His room was silent except for her own breathing. In the stillness, her knees quivered. "Can we sit?"

Keeping hold of her hand, he led her to the cot against the wall and sat. Before she could sit beside him, he let go of her hand and pulled her onto his lap, wrapping his arms around her. "Do you mind?" he said. "Please say you don't mind."

"I don't mind." She snuggled against his chest as he held her.

Her fingers began to sting again, the pain growing. She flexed them and he released her and reached for her hand. With one arm around her, he clasped her fingers gently and the pain faded again. She leaned into him. Her legs rested on the blankets on the cot. It was a narrow bed for a large man but at least he had soft blankets.

Had her ruse worked? Would he try apprenticing with Axe

again? She opened her mouth but was too afraid to ask. "Will you tell me how you met Axe?"

He shifted to lean back against the cavern wall and she fell against him. Once she was settled, he spoke, his voice rumbling against her side.

"When I was ten winters, I sneaked out of the caverns and called Axe. I didn't know what I was doing. I felt such a pull to be above ground. Guards were stationed at all the entrances to the caves, so I started a fire to distract them. It was a terrible thing to do, but I couldn't think of another way. And I didn't realize how dangerous it could have been because fire had never frightened me."

He truly had been trapped down here. Jane shuddered and his arm tightened.

"I got out into the forest and went to the clearing where I could see the stars. I'd seen the sky before—the queen couldn't stop us from celebrating the rise of the full moon. But I'd never been out alone in the dark or heard the night animals clearly. It was early spring and cold and clear out. I felt more alive than I ever had. I knew someone was coming and I was waiting for him. But Larch found me."

"Larch?"

"Do you mind hearing about him?"

"No."

"He saw me sneaking out of the caverns and followed me. We weren't friends then. No one wanted to be friends with the queen's children because we feared her. He happened to see me leaving and came after me to discover what I was doing."

She had a moment of pity for Larch. It probably wouldn't last as Rowan's story continued.

"Larch tried to convince me to return before anyone saw me, and I couldn't explain why I needed to stay in the clearing. He tried to drag me back but I was bigger. And suddenly Axe was there. The treetops swirled and both of us fell over and stared at the sky and he circled around and landed right in the clearing. I knew exactly who he was—I mean, I knew he was there for me and he wouldn't hurt me and that I was supposed to go with him. But Larch was petrified and held me back."

She could imagine the trees swirling as they had when Axe arrived at the mine camp.

"Axe waited. I wanted to leave with him so badly. But Larch was begging me not to go and saying the queen would be mad and we'd get in trouble. I remember staring into Axe's eyes and understanding that he would wait for me. And I had a vague sense of where he'd be, nearby in the mountains."

"Do you think Larch knew why a dragon had come for you?"

"I don't know."

But regardless, Larch must have known the dragon had something wonderful to offer Rowan and he'd blocked him from accepting it. "He should have let you go."

"He was scared. Anyway, we went back to the caverns. After that, Larch and I were friends. He never told anyone what I'd tried to do and I felt grateful to him. We seemed alike. Neither one of us was much good at magic. We couldn't communicate with birds or become invisible or do any of the basic things most fairies can do by the time they're a few winters old."

"Do those with fire magic usually struggle with other forms of fairy magic?" Jane asked.

"I think so. Sage did. She's a fairy elder who can use fire magic."

Rowan shouldn't compare his own lack of ability with Larch's. Larch had no excuse, unless being a twit hurt one's ability to use magic. Which might be true, given what she'd seen of how magic worked. Jane quietly huffed out her annoyance. "When did you see Axe again?"

"Two full turns of the seasons later. I never stopped thinking about him. And somehow I found my way to Sage. When I told her what had happened she explained everything to me. She demonstrated her fire magic using a candle flame and offered to help me get to Axe. It meant defying the queen, but she knew how important it was. We gathered supplies and she taught me to climb on the rock walls underground, and she explained how to use the ropes and iron pieces for safety. She had gone to the mountains many, many winters ago. She drew me a basic map, although she didn't know where Axe's den was. But he'd said he would be close. Sometimes I even thought I could feel him waiting."

"What went wrong?"

He sighed. "I should have sneaked away and not told anyone. Sage would have known where I was. But I knew Larch would miss me and I didn't want him to worry. I knew better than to tell him before I left, though, since he'd try to stop me again. So I left a note here."

"Here?"

"In my chamber. This is the same one I've always had."

Jane suppressed a shudder. Not only was Rowan alone here but he was also in the same room he'd had as a child? How many memories must haunt it? It pained her to think of him living here by himself when the other fairies were up in the forest, in the sun and breezes, especially given how alive he'd been in the open air of the mountains.

"Sage helped me escape the second time, so I didn't have to start a fire. Well, technically we started a fire but she was there to put it out. I think the fire tipped off Larch, though, because he came after me right away. I'd hoped to have a few days' head start to make it harder for him to track me. And I hoped he'd let me go, that his fear of his mother might compel him to give me up. I should've known better." Traces of bitterness laced his words.

"I reached Axe quickly. I hid in the back of a wagon part of the way and I was so nervous and excited I couldn't sleep. And once I was climbing the mountain, I knew where to go. I barely used Sage's map. Axe must have known I was coming. He could have swooped down to get me but he let me reach him on my own. And seeing him again . . ."

Jane peeked up at the small smile on Rowan's face.

"It felt like home. More than anywhere I'd ever been or anyone I'd been with. I threw myself on his neck and hugged him and cried. I could tell how glad he was that I'd come. I started to hear him in my head. His communication became clearer and clearer. I'd never had that with animals, so it made me even closer to him. He wanted me to rest and said we'd start my lessons the next morning. But when I awoke, Larch was there."

Outrage burned in Jane's chest. Larch was going to ruin everything.

"He must have started right after me. And he'd climbed up the peak in the dark—I'd left my ropes hanging because I didn't know better. I remember thinking he must really care about me to have risked climbing in the dark. He said the queen learned I was gone and threatened to hurt Sage for helping me escape unless I returned. And he said the queen was angry at me, but if I went back, he'd intervene. I was always grateful to him for protecting me from her."

"Did the queen actually know you'd gone?"

"She did. When we got back, she had Sage locked in her awful human dungeon. We had to convince her to let Sage go but Larch helped. He understood how her mind worked—he could manipulate her. I was terrified simply being in a room with her."

"But how would the queen notice one missing boy? Did she take a roll call of the children?"

"No, nothing like that."

"It doesn't make sense, Rowan. It seems like no one would notice you missing except the children. It seems like Larch probably tattled on you and then acted like a hero coming to retrieve you and clean up the mess he'd caused, when he could have kept his mouth shut and let you learn fire magic."

"Why would Larch do that, though?"

"You were his friend and he didn't want to be without you."

"But I'd return in a season."

"You'd return with a skill he didn't possess. Maybe he was jealous. Maybe he thought you'd tire of him once you could do magic."

Rowan fell silent. Maybe she was wrong about Larch, but she would malign his character all day if it helped Rowan be free of him.

Rowan stayed quiet for a long time. Jane slipped her fingers out of his and flexed them, waiting for the burning to return but it didn't. She rested them in her lap and waited.

"I was foolish," Rowan said at last.

"No. You—"

"I never should have trusted Larch. I was a fool."

"You trusted someone who took advantage of you," Jane said, quoting back to him the words he'd said to her as they'd walked through the forest on the way to Sunshine's den. "He is to blame, not you."

Rowan paused, blinking. "Axe was so sad when I left. He tried to hide it, but I could tell."

"And you never went back?"

"No."

Tears pricked her eyes and her throat tightened. "We should go back to him. Axe was happy to see you when we visited his den."

"I know."

"Has he been waiting for you this whole time?"

"I think so."

Jane put her arms around him and hugged tightly. "Give him one more chance," she whispered. She studied his face. "Please. I can't stand it if you won't."

Rowan stroked her back and kissed the top of her head. "I will."

Relief settled over her, a calm surety that things would go right now. Jane closed her eyes and let him rub her back. His bare chest was warm against her cheek.

"What are you going to do about Elle?" he murmured. When he spoke, his words vibrated against her ear.

"I wanted your opinion. Larch said there's a place here where she could learn, but I wasn't sure about bringing her back here or letting him be involved. Rose said she could send him away."

"Is that what you want?"

"I don't think I trust him with her yet."

He didn't reply but his touch soothed her and she knew he would support her decision.

"This place she can learn in—the forge. Is it . . . it's not underground?"

Rowan's arms snaked around her and squeezed. "No. I know it. It's on the north side of the enclave and open to the sky. She'd never have to enter the caverns."

"Would we live there?"

"You could stay in the treehouse village. But I think Elle would want to sleep out there with Sunshine. You know Sunshine would keep her warm and dry."

"I know."

"And you could stay out there too, if you wanted to be near her. Sunshine wouldn't mind."

"Would you come too?" Jane asked tentatively.

"I'll go wherever you want me to go."

She pushed back against his hold to consider him. "I want you to be wherever I am. But only if that's what you want. Just so we're clear."

His eyes reflected the candlelight, shining with life and muting the dull bruises around them. "That's what I want."

"You don't think you have to do this? That you owe me something for the past?"

He smiled. "I'm ready to let go of the past if you are."

Jane smiled back.

The flame reflected in his eyes flickered and then sparkled. He glanced up. Overhead, tiny twinkling lights appeared, one after another.

"What are those?" Jane whispered, and her words ended with a yawn.

"Those are the cavern lights. They come on in the winter when the fairies are living in their rooms down here. Rose must've asked Snowdrop to light them since we're here."

"Snowdrop?"

"She was sweeping in the passageway." Rowan slid Jane off his lap and onto the cot. She missed his warmth immediately. He stood to blow out the candle.

The room dimmed and the tiny lights dimmed too. They took turns pulsing like stars.

Jane yawned again, covering her mouth as Rowan turned. He reached a finger toward the splint on her wrist. "You're injured," he said.

"It's not bad."

He stared a moment longer but didn't comment. The winking lights deepened the silence but made the room comfortable and friendly.

"You should sleep." Rowan gazed down at her.

"But I left Sunshine in the backyard." Jane yawned again. The blankets were so soft.

"Was she pacing on the grass and incinerating the laundry?"

"No, she was sleep— Oh. You're teasing me."

He smiled. "She'll still be sleeping tomorrow."

"What about you? You've been awake longer than I have."

"I plan to sleep too."

"Here?" She tilted her chin up and lifted her brow hopefully.

"Yes, Jane." He brushed her bangs off her face. "Lie down."

He helped her pull back the top blanket and climbed onto the cot beside her. The lights were dimming again, and as she sank into the bedding and Rowan's heat warmed her side, her eyelids were already slipping closed.

"Not too lo-o-ong," she murmured over a yawn as the blanket covered her. Rowan kissed her cheek and pulled her body into his. She blinked her eyes open but the lights had gone out, and in the close and quiet darkness she drifted to sleep.

Chapter 22

JANE WOKE IN SILENCE, WARM and snuggled against Rowan in a cocoon of softness. His chest expanded into hers and back with his slow, steady heartbeat. The curve of his shoulder was visible over her head so the ceiling lights must be faintly burning even if she could not see them.

What time was it? What day? How did the fairies even know when to sleep or wake, living without the sun down here? However long it had been, she should get back to Woods Rest to deal with the situation she'd left for Maryanne. But skies she'd rather just lie here with Rowan and smell his comforting scent. Maybe she could fall back to sleep and not have to decide if she should get moving or not.

Only now she was breathing in Rowan's scent and rubbing the tip of her nose against his skin. His hot, bare skin, pressed against her forehead and against her shoulder where his heavy arm lay over her. And she was starting to want him.

Drat. She would *not* wake Rowan merely to slake her own desires. The poor man had been awake for three nights. He'd been kidnapped and beaten. He needed his rest.

She closed her eyes and willed herself back to sleep. Her clothing itched. Why hadn't she shed her dress before they'd lain down to sleep? She couldn't do it now without disturbing him. A shirt, maybe, but not a whole dress.

Maybe she could free her legs. She wiggled a hand free of the blankets and slid it down to her hip, where she gathered the fabric of her skirt and slowly pulled it up. The soft blanket caressed her knees and lifted to allow her to twine her legs into Rowan—who still had his trousers on. Jane quietly sighed. She had to wait for him to wake.

A light winked on overhead.

She tipped her face up to regard it. It twinkled back.

"Can you shine," she mouthed in the barest whisper, "a little brighter?" Maybe if the lights woke him slowly, waking him wouldn't be such a selfish thing to do. And it wouldn't be *her* waking him. It would be the lights.

A few more lights glowed above them. The light gleamed on Rowan's jaw near her forehead. His breathing shifted slightly.

She grinned up at the lights. "Thank you," she whispered.

Rowan's hand caught her head and his thumb stroked her cheek before tangling in her hair. "What are you doing?" he murmured in a sleep-drugged voice.

"Talking to the lights."

He didn't let her go but a stretch ran through his body, tightening and releasing. The arm beneath her shifted and the one in her hair moved in some unidentifiable pattern. "Did you sleep?"

"Yes. I'm sorry I woke you with my talking."

"You woke me with your squirming."

"I'm sorry."

"It's a nice thing to wake to." The hand in her hair was still moving. Stirring her hair, among other things.

She wiggled herself up the cot to see his face. The semidarkness hid his bruised skin, but the cut on his lower lip showed. She reached up to touch it. "Does it hurt?" she asked.

"Not enough to stop me from wanting to kiss you."

Jane smiled and caught his face in her hand as he leaned down. His kiss was soft, but he'd always been a soft kisser even when he wasn't injured. Her fingers fell away to land on his chest. He didn't shift her body around or press her for more, only kept on kissing her. Well, his hand *was* stroking down her back. And when it curved over her bottom, she pressed into him. His fingers reached the hem of her dress and found the bare skin at the back of her thighs. He stopped there and his hand cupped around her leg and squeezed.

He was awake. She could get this dress off without guilt.

"I had bitter tea yesterday," she whispered between kisses. "We could, um . . ."

"We could what?" He kissed her again.

"You know."

"I do." Another kiss. "Is that what you want us to do?" He paused and waited.

"It's . . ." Jane hesitated. She didn't want to disappoint him. But she didn't want to lie to him either. "It's what people do," she said at last.

"It's one thing people do."

"But it's like the *main* thing. The thing everyone talks about. The thing everyone wants."

Rowan leaned back, keeping her close. He watched her face. "Tell me what's worrying you."

Jane's face heated and she studied his chin. Her heart hammered, but she took a deep breath and forced the words out. "It usually hurts," she whispered.

"You mean having a man inside you hurts?"

"Yes."

"Has it always?"

"Yes."

"Have you told anyone?"

"I did when I was younger, but people just told me, try to relax. Or, have some ale first. And after the last time, I told Ladi and she took me to visit Synne, the healer in Woods Rest. Synne seemed to understand at least. She delivers babies and everything."

Rowan waited. She should tell him. He wouldn't dismiss her concerns.

"Synne said my muscles are tight down there. It makes things hurt. She taught me exercises to have better control over relaxing. And she suggested . . . some other things, but I felt so embarrassed I never did them. It will never stop hurting if I can't stop worrying about it because that only makes me more tense."

"You're anxious about it hurting before it does."

"Yes. And I know if I could stop being anxious it might help, but I can't. It's so stupid and I can't fix it."

"It's not stupid."

"But I'm making it into a problem just by thinking about it so much."

"It's still real—even if anxiety causes it."

He was listening to her. He wasn't offering useless advice. Her eyes welled up. "When you kiss me it's so good. I want you down there. The pain's not awful. You could still—"

"Jane, shh. I don't want you to hurt."

"I can handle it. It's just a little while."

"But there's no reason we have to do that. We can do so many other things."

"But . . ."

Rowan watched her.

". . . won't you be disappointed?"

"No."

Of course he'd say no, that it was fine if they didn't tumble each other *that way*, but she couldn't believe him. He wouldn't *tell* her he was disappointed with her. He was too nice. He'd go on tolerating her because he was generous or because he thought he didn't deserve someone better than her—someone whose body worked the way it was supposed to. But she'd never get him to admit it. He'd keep saying it was okay and she'd never believe him.

Rowan leaned close with his lips by her ear. "I can tell you don't believe me," he whispered. "But I promise you, Jane, I'll swear on anything you like: I won't miss it. I can think of dozens of ways I want to touch you that don't involve thrusting my penis in your vagina."

Heat flooded her at his words. He kissed her forehead, and his fingers on her thigh were light.

She nudged her way out of his arms and sat up. She could see him clearly although the light was dim. The lights warmed to golden as he shifted onto his back and folded his arms behind his head, watching her. His chest was bare but the blankets swathed his lower half. He had trousers on but she could easily pretend he didn't.

She blinked away the remains of her tears. "Does one of them involve thrusting your penis in my mouth?" she asked, trying not to smile.

His eyes crinkled. "Several of them do."

A smile broke across her face.

"And several of them don't even involve me touching you because merely looking at you is enough to make me come."

"It is?"

He nodded slowly. "And I want to learn every way I can touch you to make you feel good so—"

"Wait, looking at me?" She pursed her lips. "Without touching me? I don't believe you."

"Is that a challenge?"

Jane narrowed her eyes. "Maybe."

Rowan shifted upright. She had to stop herself from reaching for the muscles of his abdomen as they tensed with the effort and his arms came down to his sides. Only he kept moving forward, leaning into her space until she scrambled back from him but he crawled after her. He caught her by the front of her dress and gently pushed her to lie on the blankets until she was flat on her back and he was leaning over her on one arm.

"You're touching me," she said.

"I'm touching your dress."

"Lying fairy."

He only laughed in reply.

He undid her buttons with his free hand, careful to keep his fingers outside her dress. The sense of his rough fingers close to her skin and never touching her caused a familiar ache between her legs. His hair slipped into his face but he was focused on the buttons. He concentrated as he unbuttoned her all the way down her chest and over her belly. The dress gaped open and the chilly air of the caverns stole in.

When he had her dress open to her waist, he sat up and reached for her shoulders. He met her gaze as he pinched her dress material around the straps of her undergarment. He raised his eyebrows.

"Go on," she said and her voice cracked with a desperate plea. He stifled a grin. He peeled down her dress and undergarment, slowly dragging it under her shoulders and down, baring her breasts and her bellybutton until all her clothing was bunched at her hips. Cool air drifted over her skin, but the sight of her bare breasts and Rowan's sharp inhale as he took in her body made her warm up, as if his gaze were a burning lamp warming her as it roved over her.

His fingers trailed over her clothing. "Are you sure you don't want me to touch you?"

"No touching," she managed to whisper.

"How do you feel about me making a mess on you?"

"A mess?"

Rowan smirked—an actual, across-his-face smirk—and before she'd recovered her shock at the expression on his face, he straddled her, pinning her arms against her sides inside his legs. He walked forward on his knees until they hugged in at her waist and he towered over her. His meaning came clear and a hot flush spread from her neck up her cheeks and down over her tingling breasts, and the ache between her legs flared to life like an ember in a haystack. Rowan broke into another a wide grin.

She sucked in a breath and waited to see what he would do. Or undo.

He undid the top button on his trousers.

"Rowan—"

"You don't want this?"

"I do. But I could touch you." Her words ended with a whine.

"No." He undid another button.

She squirmed, trying to satisfy the longing between her thighs. If she could move her hand the littlest bit and get it over her leg, she could reach down . . .

"You're awfully squirmy." The rest of his buttons came open. "Are you okay?"

"I'm fine!" She couldn't move her arms a smidge. She rubbed her legs together, trying to ease the ache as he opened the front of his trousers and took out his shaft, already firm. He gave it a few long strokes with his hand and it visibly hardened. His gaze roved from her face to her breasts and down and he began to stroke himself.

She forgot her longing a moment as she watched his hand, transfixed. She wanted *her* hand on him, holding the end lightly like he did and working his foreskin over the head of his shaft. Or pushing his foreskin back with her lips and sucking on the tip while his hands did whatever they could do around her mouth. He took a few minutes while she ogled his hand and grew harder and hotter until she was the one aching with want and practically panting underneath him. He went faster. She *wouldn't* squirm and disrupt him, she wouldn't move, but she might climax just from watching him, hands or not.

His eyes drifted closed and his breathing grew rapid. He gasped. A beat later, he rained shining droplets down on her breasts. He opened his eyes, watching as he twisted his hips and made sure to get the drops all across her. They were hot like sparks on her skin.

He smirked at her again.

"Next time you should put it in my mouth," she said, breathless.

"Next time will be soon if you keep talking like that."

He settled back, not exactly sitting on her but not freeing her arms. He relaxed with an exhale. Was he trying to torment her? He had to know the effect he had on her.

"Let me get you a kerchief." He shifted one leg to stand beside the cot.

"No." Her freed arm darted out and held his leg. "Leave it."

"What do you want me to do?"

She nudged him the rest of the way off her until she could lift her knees and wiggle her body backward, careful not to drip anything on his blankets. She made room by her feet. "Sit," she whispered.

He lowered himself down and watched her over her knees. She bit her lip and widened her eyes up at him, and she heated just thinking about what she wanted. "Will you . . ."

"You know I will."

He rested his hands on her knees and she spread them wider. Her skirt fell up her thighs to pile at her hips with the rest of her clothing. His hands on her legs made her want him so badly she whimpered. He caressed under her knees with his thumbs and up her thighs to beneath her skirt, where he hooked her underpants and tugged them off her bottom. He drew them up her legs and down her calves and off.

She was going to go off the moment he touched her if she didn't calm herself.

He was back at her knees. "Tell me how you like it."

"Okay."

He kissed up her leg. "If you want it softer or harder."

"Okay." She curled her fingers into his hair as it came within reach. He kissed his way under her skirt and out of sight. She lay her head back and closed her eyes, left only with the press of his kisses.

His mouth found her needy body, kissing her gently until she tightened her fist in his hair. He responded with suction. As his lips played with her and the tip of his tongue nudged in and wet her, she trailed her free hand through the beads of moisture he'd dropped on her skin. She smeared the drops across one breast, circling the nipple. What would he think if he saw? But his face was buried in her skirt and besides, he'd watched her grind herself against his leg to reach a climax in Sunshine's pool and then against his face a few minutes later and he hadn't been turned off. He'd probably *like* watching her paint herself with his seed.

His hand on her hip was holding her against his mouth. She tilted her hips into him and he nudged her thigh up onto his shoulder. She rocked gently against him and he let her movement set the pace, sucking harder with steady pressure. His knuckles caressed the base of her thigh and stopped beneath his mouth, touching her lightly to let her know they were there.

She tilted higher and rubbed her opening against his knuckles with a moan. The touch sent sparks bursting and she let it happen, arching against his mouth and his hand and fisting both hands in his hair as she bucked against him, her body throbbing with shocks and aftershocks until she lay panting and twitching.

She blinked open her eyes. Lights winked down at her. She tried to smile back at the lights but gasped in another breath instead.

Rowan's face was in her skirts and one soft kiss might have fallen, but her skin was so chafed from kisses and suction she couldn't be sure. She loosened her fists and petted his hair. As he pulled back and sat up, the lights dimmed to a quiet gold.

Rowan rubbed a hand down his face and the back of it sideways across his lips. She rested an arm behind her head and stifled a grin as he turned to her. He leaned his chin on her knee.

They lay there in the quiet room, watching each other. Her chest had dried like armor and the room was plenty warm now, even lying naked. His eyes held warmth, fondness, but something else . . .

Peace. Rowan looked peaceful for the first time since she'd known him. And she shared that peace. They had each other as helpmates. They would fetch Elle and bring her here to learn her fire magic in a safe place. Or more likely Sunshine would bring her. And somehow they'd let Axe know and he could come too— if Rose didn't mind one dragon in her home surely she wouldn't mind two. Jane knew her well enough to know they'd find a way to make it work. Rowan could learn to use the magic he'd been gifted with. And after that . . . well, maybe she'd figure it out tomorrow. She had enough to manage today.

She took Rowan's hand on the blankets. "We should go."

He helped her sit up. "Do you want to wash up?"

She grinned up at him and began buttoning her dress, tugging her undergarment up under it. "Later. We should rescue Maryanne from the dragon in the backyard first."

Rowan adjusted his own clothing and leaned back on his arms to wait. "By the time we get back, that dragon will be her best friend. Sunshine will have minded the children all day while Mary- anne got a long-overdue rest and a few rounds with Wells."

"And we'll come back here for the summer?"

"If that's what you want. I can show you the forge before we go."

"I trust you. I'd rather get back. The two of us can't fly so we'd better get started. And you'll . . . you'll let Axe know?"

She held her breath. Rowan slipped an arm over her shoulders and kissed her temple. "Yes."

Happiness. That was the warmth filling her.

"In fact," he continued, "you may be wrong about flying." He grinned.

Jane leapt up. She shook down her skirt and snatched her un- derpants off the floor. "He's here?" She hopped on one foot as she tried to get the other into her pants. Rowan reached out to steady her. "You could reach him all the way in the mountains?"

"I tried."

Jane got her clothes righted and moved to the door. Rowan snagged a shirt off the shelf and followed her out into the caverns, pulling it on as they walked. As soon as his hands were free, Jane took one and pulled him to walk faster. The dark passages were empty all the way to the barrier. Jane closed her eyes and let Row- an lead her through.

Warm, summery air filtered down the steps with the sunshine. Jane blinked in the brightness as they emerged into the late morning. Bees droned in the fruit trees but the garden was deserted. Except for under the trees opposite them. A crowd of fairies gathered—all facing away from Jane and Rowan and into the clearing she had crossed with Rose yesterday. The clearing where, ten winters ago, Rowan had first met Axe. And where they'd go to meet him again today.

"I'm sure we could borrow horses," Rowan said.

Jane squeezed his hand. Across the gardens, butterflies flitted from blossom to blossom. She inhaled the scent of earth and new life and possibility. She peeked up into his face and smiled.

"This way will be faster," she said, leading him forward. "Let's go."

Six moons later

JANE UNTIED HER APRON AND hung it on the peg by the door. The fires in the firepots were banked and dying, the sacks of coal brought in for tomorrow, and the blade for Ms. Ferguson's plow waited by the back wall for her to pick it up the next morning. All the farmers had been bringing in their broken and worn tools for mending and sharpening now that the crops were in. Thank the skies the ironworks had gotten that ore from the mine and resumed processing it into the bars and plates the blacksmiths needed.

Master Smith had locked the front door when he left. She'd let Benny and James go home an hour ago to beat the sunset.

Jane fastened the back door and headed to the narrow steps tucked between her shop and the farrier's. They led to the small living space over the blacksmith shop, usually taken by one or more of the apprentices. Rowan had moved in last spring—on the day she met him—and hadn't spent even one night there before he'd left with her to find Elle. He still lived there, only now she and Elle lived with him. And now she was the blacksmith's apprentice.

She hadn't noticed the wintry chill in the air all afternoon with the fires burning and the work of hammering, but it stole under her clothes as she ascended the steps. The sky emerged a pale pink with one bright star out. Rowan and Elle were usually home by this time, but no lights shone in the upstairs windows.

How cold was it up in the mountains? The mine was running, but the miners would halt for the winter soon. Jane was eager to meet Os and Derek and the other miners again, assuming they came to Woods Rest for the winter. She had only a hazy memory of their first meeting on the horrible night when she'd found them locked up, and she'd been whisked away by Axe before she ever got to thank them for helping her. It would be nice to replace the memory of that night with new ones. Maybe they could get ales in the pub some evening and get to know each other.

After he finally met them, Rowan said he'd liked them. After collecting all of his things from Sunshine's peak, he'd stopped by the mine to retrieve the belongings Jane had abandoned in the weeds behind the shack where he'd been held captive. She hadn't needed her things back, but Rowan wasn't about to start leaving detritus throughout the forest—not like a human would.

Hopefully Sunshine was warm, curled in her cave for the winter. Jane smiled as she unlocked the door and went in. Sunshine was sticking around. She would hibernate through the cold moons and return to Elle in the spring for another season, and who knew how many more after that. Sage had told Jane most fairies with fire magic worked with several dragons throughout their lives. One dragon would return to their home among the lakes and hot mineral springs in the western mountains and a few summers later another one would arrive.

But Elle was young and she and Sunshine were devoted to each other. Sage suspected Sunshine would stay around until Elle was grown.

As for Rowan . . . He and Axe had worked together all summer and now Rowan could catch flames easily and use his magic to do basic tasks like put out a fire or make fire powder. But more importantly, the two of them had spent time together, all that time that had been stolen from them ages ago. Axe had never given up on teaching Rowan. He'd been living on his peak for eight winters, hoping Rowan would return. And Rowan finally had.

As autumn had neared, Axe had at long last returned to his home in the west. No one knew if another dragon would come to replace him.

Rowan said he was content with the skills he had learned. But he made many visits to the ironworks and kept mulling over the ways dragon fire could be used to make the blast furnace and foundry more efficient, or to make the forge hearths function without emitting the dark smoke of a human-made coal fire. Maybe someday the entire ironworks and all the other human industry in Woods Rest would be up to fairy ecological standards.

While Elle and Rowan learned magic all summer, Jane studied blacksmithing. Master Smith had taught her the steps of making a hook before she left Woods Rest, and one of the fairies at the enclave had shared basic skills. The stone courtyard at the enclave included an anvil and firepot tucked under a ledge, and with the help of young fairies to work the bellows, Jane had built fires and hammered out a few dozen hooks and then decorative leaves and towel racks and even one iron rose.

Jane hadn't seen Larch once all summer.

Now they were back in Woods Rest and she was receiving more rigorous training from the master blacksmith, and smithing was every bit as fun as she'd always imagined. While she worked, Elle was off with Rowan or Maryanne. Maryanne had accepted Rowan's help, grudgingly at first, but once she realized she could have an entire day to herself to frolic with Wells, she'd warmed up to having a fairy around as a co-parent. Wells, on the other hand, Jane wasn't so sure about. He might've preferred their former arrangement.

Over the summer, Elle and Rowan had resupplied the fairy enclave with fire powder, and in exchange, the fairies had stocked their larder (and Maryanne's) with enough herbs and medicines and preserves and root vegetables for a dozen winters, plus a few bottles of their infamous elderberry wine, which Maryanne had hidden in the linen closet to avoid Wells getting his hands on it. They'd even had enough fire powder left to start trading with humans.

Jane pulled off her boots and work clothes and hung them by

the window before pulling up the sash to let a breeze into the room. It was sparsely furnished with a basic kitchen and two beds hidden behind curtains, but it was enough. They spent much of their days out in the village anyway. And when Elle was off with Maryanne's crew, and she and Rowan were alone . . . well, they didn't need a palace for what they got up to then.

She washed up and tugged on the pair of stretchy leggings, the name the fairies finally settled on, that Rose had given her. Unlike Rose's forest-green pair, Jane's were fiery orange, and they were every bit as comfortable as Rose had said. She donned a tunic long enough to cover her bottom and brushed out her hair before re-braiding it. Beside her brush on the dresser was the letter from her brother. She'd written to her family over the summer—a real letter, letting them know everything that had happened to her—and her brother had replied. They would plan a visit soon, so Jane could see her family and introduce them to Rowan and Elle, and Elle could meet her new young cousins.

Something fluttered at the window and Jane turned. The open window was empty. A bird must've landed and flown away. But a small parcel rested on the sill.

Excitement welled up as Jane walked to the window. Had Rose sent it? It was a bundle of fabric about the size and shape of a golden melon and when she picked it up, it was heavier than she expected. A piece of twine held it closed.

Jane took the parcel and sat on the edge of her bed, pushing aside the curtain. She undid the twine and unrolled the fabric. Whatever was inside was heavy and hard—what in the skies was it? The fabric fell away and Jane stared at the object in her hand.

It was made of white stone. Or quartz crystal, she thought as she held it up and the last rays of sunshine sparkled through it. And it was shaped . . .

Jane swallowed. It wasn't exactly shaped like a man's erection but that's what it made her think of. It was smooth and long and rounded, but it had a gentle curve to it and the end had a little knob. She ran a finger down it and startled when a glow pulsed out of the crystal.

It began to vibrate.

"Oh skies!" Jane whispered. It was a fairy wand, exactly as Rowan had described it.

She'd begun to think he'd been teasing her about them. But over the summer she had spoken with Thistle, the fairies' most experienced healer, about the pain she experienced when she tried to have a man inside her. Thistle had confirmed everything Synne said—in fact, the two of them were friends from long ago—but she'd had new ideas about ways Jane could help the muscles inside her relax. And one of those ideas had been to use vibrations—like a massage on her insides.

Thistle had pointed out something Jane had never considered—that her condition wasn't inherently a problem. It only became a problem if she wanted to have things inside her. But she'd considered it all summer and she did want that. Knowing Rowan accepted her regardless was a huge comfort, but she wanted to try having him inside her without it hurting. She wanted to be able to share that experience with him.

Jane listened. The alley outside the window was silent. No babbling Elle coming home with Rowan. In fact, all she could hear was a gentle hum from the wand, vibrating in her hand.

She licked her lips and lifted the hem of her tunic. Her leggings were thin as silk. When she touched the tip of the wand below her belly, the vibrations came right through. In fact, the wand seemed to vibrate a little more forcefully. It was kind of like a purring cat. Maybe Maple the inventor had employed new helpers.

Jane lay back and rubbed the wand down a little lower and it hummed in response. She poked it between her legs and oh, skies that was nice. Her cheeks flushed and her body reacted instantly. She rolled it around against her and when she pressed harder, it thrummed in response. Hummingbird wings? It was more like a hive of bees. She nudged it down between her legs and all at once the shape made sense. As her rising climax threatened to tip over, she pressed the whole curve of the wand against her body and the knobby end fit right in against her entrance, and the buzzing sensations overwhelmed her. She gasped and rubbed as much as she could with the barrier of her clothing, and her body heated and shook until the waves passed.

The wand went still in her hand. Jane caught her breath, staring at the open window. That had been way too easy. And she had wanted that knobby end inside her. Next time she was doing this with her leggings off.

Footsteps sounded below. Jane flew up off the bed and across to the dresser. She yanked open the top drawer and nestled the stone wand and its packaging in among her underclothes before pushing the drawer shut and turning.

The door opened and Rowan burst in. "You have to—"

Jane smiled brightly and lifted her brow.

"Are you okay?" he asked, coming inside. His hair was shaggier than it had been at the start of the summer. He wore it pulled back in a tie and his hair stayed tucked behind his ears now. He left the door open.

"Yes!" Her voice came out a pitch higher than usual. She cleared her throat. "What's going on? Where's Elle?"

"She's staying with Maryanne tonight. There was a casserole and something about apples?" He shook his head.

"Ah, Maryanne's famous apple squares."

"That's it."

"She waited to make them this fall until we were home from the fairy enclave, so Elle wouldn't miss it. What were you excited about?" She stepped away from the dresser and smoothed down the front of her tunic.

"Come see," Rowan said and held out a hand.

Jane followed him out the door and down the steps. Behind the shop, he led her across the stubbly meadow to the edge of the forest.

"Maryanne told me about the big persimmon tree. I wanted to find it and I spotted . . . there."

Jane followed his pointing finger to a small, smooth trunk with a branch poking out. A silver-white strand hung from the branch like a fat piece of yarn but shiny, and it twisted back and forth. She followed it down a few hands' widths to the bottom where . . . something hung on the end.

"Is that a snake?" Jane asked, peering closer. It had the narrow gray body of a snake but wrapped up on itself, all twined together and wriggling as she watched, and spinning. The strand of . . . whatever that material was that it hung from was spinning back and forth from its motion.

"Look closer."

One bit of the mass pulled back. It was speckled and it had tiny antennas.

"It's a slug!"

"Two slugs."

Now she could see the two bodies. They were wrapped around each other in a slimy embrace, coiling and sliding in goo.

"Are they mating?" Jane whispered.

Rowan's arms came around her and he pulled her back against his chest. "They're about to," he whispered in her ear.

The slugs settled into a rhythm that twisted their strand of goo farther, coiling it up one way before unspinning it the other. Their two bodies tightened around each other and locked into place. Something poked out the end of each—iridescent blue—and grew longer and weirder until the two protuberances met and *they* wrapped around each other. Jane leaned forward against Rowan's hold to observe the coiled slugs as they twisted and writhed, on and on, spinning madly as a minute passed, and another, until they abruptly stopped moving.

They held on as the motion caused by their coupling faded. The blue extensions retracted and the tops of their bodies broke free. Their heads peeked up from the coil, looking about.

Jane steadied her breathing. Hopefully Rowan hadn't noticed—

He kissed behind her ear. "You liked it," he murmured.

She exhaled one last pant. "Fine. Yes."

"I told you it was romantic."

"The way they held on to each other . . ."

Rowan kissed her more and her heart rate picked back up. Over on the tree, one of the slugs had crawled onto the trunk while the other still hung from the strand. Maybe it needed a moment to recover. She would have, after that.

"It's late in the season for slugs to be out," she pressed on, trying to distract herself even as her fingers found Rowan's leg behind her and dug in, holding him against her. She couldn't tumble Rowan now—not here on the damp autumn leaves after the sight of two slugs fornicating had turned her on. But twilight had fallen and no one would see them in the fading light. And the slugs weren't watching. The first had slithered out of sight and the second was crawling back onto the tree.

"Maybe they only recently found each other," Rowan said, licking her ear.

"Maybe."

He kissed her ear and let her go with a sigh. She stopped herself before she whimpered.

"I meant to tell you," Rowan said as she turned to face him, "a package is coming."

"Oh?" Her attempt at surprise sounded like a squeaky hinge.

"It's a present for you."

Jane whistled out an exhale and stared into the forest. "It, um, it might have arrived."

"Did it?" Rowan was hiding a smile.

"Yes, all right, it did."

"You opened it."

"Yes. It wasn't labeled to you."

He tilted his head. "What did you think?"

She scuffed at the grass but broke into a smile. "I liked it. Thank you."

"You tried it?"

"Yes."

Rowan's hand curled around the back of her neck and he kissed the top of her head. "Maybe sometime you can show me how you used it. If you want."

"Sometime?" She gazed up with wide eyes.

He grinned. "Or now."

Jane took his hand and tugged him back toward the smithy.

A Note from the Author

Dear Reader,

Thank you so much for reading *The Fire Apprentice*. After I introduced Jane in *The Forest Bride*, I left her hanging. I wanted her to reach a happy ending, but I couldn't come up with a plot until I decided *not* to pair her with Cedric/Larch. Trying to find a way to redeem him after what he did was the hurdle holding the story back.

I had been considering writing a heroine with pelvic floor issues that cause pain with sex. I'd never seen this in a romance novel, or any novel; for a long time I hadn't even realized such pain could occur continuously, beyond someone's first time having sex. Even when actively looking for information, it took me years to find any, as this "women's issue" is little researched or understood. Two helpful resources are the chapter on pelvic floor muscle spasm and vaginismus in *The Vagina Bible* by Dr. Jen Gunter and *The Musculoskeletal Mystery* by Ingrid Harm-Ernandes, a pelvic floor physical therapist.

I had also noticed that cis-het M/F pairs in romance novels with love scenes commonly have penis-in-vagina sex, usually with lots of thrusting that feels amazing to her and ends with an orgasm. Never mind that 70% of women don't reach an orgasm with such thrusting (Solot and Miller, *I ♥ Female Orgasm*, p. 115). If someone can't enjoy that type of sex at all, reading about it in every single story can feel alienating. And it perpetuates the idea that this particular form of sex is better or necessary or "the real thing." I wanted to write a romance between characters who find a happy ending that doesn't subscribe to that norm.

A love story with no intercourse might not be for everyone. If you did like the story, please consider leaving a review online to help like-minded readers find it. I would truly appreciate it.

I'm hoping to have the next book in the Sylvania series, *The Magic Seeker*, out in 2026. It is Snowdrop's story. You can subscribe to my email list at https://janebuehler.com for an email when the new book is available. I send only a few emails each year, so I won't crowd your inbox. When you subscribe, I'll send a link to bonus material, including a video (shot in my backyard!) of two slugs mating.

You can also connect with me online on various social media sites and author pages listed at my website. And you can email me at jane@janebuehler.com.

Until next time,

Emily Jane ♡

Acknowledgments

As always, I want to give a big thank you to my friends and family. The supportive network you provide keeps me going, as a writer and otherwise.

Thanks to all my classmates in the March 2023 "Smithing Made Simple" blacksmithing class at the John C. Campbell Folk School, and especially teachers Caitlin Morris and Steve Wilde. Caitlin runs Miss Caitlin's School of Blacksmithing in Frederick, Maryland. If you want to learn the basic steps of building a fire and forging a hook, she offers short classes at her shop. Her website is https://mscaitlinsschool.com.

Thanks to Lauren McLaughlin (Conscious Strong) and Ingrid Harm-Ernandes for the insights about the workings of the pelvic floor. In 2024, they co-taught a workshop I attended in February, the same month I began revising this story.

Thank you to Christy R. for reading the first draft and helping with the "mom" perspective. Thanks to Grace C. and Erin C. for being my back cover beta readers. Angie M. provided great insights to help me improve the story—thank you for all your encouragement over the years. You all are my favorite fans!

Autumn Brown at Write & Whimsy Book Editing (https://autumnbrownux.com) provided helpful feedback and was a delight to work with.

And finally, I'm grateful to have Kelly Urgan (https://www.editegrity.com) as my editor and Cory Podielski (https://podielski.com/) as my cover designer.

About the Author

Emily Jane Buehler was adrift for many years before realizing she wanted to work with words. She published two nonfiction books—one on the science and craft of baking bread, the other a memoir of her bicycle trip from New Jersey to Oregon—before venturing into fiction. She now writes cozy fantasy romance: lighthearted stories that focus on a protagonist finding their courage and happiness, as opposed to plots with a lot of fighting and darkness. She also copyedits (mostly science papers) and teaches bread-making classes.

Emily lives in Hillsborough, North Carolina, with a bossy cat named Coco. Her favorite things include letters sent through the mail, her fair-trade wool leg warmers, and chocolate cake with frosting. She is passionate about living waste free and supporting locally owned businesses.

Emily publishes fiction using her middle name, Jane.